THE OUTCASTS

Life After the Great War of 2042

Bill Thompson

Published by
Ascendente Books
Dallas, Texas

Published by Ascendente Books

ISBN 978-0996467179

Printed in the United States of America

Books by Bill Thompson

Apocalyptic Fiction

THE OUTCASTS

The Crypt Trilogy

THE RELIC OF THE KING

THE CRYPT OF THE ANCIENTS

GHOST TRAIN

Brian Sadler Archaeological Mystery Series

THE BETHLEHEM SCROLL

**ANCIENT: A SEARCH FOR THE LOST CITY
OF THE MAYAS**

THE STRANGEST THING

THE BONES IN THE PIT

ORDER OF SUCCESSION

Middle Grade Fiction

THE LEGEND OF GUNNERS COVE

INTRODUCTION

I'm Nathan Dax. It's 2094, I'm seventeen years old and I'm an Outcast. It's not something I'm ashamed of. It's just the opposite. I'm proud that my mom and dad followed their consciences and beliefs instead of doing what everyone else did. Dad always said he'd have been a hippie if he had lived in the twentieth century. He was once an Outcast too – they didn't kill them back then – so there's this streak of rebellion that goes way back in the Dax family.

"Nate," Dad told me when I was younger, "life's going to be hard for you, but your mother and I will teach you everything you need to know. Someday, somehow, being an Outcast will allow you to make a difference. I don't know what it'll be, but I'd bet my life it'll happen."

Now that my parents are gone, I wonder if Dad actually did bet his life on me, if they went missing because their son was an Outcast.

CHAPTER ONE

Historians go back seventy-five years to explain how things are today. The US presidential election of 2016 was unprecedented – two candidates whom almost everyone disliked battled it out for the White House. The choices were the lesser of two evils: bluster, bombast and bragging on one side and a blatant disregard for the law on the other.

When all the votes were counted and the Electoral College had convened, the Republican party controlled the White House, Senate and House. That should have allowed for sweeping changes but instead America's politicians seriously misjudged their constituents. The manner in which the majority party governed was met with bitter resistance. As had happened during the campaigns, there were riots more and more often across the country.

Dissatisfied citizens sent another message in the midterm elections of 2018. Many incumbents lost their seats, and the leadership in both houses of Congress switched to the Democrats. To say people were upset would have been a massive understatement, and a social revolution began to materialize.

The 2020 presidential election was the last straw. Once again ignoring what people wanted, Hillary and Donald were the candidates once again. Neither the brash, bullying Republican nor the female Democrat whose private email server created such a fuss last time had approval ratings of more than twenty-nine percent. Polls reflected that ninety percent of likely voters wanted something different. A new political party seized the opportunity to give people what they wanted.

The movement started with young voters – those between eighteen and thirty. They rallied behind a third-party candidate – a likable, sincere individual who reminded some of Bernie Sanders four years earlier. He was an honest man, an outsider with a solid business background, and his party – the Social Democrats – built a huge cadre of volunteers who helped tens of thousands of young people register to vote for the first time.

The positive words of a candidate who offered a refreshing change resonated with the people while the Democrats and Republicans kept up the mudslinging, snide remarks and derogatory slams. The Social Democrats promised if they were elected that things would never be the same in America again. When it was over, the Socialist candidate won by a seventy-seven percent majority, a clear mandate that would entrench the party in the White House for the rest of America's existence.

The people's dislike for politics as usual spread much further than the White House. The Social Democrats had come into the 2020 election organized and prepared. They ran candidates for public office in all fifty states, and many of them won handily. Of the four hundred and thirty-five mostly incumbent representatives on the ballot, every single one with more than four years' seniority was removed. It was worse in the Senate. Thirty-four senators ran for re-election and all thirty-four were booted out of office.

The freshman class of the 2021 Congress contained nearly three hundred and fifty men and women, half of whom were Social Democrats. It was a strange and unsettling time in America. Many people were jubilant and optimistic. Many others, especially those over fifty, were very worried.

Things went more smoothly than many predicted. Even critics ultimately agreed the one-fell-swoop wholesale removal of the old guard was a positive thing. From committee assignments to new alliances, the nation embraced the concept of a true third party.

The Social Democratic platform was a blend of capitalism and socialism. Spending cuts in the military budget meant a smaller army and a corresponding withdrawal of US troops from the foreign battles this Congress was no longer willing to support. The moves were meant to demonstrate America's desire to promote world peace, but nations that were not our friends watched with interest as America deliberately emasculated itself.

Beginning in 2021, the government implemented corporate nationalization. From automobile manufacturers to railroads, from utilities and telecommunications to pharmaceutical companies, from banking to technology, the government nationalized and combined one industry after another. By 2040 more than half of what had been private corporations were now owned by the United States government and the country was truly a socialistic state.

CHAPTER TWO

On January 2, 2042, at 4:48 a.m. local time, strong earthquakes jolted people awake along the West Coast from Seattle to San Diego. They ranged in intensity from a 7.0 on the Richter scale in Washington state to an 8.2 in the vicinity of Los Angeles. It was enough to rip overpasses apart, crippling the interstate highway system in this densely populated area of Southern California.

Within a short time, news reports began streaming in. This wasn't an isolated event – there were tremors all along the Ring of Fire, an earthquake zone encircling the Pacific Ocean from Indonesia to Siberia, across the Bering Strait then down the west coast of the Americas from Alaska to the southern tip of Chile.

On the western side of the ocean, an 8.9-magnitude quake had struck. Tens of thousands were homeless in the western Pacific islands, and buildings in Auckland, Manila and Tokyo sustained heavy damage. Other tremors, each over 6.0 on the scale, crippled cities and villages in Ecuador, Peru and Chile.

The damage was vast and estimates placed the loss of life at over three hundred thousand, although those numbers would surely rise as rescue efforts continued, the news agencies reported. Over ten thousand people in the United States had died and a hundred thousand were in hospitals.

Both sides of the ocean experienced strong aftershocks each day, hampering rescuers and increasing the death toll. When the world thought things could get no worse, six days later the full fury of hell was unleashed on California.

At 11:25 on a sunny morning, the thing Californians had nervously joked about for generations finally happened. The Big One – the grandfather of all earthquakes – ripped apart the earth along the San Andreas Fault, creating a rift through the lush central California farmland. Horrific sounds – one enormous boom after another that reminded witnesses of the bombs of war – accompanied the opening of the bowels of the earth. A vicious gash five miles wide and a hundred feet deep in places zigzagged southwards, pushing everything west of it towards the Pacific Ocean. The rift tore through downtown Bakersfield and continued south to the Mexican border. This time the Richter scale was useless – this wasn't a measurable event on any scale known to man. There were massive earth movements all the way down the fault line from northeastern Los Angeles County through San Bernardino and Riverside Counties. Although the gaping trench itself lay twenty miles east of Los Angeles, the massive earthquakes brought down nearly every multistory structure in the city.

Disaster relief was underway from the quakes six days before, but there was nothing that could be done this time. The destruction was massive and total. With all utilities down, there was no means of communicating with whatever survivors there might be.

Hawaiians had been spared the Ring of Fire earthquakes, but this time their luck had run out. The Big One caused a tsunami of epic proportions. NOAA and FEMA advised governmental officials in Hawaii that it was coming and it would be monstrous. There were only hours to plan; evacuation procedures were put into place immediately. *Get as high as you can, as quickly as you can*, everyone was told. Tens of thousands of tourists were herded onto sightseeing buses and taken to the mountains. Residents loaded families and keepsakes in their cars, and everyone started driving into the hills at once. Honolulu would suffer the worst losses because of its dense population. Many people would die stuck in traffic when the tsunami hit. It was better on Maui, Kauai and the Big Island, where the population was smaller and many already lived at higher elevations.

Six hours after the massive earthquakes in Southern California, aerial reconnaissance planes over Hawaii shot video that horrified the world. A wave six hundred and forty feet high screamed westward across the Pacific, hitting the beaches of Waikiki with the force of a hundred atomic bombs. Everything in its path was utterly and completely demolished. It resembled the horror of Pompeii two thousand years earlier. Everyone who hadn't made it to high ground perished in seconds.

It took weeks for federal investigators to assess the damage, and what they reported was more terrible than anyone could have imagined. On the mainland, nearly every building in the cities of LA, Ontario, Riverside, Bakersfield, Palm Springs and Palm Desert lay in ruins. Hilltop mansions in Beverly Hills tumbled down. Homes perched on the cliffs in Malibu fell into the ocean like a child destroying a Lego building. The infrastructure in Southern California was in ruins; there were no intact freeways or surface streets anywhere west of the fault line. Area airports – LAX included – didn't have a single working runway. It wouldn't have mattered. There was no one there to direct traffic. The control towers had all toppled, killing everyone inside.

On a per capita basis, Hawaii suffered the most loss of life. The islands looked completely different now, since what had been dense jungle six hundred feet up the mountainsides was waterfront property today. Many survivors joined together, sharing what meager possessions they'd managed to bring. But even in the lush mountains and temperate climate, thousands who survived the initial devastation would themselves die within weeks. Some starved and others perished at the hands of their fellow humans who had become animals, murdering to take what they wanted. Any thought of government and democracy was swept away with the tsunami, and life degenerated into an abyss of fear, danger and tyranny.

Death counts would never be more than estimates since the waters wouldn't get back to normal levels for months. There was no way for survivors to communicate with loved ones. Educated guesses on Hawaii's death toll put it at 1.3 million, sixty percent of whom were residents and the rest tourists. Hundreds of thousands were missing and presumed drowned. Most would never be found.

In California seventy thousand were killed in San Bernardino, Riverside and San Diego Counties, but in the more populous ones – Los Angeles and Orange Counties – it was far worse. Nearly four million were unaccounted for and presumed dead. In the United States, the total number who perished was estimated at six to seven million.

The president and California's governor spent two hours flying over the greater Los Angeles area two days after the destruction. The surreal scene below displayed unbelievable devastation. There was no traffic because there were no roads. There were no neighborhoods because every house was flattened. There was no downtown or Century City with skyscrapers touching the clouds, because not a single building over one story remained standing.

As the helicopter flew low, the two chief executives saw people moving about, picking through the rubble of ruined stores. These were not looters; these were rational, everyday Americans who simply wanted to live another day and who were using any means at their disposal. There were fires going in almost every intersection and human beings huddled around them, apparently cooking food they held out on sticks like kids roasting marshmallows at a picnic.

The president had ordered the National Guard, Army Reserves and thousands of full-time soldiers to mobilize, but he cancelled that order after the flyover. There was nothing a few thousand troops could do. These people didn't need law and order anymore. They needed food, water, a place to live – or they would die quickly.

Subcommittees in Washington somberly discussed how best to help, but the magnitude of the destruction made execution impossible. FEMA – the Federal Emergency Management Agency – had neither the budget, the personnel nor a plan for something like this. The president urged

Americans to pray because there was nothing else that could be done for weeks or months.

CHAPTER THREE

America had never been at a lower point than in the winter of 2042. After the January earthquakes and floods, the world's financial markets collapsed. Oil, silver and gold prices skyrocketed and so did the sales of weapons. The number one book on Amazon was a how-to guide called *Emergency Stockpiling: Prepare Now and Be Safe Later.* But for many it was too late.

The Department of Energy, which bore national responsibility for the government-owned utilities, struggled to cope since there was no power or telecommunication infrastructure in thousands of square miles of newly created wasteland. No disaster plan could have contemplated the utter destruction of Southern California and the loss of millions of Americans.

For a nation just beginning to recover from its greatest crisis in history, the gods weren't finished yet. In late January ice storms swept southward from Canada, bringing record low temperatures and massive blackouts as far south as San Antonio and Shreveport. A six-inch snow in Phoenix on January 25th didn't melt for two months. This would go into the record books as the most severe winter ever. And it couldn't have come at a worse time.

Experts believed the storms were an effect of the earthquakes and tsunami three weeks earlier. Whatever had caused them, record low temperatures and ice-covered roadways led to even more deaths. Thousands of trucks loaded with critically needed food and supplies became stranded on jammed interstate highways. By the end of February five hundred thousand more Americans were dead, many from exposure. Some had been stranded outdoors, others were homeless to begin with, and still others, including many families, were eventually discovered huddled together under blankets in homes without power, frozen solid in subzero temperatures.

America's situation was becoming more critical by the minute, and some opportunistic nations followed its woes closely. Inevitably, one seized the opportunity. On February 21 the Secretary of Defense reported to the president that seven Severodvinsk-class submarines, Russia's newest nuclear attack vessels, had reportedly been taking advantage of the unprecedented winter weather to engage in deep-water test dives. He added that the subs were almost certainly armed with cruise missiles, probably nuclear.

American jets kept an eye on them as they maneuvered in seas off the coast of Iceland, but suddenly one morning they were gone. Recon aircraft saw nothing and assumed they'd left the area, but there was so much ice in the north Atlantic nowadays that underwater submarine tracking – a tricky situation in even good weather – was impossible now.

On March 2nd, just ten days later, the mystery was solved and the future of the United States of America became perilous.

The seven submarines that had gone silent since they left Iceland resurfaced at last, much further south. Satellites recorded intermittent transmissions in Russian, originating off the Eastern Seaboard of the United States. This wasn't the first time it had happened. In a blustery show of force during the Cold War, the Soviets had positioned Akula-class subs two hundred miles out in the Atlantic. This time it was perilously different. There were four groups of subs, each twenty miles offshore and each near a major US city.

Militarily, the federal government was in a uniquely bad position to deal with such a show of force. Its armed forces were a fraction of what they had been. The defense budget had been slashed time and again over the past twenty years as resources were reallocated to fund social issues. Five years ago the US signed nuclear standoff treaties with China, Russia, India and Iran. As a show of good faith and to comply with the letter of the agreements, America immediately began dismantling its nuclear weaponry. But as the government had seen time and again, the others had no intention of complying. Each annual inspection revealed no changes. Every signer of the treaties but the USA still had a full nuclear arsenal. There were threats and demands, but a weak America could no longer force its enemies to comply.

As decimated as its arsenal was, the country fortunately had a little firepower left. Eleven Ohio-class submarines in America's fleet were still operational. Five of those were on a training operation in the eastern Mediterranean and four others were in the Sea of Japan, attempting to show force in response to saber rattling by North Korea that happened ever more frequently these days. Each sub was loaded with fifty AGM-86 cruise missiles armed with nuclear warheads.

Although the Social Democratic government was composed primarily of pacifists, they were also realists. The secretaries of Defense and Homeland Security advised the president to raise the threat level and prepare to retaliate if the nation were fired upon. The Russian subs were so close that responses would have to be instantaneous. The president took their advice, ordering the nation to prepare to defend itself.

At midnight on March 3, 2042, ten cruise missiles soared into the sky from a Russian submarine off the coast of Massachusetts. There was no time for a response; within moments Boston was utterly destroyed.

The president himself was the biggest pacifist of all – a man who abhorred even the thought of war, but now he had no choice. He ordered US submarines to strike. Two hundred missiles were launched against Moscow and St. Petersburg, and fifty more hit Novosibirsk, Siberia.

Seconds later a barrage of missiles screamed away from a military base near Shanghai. Tokyo soon lay in ruins. Realizing the immediate danger facing his country, Japan's president retaliated, using the nuclear weapons his country had obtained at the end of the longstanding nuclear non-proliferation treaty with the USA.

Israel's prime minister watched one assault after another and implemented the aggressive plan the Knesset had approved months before. Israeli missiles struck Damascus, Tehran and three other Iranian cities. On the other side of the globe, Russian subs in the Atlantic continued their mission. Missiles were launched at Washington, New York and Philadelphia. Knowing he had only seconds left, the desperate US president launched every remaining missile at Moscow. That was America's last stand. All communication ceased as the nation's capital was decimated. No more orders would be issued. The Capitol building and the White House burst apart in white-hot direct hits, and the federal government of what had been the greatest nation on Earth ceased to exist.

In only twenty minutes the world war was over. It all happened so quickly that people in the Midwest only learned there was something wrong when TV news feeds went blank or they lost power. After the nuclear holocaust, New York, Washington, Philadelphia and Boston were in ruins and their populations were totally annihilated. The same situations existed in Beijing, Shanghai, Tokyo, Moscow, St. Petersburg and Novosibirsk. Damascus, Tehran and three other major Iranian cities were gone too.

Some places, including the United Kingdom, most of western Europe and Israel, were spared but now faced a world much different than it had been when this day began. Millions upon millions were dead, and radioactive fallout would kill that many more within days. The national governments of four superpowers were gone, and any sense of world order was replaced by chaos and fear.

Who would take the reins? Who would assume responsibility for normalizing the world's nations and ensuring that those with ulterior motives were kept in check during this time of uncertainty, danger and doubt? Around the globe people trembled, prayed and prepared for the worst. An anxious world waited for someone to come forward with a plan.

CHAPTER FOUR

What had been dark times before were truly mind-boggling now. In the months following what became known as the Twenty-Minute War, many countries that were spared did what little they could to help the others cope and rebuild. The handful of congressmen still alive – the sixty or so who were out of town when the attacks came – demanded that any allocation of funds for reconstruction of ravaged nations must include America.

But now America could make no demands. It was no longer a player. The powerful, ultra-wealthy rulers of the Middle East immediately pledged billions of petrodollars to restart the governments of China, Russia, Iran and Syria, completely ignoring the former Western superpower.

Radiation had contaminated everything for a hundred miles from the epicenters of the bombings in the four US cities. Hospitals attempted to treat gravely injured survivors, most of whom died quickly. In this situation, death was preferable to living with no ongoing means of treatment. Once supplies and generated power ran out, the medical centers had to close their doors.

Hundreds of thousands of people who were outside the radioactive area had to make plans quickly. Some banded together, pooling food and supplies with neighbors and friends in order to survive until order could be restored. Others saw the baser instincts of human beings manifest themselves. Men turned on their next-door neighbors and football-watching friends, killing entire families in cold blood for whatever was in their garage freezer. Gangs of thugs from impoverished areas stormed affluent gated communities during the long nights, shooting and stealing and raping. Bankers, lawyers, accountants and people from

17

every other occupation couldn't believe that in a few short days they'd gone from normal suburban life to sitting sniper-style in second-floor windows of darkened houses, cradling rifles and ready to kill truckloads of would-be thieves before their own families could be murdered.

Many decided to leave everything behind and head west, where there had been no earthquakes or bombed cities. People chose carefully what they loaded in their cars for a trip from which they might never return. There was only so much room. It meant leaving a lifetime of once-important things like artwork, family albums, stamp collections, and childhood trophies. Memories were suddenly far less important than canned meat and vegetables, batteries, warm clothing, tents and survival gear. As families backed down driveways and went past house after house where friends and neighbors lived, everyone wondered when or if they'd see this place again. If they did, would their houses still be there?

Interstate highways 70, 80 and 90 westbound were clogged with traffic. Breakdowns and accidents made things worse and makeshift camps sprang up everywhere along the roadsides. At night the communal areas were lit by small fires, and the sounds of guitar music, babies crying and dogs barking mixed together as people tried to make the best of an awful situation.

A lucky few had packed tents. They survived the cold and wet weather better than those who slept in their cars or huddled outside under tarps and sodden blankets. Some people gave up their relatively comfortable, dry tents to mothers with small children. The common thing almost every family had packed was a weapon or two. After dark, everywhere one walked in the camps they passed stone-faced fathers sitting alert with shotguns in their laps, guarding their sleeping families and what precious little possession they had left.

Inevitably these camps became permanent residences for many of the refugees. Cars ran out of gas, or were stolen by others fleeing the devastation, or simply broke down. Gasoline had been available when the mass exodus to the Midwest began, although many stations priced it at fifteen or twenty dollars a gallon. Station owners assumed there wouldn't be more deliveries for a long, long time and some gouged whatever profit they could from the unfortunates. The wealthy refilled their tanks whenever they stopped, despite long lines and angry outbursts from those who couldn't afford gas. After two days there was no more fuel anywhere on the highways, so many were forced to live wherever along the road their cars had died.

Level-headed men and women struggled to maintain order while some of their fellow humans took advantage of the weak. Theft, rape, extortion and murder were what rational people feared once the sun went down each evening. Screams, gunshots and drunken laughter could be heard in every camp, every night. Terrified parents tried to keep their children from hearing and seeing what was happening around them.

A few men in each camp assumed an awesome, terrible and necessary responsibility, becoming an on-the-spot judge and jury. If a man was caught stealing or worse, there would be someone in the camp who'd handle the matter. The criminal, hog-tied like the days of the wild West, would be delivered to one or two individuals who'd haul away the perpetrator. No one wanted to know exactly who they were because what they were doing had to be done. In reality they were the people who worked, played and existed next door to everyone else. But in these times they filled a need. As men dragged a lawbreaker off into the trees and a gunshot echoed into the night, even those in the camp who had bitterly opposed capital punishment now understood that this was absolutely necessary for the survival of the group.

Evangelical groups called the Twenty-Minute War Armageddon, and in many ways it was exactly that. The United States was a fractured shell. Japan, Indonesia, North Korea and Vietnam were crippled from the earthquakes, and Tokyo had been bombed into oblivion. For now, Russia, China, Syria and Iran no longer posed a threat to Israel or the West, although within weeks the leaders of Saudi Arabia and the UAE would be pouring dollars in to help rebuild their economies.

With Los Angeles and New York decimated, the national television networks moved operations to Chicago. There was no Federal Communications Commission left, so leaders of the top broadcasters agreed among themselves what and when to air. Except for emergencies, broadcasts began at five a.m. Eastern and ended at eleven p.m. Sitcoms and talk shows were limited to reruns because most of the actors who'd appeared on them were dead and there were no studios on either coast. There was mostly news during the day, but in the evenings some networks aired shows covering religion, the end times, apocalyptic events and the future. Radio became a bigger medium than television or the Internet because the refugees – and many who still lived in the cities – no longer had power, but they did have hand-cranked radios bought for weather disasters, and the fortunate who ordinarily stockpiled batteries had a temporary fix.

As much as commentators tried for a positive spin, there wasn't much positive to talk about in the world. It was a time so unusual and so sobering that nightly news shows around the world began and ended with prayer. The broadcasts no longer focused on infighting or war or petty politics or economics or mundane human interest stories. All the stories were about an uncertain future and how – or even if – the world could move forward in peace. Or at all.

Despite having no national structure anymore, leaders emerged, joining to discuss the creation of a provisional federal government. They had no national mandate, no legal justification and no motivation except survival, but the mayors of Houston, Phoenix, Indianapolis, Jacksonville and San Francisco convened a Constitutional Convention in Chicago. There were functioning cities larger than some of those, but the men and women who called the meeting wanted geographic and economic diversity. It wouldn't have worked for three cities in Texas to be included, they decided among themselves, even though those three were among the nation's largest now. The future of the nation was literally hanging in the balance, and everyone cooperated.

Discussions on unification were also underway in London, Brussels, Berlin and Tel Aviv. The focus now wasn't on politics or religion or one group's issues with another. It wasn't even a matter of protecting national borders anymore. It was about continuing to exist.

The Armageddon doomsayers preached hell and damnation, cautioning people to watch closely for the emergence of the Antichrist, a man – or a woman, perhaps – who would lead the world into what would appear to be peace and unification. *Don't believe it!* they shouted as they picked apart every word of the Book of Revelation on the nightly talk shows. They predicted that the Antichrist was already on Earth, ready to dominate the world and face Jesus Christ in the last great war between good and evil. Many people laughed at the thought, but countless others took the Bible scholars seriously.

As could be expected, a few countries decided to use the situation to further their agendas. Once air traffic was reestablished, the president of Venezuela invited the leaders of Yemen, North Korea, Afghanistan, Saudi Arabia and Pakistan to a strategic meeting in Caracas. They called it a conference on world unity, but there was no mistaking the message. These enemies of the West, some of which had birthed the world's worst terrorist groups, were hell-bent on creating a strong, unified partnership of hate. The Caracas Coalition, as the group would be known, began planning its first move.

CHAPTER FIVE

The fledgling government of the New United States of America was led by a president elected not by the people but by the delegates at the Chicago Convention of 2042. She happened to be a Democratic Socialist, a member of the same party that had ruled America since 2020, but political parties didn't matter anymore. There was accord and agreement among convention delegates instead of discord and enmity. These people had no choice except to coexist and cooperate.

The European Union was intact and there was a push for unity in that body as well. Faltering economies and immigration were no longer issues worth fighting about when the future of the world was at stake. The president of the European Council, the man who headed the EU, was a former prime minister of Britain. He was a hawk, a man who favored a strong military. At his direction the EU issued harsh warnings to the Caracas Coalition, which was rumored to be planning a strike against the United States. Europe would not tolerate another war. Any attempt to create friction would be dealt with quickly and decisively, the EU leader promised. For now, the Coalition backed down, but no one believed their mission was in any way less certain to be carried out.

In 2044 the EU convened a meeting of world leaders in Geneva, historically a place of peacemaking. Its goal was to unify the world and create a harmonious existence among its countries. The United States, Russia, Japan, China and many others were struggling. They had little input into the establishment of the World Union. Every country on Earth would be united under one government. Many nations vociferously condemned the plan, but in the end all but twenty joined the union voluntarily, and those holdouts – all members of the Caracas Coalition – finally capitulated. Despite their apparent change of heart, those countries were still hell-bent on destroying the West.

The new governing body would be located in Israel, a place considered holy by three world religions. That move was also a concession to countries who believed the World Union was simply the EU all over again. Temporary space was secured in Tel Aviv and construction began on a headquarters building.

It was decided that a simple election would be held in which the leaders of the world would cast ballots to elect a president. The person with the most votes would win outright, majority or not. There would be no campaigning, and any person of legal status in his or her own country was eligible to be nominated.

The World Union recognized one hundred and ninety-six countries, each of which would have one vote. Despite a no-campaigning mandate, behind-the-scenes lobbying efforts began with a frenzy. This election was completely different than any other had been. There were no television advertisements and no debates or public discussions to persuade voters, because the citizens had no say in this election. It would have been preferable for them to have voted, newscasters opined, but with much of the world still in chaos, it simply wasn't possible. The logistics – the infrastructure for getting out the vote, counting the ballots and coming up with a leader in a reasonable time frame – just didn't exist.

Six weeks after the World Union was created, its first president was elected. Konrad Bauer had been Chancellor of Germany and he received fifty-six of the one hundred ninety-six votes cast. The prime minister of Israel received the second largest number of votes, twenty-one. The president of the United States received only three votes – her own plus those of Canada and Mexico. The once-powerful nation was ignored in the choice of a world leader.

CHAPTER SIX

Now, more than fifty years after the Twenty-Minute War, I'm living in the mountains as an Outcast. If my parents had had any friends, which they never have, those people would never know Dan and Melanie Dax had a child. Nate Dax, their son, was the biggest secret my family ever kept. Telling just one person about me – trusting even the closest friend or relative – could easily be my death sentence. It's a big deal when someone turns in an Outcast. The reward is fifty thousand World points, more than working people make in a year, Dad told me once. That'll buy you a lot, and there are people out there looking to make a killing – so to speak – by turning in Outcasts like me.

I was around eleven when my parents explained the whole Outcast thing – my father's and mine. He was an Outcast as a kid too. My dad's family were staunch Republicans way back before the Twenty-Minute War ended politics. According to the stories, my grandparents lived on a farm in what was once Nebraska. They were at the end of a dead-end road and they could see the dust swirling as the EP – the Enforcement Patrol – drove their black Suburbans toward the house. Granddad hid my father in a cellar and the EP never found him.

He finally got chipped when he met my mom, or so the story goes. She wouldn't marry him unless he was legal. Paying the penalty for late chipping cost a fortune, but my dad still laughs when he calls it the price of love. At least he got to pay to get chipped. Now the law's different. Now they don't allow Outcasts to live once they're located. They simply euthanize them. That's what will happen to me someday if I'm not careful. I don't worry about it. I just have to stay out of sight.

25

The chip program – formally called the Comprehensive Identity Protection (CHIP) Act of 2049 – authorized the worldwide identity-tracking devices. Every person is injected with a sensor a hundred times smaller than a pinhead that stays inside you forever. When the program began, everyone was allowed six months to get chipped. Now babies get it when they're born and it stays with you until you die and they remove you from the database. As you grow up, a lot of things are added to the unique ID number and lottery number you get at birth. Your medical history, personal information, arrest and military records are all on it.

Unchipped people – Outcasts like me – can't do the most basic things, like work, buy things in a store, or recharge a car. I couldn't buy a bus ticket or go to church. And anywhere there's a metal detector, even one of those things at store exits that beep when you've forgotten the antitheft device, your chip is scanned. That's the end of the line for Outcasts.

CHAPTER SEVEN

In 2044 the World Union adopted the System of Laws – the rules that govern every nation on Earth. Those laws brought sweeping changes. There were no more individual countries or constitutions. The world was divided into four regions: Eurasia, the Americas, Africa and IndoAustralia. Each region was overseen by a governor – the first one in the Americas was the woman who had been president of the USA when the country was abolished. The governors reported to the president of the World Union.

The System of Laws changed a lot of things, but one thing it left alone was religion. I think it was smart of the leaders to realize most people didn't want the government getting involved with religion. I heard that many people became atheists, but a lot of people still worshipped a god, whichever one worked for them. The System of Laws decreed that there would be no conflict in the name of religion. As long as everyone was willing to live in peace and harmony, they could believe in whatever they wanted to. If some group decided to hate some other group because of its religion, the World Union would shut the aggressors down. For the last fifty years that's worked fine.

When they started the CHIP program, it was a big deal. Every person was allowed six months to go to a center where they would be injected with a tiny chip. It must have been difficult to enforce, since remote tribes in Africa and South America had to be dealt with, as well as the teeming ghetto populations in places like India and the Middle East. Apparently most people obeyed the law and got signed up by the deadline. Billions of chips were monitored by the new Population Control Council in Tel Aviv. Since everyone knew there were still millions of people out there without a chip, severe penalties for noncompliance were adopted. That was when the term Outcast started being used. It isn't an official World Union term, but everyone uses it, even the cops.

After the six-month grace period, an Outcast who turned himself in could pay a fine of five thousand World points for late registration and be chipped. A year later the government cracked down. Outcasts could still come in voluntarily, but an unchipped who was caught would be euthanized, and anyone who harbored or assisted an Outcast would die too. No trial, no excuses, nothing. There was also a huge reward for turning in a fugitive, so some people became bounty hunters. Suddenly Outcasts started showing up for chipping in droves. But still there were holdouts.

Over the next five years, chip readers were installed everywhere – in point-of-sale machines at stores, in every single metal detector and store-exit theft detector in the world – so now you couldn't buy things without a chip. There were no more credit or debit cards, no more bank accounts or savings and loans. It was a point-based society with a lot of bartering and trading on the side. That kind of thing wasn't addressed in the System of Laws, but the Enforcement Patrol didn't hassle people who bartered. I guess they figured it didn't really matter, although it was one of the few ways for Outcasts to survive.

CHAPTER EIGHT

The worst part of the System of Laws – the part that most affects Outcasts – is the decree about managing the population. Apparently this was the most controversial part of the Laws. It was debated for several years until it finally passed in 2049. No one could argue that the world population was getting out of control, and most people were in favor of controlling it, although once the laws were passed, I'd bet a lot of citizens were sickened at how it would be done.

A law was passed setting the maximum population of the world at the 2049 level, or eleven billion people. The World Union is responsible for maintaining the level.

Ever since, the Population Control Council – the PCC – meets twice a year in Tel Aviv. The world population is easy to determine because of the chips. Except for the Outcasts – and no one knows exactly how many of us there are – the population number can be determined with one keystroke on the World Union's massive Galaxy computer storage system.

If the population is less than eleven billion people on the day the Council meets, nothing happens. I guess they have lunch, play a little golf, chat about soccer and cars, and go home. However, if the population is greater than eleven billion, then the control mechanism kicks in. Every legal person on Earth has a CHIP lottery number, a number that's auto-generated when the chip is inserted. The numbers range from one to five hundred.

The mechanics of it goes like this. Say the population is one hundred thousand people greater than eleven billion. A chip lottery number is drawn – say it's the number four – and the PCC's computer shows how many people in the world have the number four on their chip. If it's more than one hundred thousand, then every person with the number four is ordered to report to an EC camp. If it's less, then another number is drawn, and it keeps going until there are at least a hundred thousand people selected to be killed.

Euthanization Camps, ECs for short, are located in a lot of places around the world. The closest one to us is in Denver. The leaders tell everyone it's a painless, humane, fair and simple way to adjust the population back to eleven billion. Every person with the number that was drawn must report within two weeks to be "put to sleep," which I guess makes it sound better, like they were doing it to a dog or cat. As the people report to ECs and the job gets done, their chips deactivate. Since the government has the personal history for everyone who is supposed to show up, they know who didn't come in. Sometimes they can hide for a while, but their names and photos are shown on TV every night and bounty hunters are always on the lookout for them. So are the Enforcement Patrolmen, the ones who also search for Outcasts.

Logically, the lottery sounds like an effective way to control the population without singling anyone out. No one except the president and the four governors of the World Union are exempt, and they only get a pass while they are in office. But think about what it really does. It means taking your seven-year-old child, or your grandmother, or your husband or wife, to a Euthanization Camp if their number was selected. It's a horrible concept and there's really no way to hide your friends or relatives, since the government not only knows who and where the selected ones are, they also know who their families are. Aiding a person selected for euthanization, like harboring an Outcast, is a capital offense. The offender will die, but anyone who helped him or her dies too. It's a big deal, and a huge part of the World Union budget is spent on Enforcement Patrols worldwide.

As soon as euthanization was implemented, people began coming up with ways to outsmart the system, like they always seem to do in difficult situations. The only way to keep the government from knowing about you was if you never existed at all. You had to be born with no doctor or hospital involved, live in hiding forever, and be dependent on help from another who will lose his own life if you are discovered.

Why would people do this? Why would a parent hide a child for years? Why would others spend lots of wasted time trying to learn how to remove or disable a chip? As "big brother" as euthanization is, isn't it preferable to being on the run the rest of your life? Most people eventually said yes.

Although it's illegal to criticize the CHIP program, many people, including my parents, think it's despicable. Besides the horrible fact that you lose someone you love, the chip takes away your freedom of personal choice and goes against the American way of doing things. My mother has said those words a thousand times. It's interesting that even though there hasn't been a country called America in years, people still cling to that outdated sense of nationality – the "American way."

And it's far more personal than that to my family, just like it is to so many others who've been through the grief. For Mom and Dad, it meant kissing my dad's sister Julie goodbye at the bus station in Vail one day. Aunt Julie was living there three years ago when her number was drawn. Everyone cried and my father and mother screamed and ranted at the injustice of the system, but my aunt said she was at peace. She told my folks not to worry. They sat in the station with her and said goodbye when she boarded to go to Denver, the closest city where there was a Euthanization Camp. The government killed her two days later, according to the generic "Dear Friend or Relative of (insert name here)" email notification my father received from the Population Control Council.

And that's a major reason there are Outcasts.

CHAPTER NINE

We live in the Rocky Mountains twenty miles from the town of Leadville, NWA – the Northwest Americas region. We have a four-thousand-acre ranch that's been in my mom's family for two hundred years. The house was built in 1878, and there's an old fort in the woods a couple of miles away that the military used to keep an eye on the Indians back then. It was built in the 1850s and abandoned around 1900. In the past two hundred years a dense forest has grown up around it, so it's completely hidden now. I spent a lot of time as a kid playing there inside its mazes of tunnels and rooms, and my mother told me she did too. For the past couple of years, it's been my home.

Before my parents figured a way around it, food was frequently a problem. Every adult in the world has the same monthly food allotment – four hundred and fifty World points. Children have an allotment too; the amount is based on the child's age. There's none for me, of course, since I don't exist.

Once a week my parents drive into town and go to the government store to shop. Every store on the planet charges exactly the same prices, so if you could travel to the European sector, say London, which, of course, you can't, the food would be different, but you could get the same quantity for the points as you could here in NWA. My folks buy produce, bread, dairy products, Cokes, beer and wine – whatever they want for the week. Every couple of weeks they go to a restaurant for lunch before coming back home. That's Dad's little treat for Mom and she really looks forward to it. They tell me all about it when they get home. It sounds neat, sitting down and having someone serve you food instead of eating in your own house. I've only been to town twice and I've never been inside a restaurant. I don't know if it can ever happen, but it's a goal of mine to walk down the street and go wherever I want just like the chipped people.

You may wonder how three people live on an allotment intended for two. That's where living on a ranch comes in handy. I read that when marijuana was illegal a long time ago, people used to cultivate it in secret fields in the woods. That's what we do now, only it's not pot we're growing – it's food. My father cleared a couple of acres in the middle of the dense forest where the fort is. We walk in and out on foot, and we're careful not to leave a trail when we go up there to harvest. Just like the fort itself, the Enforcement Patrol will never find it unless someone tells them it's there.

Dad grows potatoes, corn, onions, tomatoes, beans and carrots. Some years the crops are better than others – our weather can be tough here – but we have plenty to eat all year round thanks to Mom's clever ways of preserving things. We have chickens, cattle and pigs too, so there's no shortage of meat, milk and eggs.

My dad keeps some of our farm animals near the house in a corral, but he keeps more up in a pasture far, far away from the house just in case the EP comes nosing around. We want them to think the allotment's almost all we have to depend on. It's not illegal to have a garden or to slaughter your own animals, but they'll reduce your allotment if they find out you have access to other food. When they make their occasional inspections, the EPs can see we have a few farm animals by the house, like any normal ranch would, and so far, they haven't said anything. That's good. Since my parents are harboring a seventeen-year-old Outcast, they need everything they can get.

CHAPTER TEN

As amazing as this might seem to people with a chip, until my parents recently disappeared, I'd only been off this ranch twice in seventeen years. My folks didn't have nearby neighbors or close friends, so it was easy for Mom to disguise her pregnancy. I was born in a room in the old fort my dad fixed up just for that purpose. According to the story I've heard a hundred times, he was the midwife, which I guess means he helped her have me. Everything apparently went fine and I lived in the main house most of the time as a child.

We don't have visitors except once or twice a year when the Enforcement Patrol comes out for their routine check. Back before the government outlawed purchases of security equipment, my dad installed sensors on the trees by our front gate a couple of miles down the road from the house. Whenever someone comes through, we get a loud ding. We also have wireless cameras inside and outside the house and we can view them from our phones and tablets. Usually when someone came, my mom and I would jump in the ATV and take off for the woods. Dad would honk the horn when it was safe to come back. Sometimes they'd do it the other way around; my father would take me and she'd tell the EPs he was working the cattle. Other times we used the hole. It wasn't as safe, but it never failed us.

Twice a month or so Dad goes to a meeting somewhere off the ranch. Some nights he's gone for a couple of hours but usually I'm asleep before he returns. He and Mom don't talk much about what the meetings are about. I think it's some kind of committee to help make sure people like us who live in remote areas have adequate security to protect their families and property.

In seventeen years we've only had two close calls and fortunately Dad was home both times. The first happened when I was six. We heard the ding and saw the familiar black Suburban heading up the mountain along our narrow dirt road.

"Run, you all. Go to the hole!" my dad said. Mom and I hurried to the back bedroom where I slept. She gave it a quick once-over to be sure it looked unused, like it always did except at night when I slept there. In my whole life I had never had toys or stuff like that because there wasn't supposed to be a child in this house. They couldn't risk someone showing up unannounced and finding something that would give me away. We went down the ladder in the closet and soon we were hidden.

It was scary in the hole, even though Mom was with me and we had practiced this over and over. Doing it for real was hard for a six-year-old. Mom held me tight in the darkness and I whimpered quietly as we waited and listened.

After it was all over, Dad told us what had happened. Two EPs came to the door and said they wanted to do a complete house search. "Just routine," they assured my dad. He said his heart sank as they began to look around. This wasn't normal; they were being way too thorough. He wished he'd gotten us out of the house this time, but there was no way around it now. It was too late.

Dad said the EP leader acted really cocky as he glanced at a sheet on his clipboard. "You have a wife, Melanie Dax. Where is she?"

"She's gone to town for supplies."

He consulted the sheet again. "You have one car, the Jeep that's sitting outside. How'd she get to town?"

"Her friend picked her up." He was getting nervous. He hoped the guys wouldn't ask which friend, since there weren't any. "What's this all about?"

"Purely routine. Why do you ask, Mr. Dax? You seem a little jittery. You don't have anything to hide, do you?" Dad said he shook his head and tried to act like things were fine.

My father said they looked pleased with themselves when they discovered the trapdoor in the back closet floor, pulled it open and saw the ladder leading down into darkness.

"What have we here? A hidden room?" the leader said with a smirk.

"It's an old root cellar. We store stuff down there. It's nothing special; a lot of these old houses have them."

"I'll be the judge of what's special," the EP said with a satisfied smile. "Let's take a look at what's down there in the secret room." The cop obviously believed he was onto something; my dad held his breath as the officers went down into the cellar.

Mom and I heard some noise, then the muffled sound of men talking in the cellar as we sat in the dark in our little hiding place. Dad waited upstairs and listened.

"God, this room stinks," one cop said as he got a big whiff of the musty odors that permeated the damp room. Wooden shelves lined the walls, full of dusty wine bottles and jars of vegetables and fruit my mom had canned.

"And it's a perfect place to hide things you don't want anyone to find," the cocky one answered as we heard loud banging. They pulled out a couple of wine bottles and were using them to poke the back of the shelving, trying to see if anything sounded hollow. Fortunately, Dad had planned ahead. First he lined the back of the shelf that moved with aluminum foil. Then he tacked on pink insulation, the kind you roll out in your attic. He layered it so the shelf we were behind sounded muffled – nice and solid – exactly like all the others did.

"Run the locator," the leader said. Each EP carried a sensor that went off when a chip was nearby. That was how they searched for people who were lost or in hiding. We heard them test it on themselves; it gave out a solid beep like a stud finder on a wall. We didn't hear anything for a couple of minutes; they were probably going around the room, aiming the sensor at each shelf and looking for a hidden area – the one we were sitting in. The aluminum foil worked perfectly just like it had when Dad tested it. It was the only thing he'd ever found that blocked the sensor from locating a chip. If the foil hadn't been there, they'd have found us, and that would have been the end for me. Instead they went away empty-handed and we never had another house search.

The other scary situation came when I was twelve, and it turned out to be far worse than the first one. It was winter and it was pouring rain with a forecast for overnight snow. I slept in the main house back then, and everybody was in pajamas, watching a video. Around nine we heard the ding of the sensors way down at the entrance to our ranch. Someone was coming up the road.

We all jumped up and my dad yelled, "Take Nate to the fort!" My mother looked out the front window just as a huge bolt of lightning lit up the sky like it was daytime.

"There's no one on the road, Dan," she said. "The lightning must have set the sensors off."

He joined her at the window. I walked over too, but he grabbed my arm. "Stay back! If someone's out there, we can't let them see you." He stepped away, drawing the curtains tightly shut, and we all sat on the couch. A few minutes later Mom got up again, pulled the curtains apart just a little and stifled a scream.

"Dan! There's someone on the porch!"

"There's no time now! Go to the hole!" my father whispered to me. "Melanie, go out on the back porch. If I don't come for you in five minutes, run to the woods!"

Other than for drills I'd never been in the hole alone. I ran into my walk-in closet, pulled aside a large box and went partway down the ladder. I stopped to reposition the box on top of the hole so no one would see it and went on down into the root cellar. I ran to the movable shelf and carefully swung it out so the cobwebbed jars wouldn't fall. I went into the small space that was behind it, pulled the shelf shut, hooked the lock and sat on a bench in the dark to wait. The only light came from the dim green dial of a clock.

I thought I heard muffled sounds from somewhere, but I wasn't sure. I figured my dad would come down and get me, but as the minutes ticked by, I began to get concerned. Dad always told me to never ever come out of the hole until he or Mom came to get me. I sat alone in the dark and got so scared that I decided to go check on things. I quietly pushed the shelf open and stepped into the root cellar. The sounds were louder now. My dad was yelling; I couldn't tell what he was saying, but I knew something must be really wrong. I was terrified, but I had to see if he was in trouble. I crept up into my closet. Now I heard the sound of something breaking, like there was a fight going on. I tiptoed to the living room door and saw a scrawny-looking man getting ready to hit my father with a baseball bat that Dad kept behind the front door. The man's back was to me. One of Dad's arms was hanging by his side. He was trying to ward off the blows, but I was sure he'd be dead before it was over. I glanced at the fireplace and saw a heavy brass poker. Without thinking, I grabbed it.

My father yelled, "No, Nate! Just run!"

The man turned to me and bellowed, "I'll kill you too!"

I swung the poker as hard as I could. I heard a cracking sound as it connected with the side of his head. He immediately fell to the ground and lay still.

"You won't kill anyone now," Dad said quietly. "You won't kill anyone anymore."

"Is he ... is he dead?"

Dad knelt down and felt the man's wrist. "Yes, son. You did the right thing. You saved our family. It was him or us. He was going to kill us and take our things."

I'd never seen a dead person before. He had a full black beard and a mustache and he was wearing overalls and a tattered red shirt. I felt acid rising up in my throat and knew I was about to throw up.

Dad was rubbing his arm and wincing in pain. "Are you okay?" I asked, concentrating on helping him instead of being scared.

"He may have dislocated my shoulder, but I don't think he broke anything. He grabbed the damned baseball bat before I knew what he was up to and started hitting me with it. That's when you came to the rescue," he said, putting his good arm around me. "He would have killed me if you hadn't. Now run to the woods and get your mom."

I called her name, and she came out of the trees, soaking wet, shivering from the cold and crying. We hugged and then we ran through the rain back to the house. Dad had brought a tarp into the living room. It was lying open on the floor next to the man's body. He told her what had happened and said, "Help me pull him onto the tarp." We did, and Dad wrapped him up and dragged him out onto the porch. The storm was easing up a little now, but it was still raining steadily.

Mom broke down in convulsive sobs. "God, Dan. What happened? What are we going to do with him? Unless he was an Outcast, they'll come looking for him." When I heard her words, I began to cry.

Dad always knew what to do. "I know that. I have to get him away from here. As far from town as we live, they might not come for days, if ever. But they could come tonight."

"Tonight? What if ..."

"Melanie, I know you're upset, but this isn't helping." He glanced in my direction. "It's not helping Nate either. We have to be strong. I need to get the body as far away from here as possible. Come help me get it into the pickup and I'll take things from there." Dad struggled to help pull the tarp and winced in pain as he tried to use both his arms.

Mom said, "I should go with you. You're in no shape to do this alone." Selfishly I hoped Dad wouldn't let her go. I was scared enough already. What if this guy had a friend hiding somewhere? I'd protect Mom, but I didn't want to have to stay by myself.

"I can handle it, and it's better if you stay and clean up." He left a few minutes later and didn't come back for a long time. Mom scrubbed up a few bloodstains that were on the living room floor, and I straightened the furniture and the rug.

Suddenly I was overwhelmed with fear, guilt and the sheer horror of what I'd done. I began to cry – slowly at first, then like I would never stop.

"I killed a man. I killed a man, Mom," I sobbed. "They're going to euthanize me!"

She grabbed me and wrapped her arms around me tightly, rocking me like I was a baby. "Shh. Don't do this to yourself. Your father's a good man and so are you. Neither one of you did anything wrong. Dan will handle this, and we're not going to let anything happen to you. He was a bad man and you did what you needed to do. No one will ever take you, I promise." We sat like that for a while. Even though I was twelve, it felt really good having her hold me like that, and soon I felt better.

"What did you mean when you told Dad that unless that guy was an Outcast they'll come looking for him?"

"Because of his chip. When someone dies, the chip deactivates within an hour or two. At the end it sends a final signal to the nearest Enforcement Patrol office so they can tell where the body is. If it's at a hospital or a nursing home – someplace where people die – they ignore it. If the signal is somewhere else, maybe in a house or the woods, they sometimes follow up to see what happened. It could have been a car wreck or a house fire – people might need help.

"Nowadays they usually don't come looking because nearly all deaths turn out to be routine and they have other things to do. But the point is, they *can*. If we hid his body here on our property and they found it, we would be in serious trouble."

"Where did Dad take him?"

"I don't know, son. I'm so sorry about this. I've worried for years about something bad happening way out here. We're so far from other people, but there's nothing we can do –"

I interrupted. "You have to live out here because of me," I said bitterly. "All this wouldn't have happened except for me." It was the truth, even though nobody ever talked about it. Life would have been so much easier if I were normal. Or dead.

"No! We ... well, yes, of course, you're partly right, but we love living out here in the mountains, where it's usually quiet and peaceful. This had nothing to do with you and it could have happened even if we lived in a house in town. How about for now we stop worrying about things we don't know about and wait for your father to tell us what really happened."

It was after eleven when we heard the ding of the sensor. I looked out to see headlights coming up the road. They blinked off and on a couple of times, our prearranged signal.

"It's Dad," I yelled, feeling a rush of relief.

He walked in completely soaked and he looked really tired. He went straight to the bedroom and I heard the shower going for a long time. He came out in his bathrobe and sat at the table.

"Do you want to talk about it?" Mom asked hesitantly.

"No, but I guess I have to. I threw him down the ravine at the top of Johnson's Pass."

"That was a good idea."

We talked with Dad for a while, and it was the most surreal conversation I'd ever heard. He'd committed a crime that was punishable by death, and so had I. But he was talking about it like he'd taken out the garbage.

Dad said it was a good thing our pickup was four-wheel drive. Johnson's Pass was miles from our house, at the top of a twelve-thousand-foot mountain where there was snow all year around. In fact, it had been coming down hard up there tonight, he said, and that would erase the tire tracks. At the very top there was a mountain on one side of the narrow two-lane road and a steep canyon on the other that dropped half a mile to a river. Even though it was April, the ravine would be full of snow for weeks longer. Dad said the road to the pass hadn't been opened yet because it wasn't plowed, but his pickup made it with no problem. Dad had thrown the man's body down the ravine, and it might not be found for months.

"Do you want some coffee?" Mom asked him.

Dad shook his head. "I'm exhausted, and I'm sure you both are too. My arm's killing me, although I don't think it's broken. I need something for the pain and some sleep. We can talk more in the morning. Nate, I want to tell you how proud I am of you. You saved my life and probably Mom's too. That guy was going to kill us. He was crazy and he was drugged up or something. You're my hero, son. You did a good thing tonight."

I ran to him and hugged him tight. He wasn't much of a hugger; I couldn't recall many other times he had held me, but he did it for a long time. When I heard a little sniffle, I pulled back and saw tears flowing down his face. I'd never seen my dad cry and it made me cry too. It also made me feel really good inside that I had saved our family and made my father proud. In bed I forced myself to stop thinking about it, and finally I fell asleep.

Dad was sitting at the kitchen table with his coffee when I walked in. Bright sunshine cascaded through the windows. Like up in the pass, snow had fallen here too during the night. I always loved to see the blanket of white stretching as far as you could see, all the way up into the mountains.

"Morning, sunshine," my mom said like she always did.

I sat next to Dad and asked him how his arm was.

"Better, but look at these bruises." He pulled up his sleeve. They looked awful. "I don't think I'm going to be in a wrestling match any time soon, but at least it's not broken."

Mom cooked breakfast as he told us more about what had happened.

"This morning before you got up, I went down to the gate and found an old pickup parked in the woods. He obviously walked up to the house in the storm. He must have been totally strung out. There was a bag of icy-looking stuff – meth, I figure - on the seat. I also found this." He pulled a prescription bottle from his pocket. "It's for hydrocodone."

Dad saw my quizzical look. "It's a narcotic prescribed for pain. There's a woman's name on the bottle. No idea who she is; maybe he stole the pills from her. Who knows? The guy was acting crazy from the minute I opened the door. He barged in and demanded to use the phone. He said his truck broke down. Before I could react, he rushed me and grabbed the baseball bat. He hit me on the shoulder and it hurt like hell. I almost passed out, but I was afraid he'd kill you both if I did."

Mom put plates on the table. The smell of over-easy eggs, crisp bacon and French toast – Dad's favorite breakfast – made my stomach rumble in anticipation.

"Enough talk," Dad said as he picked up his knife and fork. "Look at this feast! I'm ravenous!"

Later on he and I went down to see the pickup. It was an old Ford from before the war that ran on gasoline. You didn't see many of those anymore, and this one was in really bad shape. I rummaged through the glove box and found a half-empty pack of cigarettes and a registration card that said the pickup belonged to some guy in Wyoming. I showed it to Dad – there was no way to know if the name on the card was the guy I'd killed, and Dad said it didn't matter anyway if the pickup was stolen, because we were going to get rid of it.

There were two empty half-pint whisky bottles under the driver's seat along with a filthy, oil-stained rag and a little square foil package.

"What's this?" I asked, showing it to my father.

"It's a condom," he replied, telling me what a condom was used for. I made a face at the thought of that scuzzy guy needing a condom.

Dad laughed out loud when I told him I was twelve years old and in all my home-schooling Mom had never mentioned a condom. "I guess she thought you didn't need that kind of education," he said with a wink.

We took everything out of the pickup and then Dad explained what we were going to do. I drove the Jeep down to the gate and followed Dad as he took the old pickup along back roads for miles. At last we turned off into a field and went into the forest. We hadn't passed a house in ten miles and we were about as far from civilization as you could get. He got out, removed the license plates, took a five-gallon gas can from the bed of the truck and poured it everywhere.

I pulled our Jeep back and Dad made a Molotov cocktail from a Coke bottle filled with gasoline and a rag in the top for a wick. He lit it, tossed it through the front window and ran like hell. He made it to the Jeep as there was a huge *whump* sound and a column of fire shot into the air.

Given how far away from civilization the fire was, even when people saw it, Dad figured no one would check it out. If someone did, the truck would be burned beyond recognition by the time they got there.

We drove back home and, like the body up in Johnson's Pass, we never heard anything else about the truck.

CHAPTER ELEVEN

One day six months ago my parents made their usual trip to Leadville to buy supplies and have lunch in town. They were always home by three, but today they were hours late. By the time the sun dropped behind the mountains, I knew something was terribly wrong, but I had no idea what to do. Should I call Dad's phone? Or go to town? If the EP had my folks, they'd have the phone too, so it would be dangerous to make a call. They might force my parents to tell them who was calling. That wouldn't work, but I knew what would. I used the location feature on the house iPhone to see where Dad's was.

The phone was near the intersection of Sixth and Harrison in downtown Leadville. Harrison was the main street and the map showed there were several restaurants nearby. There was also another place – the Lake County Sheriff's Office, where the Enforcement Patrol was headquartered. If the phone was there, my parents probably were too. There was no way I could call Dad's number. It was too risky.

There was no choice now but to go to town, which was a terrifying thought. It had been years since I'd been there and it was twenty miles away. I had no idea if they'd built guard towers or checkpoints, how many EPs there were – any of that. Leadville was small – it was the only town in Lake County and had less than two thousand year-round residents. Still, I had no idea what to expect. I went to Google's EarthSat program and saw that it was the same little place as when my dad had sneaked me into town four years ago just so I could see it.

Was it better to go to town at night or wait until morning? What if there was a curfew? What if I was stopped? It would only take a second for someone to find out I was an Outcast, and my search for my parents would be over. But if I waited until tomorrow, I'd be there in broad daylight. Was it better to wait because there would be more people around and more activity on the streets? If I stayed away from stores, ATMs and point-of-purchase machines and didn't run into the cops, I should be okay.

At nine p.m. I decided I had to go, but I didn't know how to do it. I could ride my horse Dixie, but it would take a couple of hours each way, and what would I do with her once I got to town? It was better to take the ATV. I checked the battery; Dad always kept things fully charged. I grabbed the extra set of Jeep keys and the house phone and I was on my way. I hoped there wouldn't be traffic on the main highway, and I was relieved to see it was almost deserted this time of night. Every time I saw headlights behind me or ahead, I pulled off the road far enough to hide until they went by. Just over an hour after I left home, I pulled into the outskirts of Leadville, parked the ATV behind a boarded-up store and went along side streets about a mile to Sixth and Harrison.

There it was. There were only two vehicles in the entire block, and both were parked in front of the Silver Dollar Café. I stood in the shadows across the street and watched a man and woman come out of the restaurant, turn off the lights and lock the door. They got into a pickup next to Dad's Jeep and drove away. Other than the lights from the sheriff's office three doors down, the only illumination was a streetlight at the corner a hundred feet away. The Jeep was shrouded in darkness and the block was quiet.

Although I had brought the spare keys just in case, I knew the Jeep would be unlocked. It always was. These days with penalties so severe, crime was almost nonexistent and nobody locked cars anymore. Dad always tossed his keys on the floorboard. I opened the driver's door, reached inside, flicked off the dome light, closed the door again and ran across the street. I hunkered down for five minutes to make sure no one had seen me.

I hadn't really thought about what I'd do if I found the Jeep. Regardless of whatever had happened to Mom and Dad, I had to take it. Whatever was going on, it didn't look like my parents were going to just show up and drive it home, and I needed the transportation.

Dad's phone was lying in the console. I glanced at the backseat. My heart sank when I saw sacks of groceries and our blue Igloo cooler. It was pretty obvious what had happened. They'd bought their supplies and then stopped at the restaurant for lunch. Sometime right after that they disappeared.

I drove to where I'd left the ATV. It had a front tow bar that wasn't intended for long-distance hauling, but if I took it easy, things would be fine. I hooked it up and headed home. As I crept along the highway, I had I had some time to think.

I felt as though I was being bombarded with terrifying situations. Something I'd always feared - both my parents dying at the same time and leaving me alone - had come to pass in a way. They weren't dead - I had to keep believing that. But I was alone, ill-prepared to go out in public but having to do it to find them. I was afraid whatever was happening was because of me. My parents were just regular people but the state would call them criminals if the cops knew I was at the ranch. Had they found out? What if it wasn't the cops at all? What if they'd been kidnapped or killed? It hardly happened - there hadn't been a violent crime in Leadville in twenty-five years. But what if it had? Something was seriously wrong.

By the time I got to the turnoff, it was a little after midnight and I had created a plan. If Dad and Mom came home, I could undo everything, but for now I had to prepare for life on my own. They were gone and I couldn't even ask anyone to help me find them.

The fort – the place where I have lived since I was fifteen – is two miles from our house. Dad and I worked on it a few years ago, clearing out the tunnels and opening up underground rooms that had served as storage areas for the military back in the 1800s. We waterproofed it, installed

49

running water, hung solar panels for power and camouflaged the entrance so perfectly no one would ever notice it. I had a bedroom, a bathroom with a shower, sink and a toilet that tied into a septic system in the woods. There was a storeroom where we stocked up a two-year supply of emergency food and drinking water. I was self-sufficient, but I was growing more and more lonely and concerned about my future – and my parents' too.

I stayed up all that night working because I might have very little time. I made a dozen trips in the ATV, hauling things I'd need from the house to the fort. All of my personal stuff was already up there, but now I had to plan for being alone. I opened the secret place in the floor of our barn and took all Dad's guns and ammunition. I'd spend years in prison if they caught me with a gun, I thought to myself. Then I laughed. I guess being euthanized as an Outcast would come first, so I wouldn't be in jail after all.

I loaded Dad's tools and equipment, almost all the food and my mother's preserved fruits and vegetables from the cellar. There was a freezer in the fort and I packed it full, leaving just enough in the house so it looked like Dad and Mom were still living there. If the cops had my parents, they'd go there, and I didn't want anything to look suspicious.

At daybreak Dixie and I moved most of the cattle to the western pasture on the other side of the mountain, miles away from the house. I was lucky that it was already April; they'd be fine up there for months before I had to worry about feeding them. This would all be over by then. I had to believe that. Maybe it'd even be over really soon, but in my heart I knew better.

There was a small corral behind the fort and I left Dixie there while I drove the ATV back down to the house for a final run. Then I spent the rest of the day organizing what I'd brought up. Every hour I'd take a break and drive to the ridge. From the trees I looked at our house about a half mile down the valley. So far there was no activity.

I had decided what I would do if I didn't hear from my parents by dark, and finally it was time. After the sun set, I moved the ATV up to the fort, walked back and drove to town in the Jeep. I parked it behind the same vacant building where I'd left the four-wheeler last night and walked to the café. I stood in the shadows across the street and watched the man and woman wiping down tables, arranging chairs and mopping the floor. Just like last night, they walked out a few minutes before ten.

They went toward their pickup and I put myself in the greatest danger of my entire life. I walked across the empty street toward them.

"Hello." I used as friendly a voice as I could muster. All I needed was for one of them to panic, since we were a hundred feet away from the brightly lit headquarters of the Enforcement Patrol.

The man jerked around. I saw him tense up, then relax as he saw a skinny teenager in front of him.

"What do you want?"

"It's about my friends. I can't find them. Can I ask you a question?"

Keeping a close eye on me, his wife climbed into the truck.

The man was curious about what I wanted. "Sure, kid. What do you want to know?"

"Dan and Melanie Dax. Do you know them?"

Although it was almost hidden by the shadows, his face changed just a little. His eyes clouded over for a moment and he shot a glance at his wife.

"Sure. They were here for lunch yesterday. They come every two weeks. What about them?"

"He's my uncle – my dad's brother. I was supposed to spend a few days with them, but when I got to their house yesterday, they weren't there, and they didn't come home last night either. I remember Da ... *Dan* saying he went to town every so often for supplies, and I just wondered if you saw them. So they were here yesterday? Do you know where –"

The man interrupted me, his words harsh and clipped. "Dan and Melanie's Jeep was sitting here last night when we closed up. Right here next to our truck. Did you take it?"

"Uh, no, sir," I stammered with a gulp. "I wasn't ... I wasn't here last night. Where do you think it went?"

His wife suddenly piped up. "The EP took it, Henry. Isn't that obvious after what happened with them?"

The EP!

"Shut up! I'll handle this," he snapped. "Son, I'm going to take you right down here to the sheriff's office. I think they can help you out." He reached out and grabbed my arm, but I jerked it back.

"Does the EP have them?" I said more loudly than I intended as I backed away into the street.

Suddenly he shouted, "Sheriff! Come out here, Sheriff!"

I heard a jingle, the sound of a door opening nearby. I started to run as fast as I could, keeping to the shadows. As I turned the corner, I heard the man yell, "There's a boy – sixteen maybe. Tall. He was asking questions about the Dax couple. He ran that way!"

As I zigzagged block to block towards where I'd left the Jeep, I heard the sounds of powerful engines getting louder and louder. They were the Enforcement Patrol's Suburbans and they were after me.

I turned a corner just as headlights swept into the other end of the block. I darted into a pitch-black alley, hoping they hadn't seen me. I ran halfway down and dropped behind a dumpster. A vehicle crept by and I saw a bright beam of light sweep slowly back and forth, illuminating the alley like it was daytime. I hunkered down even more until it was dark again. They were gone.

When I reached the old building where I'd left the Jeep, I moved stealthily to a place two hundred feet away where I could watch it. It made no sense to start driving when there was almost no traffic anywhere around: I'd be a sitting duck. My plan was to give it an hour, then assess my situation. Hopefully they'd give up on me by then.

I stood up occasionally to ease my aching joints. After forty-five quiet, uneventful minutes, I decided it was okay to move. I stood but immediately ducked back down as I heard the crackle of a two-way radio. A Suburban slowly rolled into the parking lot where the Jeep sat. It drove up close and I saw a beam light up its license tag. One of the cops in the car read the numbers aloud.

The radio crackled again. "It's registered to Daniel Dax. Report your location and stay away from the vehicle. I'm sending backup."

Damn.

Within minutes another black SUV pulled into the lot. I was a safe distance from them, so I stayed put. Whatever had happened to my parents, this was all part of it.

Obeying the order to stay clear, all four officers looked through the Jeep's windows with flashlights until another man arrived and began swabbing for fingerprints.

"How the hell did it get here?" one of the patrolmen asked. "Henry said it was parked in front of his café when they closed last night, but this morning it was gone. How'd that happen? Who took it?"

"That kid, maybe? That kid that asked Henry about the Dax couple?"

I knew I was in big trouble, the least of which was that I'd lost my means of transportation back to the ranch. The good news was they could check for fingerprints all day long. They'd find mine everywhere, but I didn't exist. The problem was they knew there was a kid out there asking questions about Dan and Melanie Dax, a kid who'd said he was staying at the ranch. I had made a huge mistake. They'd come looking for me next.

Whatever was going on, it was a really big deal to the cops. My parents had to be in serious danger. I could feel it, and I had to find them fast.

CHAPTER TWELVE

Shortly there were cops swarming all over the Jeep. The fingerprint guy swabbed the steering wheel, gearshift and dashboard. Next he did the door handles inside and out, and I heard him say he got lots of good prints.

I heard them put out an APB – an all-points bulletin – on me, but they had a poor description. Every cop in a hundred-mile radius was instructed to watch for a white male wearing a baseball cap, a dark T-shirt and dark shorts, five-nine to six feet tall and thin, fifteen to eighteen years old. Perfect. That description would fit nearly every male teenager in SWA.

My original plan had been to talk to the restaurant owner and be back at the ranch before midnight. I had gotten no sleep last night, and this one was turning out exactly the same way. I was exhausted and my legs were cramping. I snaked my way noiselessly around a corner of the building and stood up to stretch. I was wondering how I'd get home when I heard the radio crackle again. They were sending officers to the ranch. I was glad I'd spent the last twenty-four hours preparing. There was nothing left in the house that I needed except a lifetime of memories. And there nothing I could do about those.

I'd heard enough. It was after two and the cops were still at work. They'd strung crime scene tape all around the Jeep. I couldn't use it now anyway since it was hotter than a firecracker. I crept away; since I was already on the edge of town, I began to walk along the highway that led home. After a half mile or so I stopped, went out into a field full of tall cornstalks, dropped to the ground and fell asleep in seconds.

A loud cackle woke me up. It took a second to recall where I was. I noticed a huge black crow thirty feet away,

55

pecking at an ear of corn lying on the ground. He couldn't have cared less about me. I glanced at my watch; it was almost nine a.m.

I sat up and peeked out of the corn rows. There was a lot of morning traffic on the highway and I saw a dilapidated, unpainted house a hundred feet away. A barn nearby was in the same condition. Two cars were up on blocks, a refrigerator with no door stood on the porch, and a thousand pieces of rusty junk and trash littered the yard. The place looked abandoned, but it wasn't. There was a woman in a long dress, hanging clothes on a line stretched between two trees in the backyard. It was perfect.

She went into the house. A few minutes later she came out the front door and began to sweep the porch. I idly wondered how she could think sweeping would help anything in this awful mess. I ran to the clothesline, grabbed a long-sleeved work shirt and a pair of jeans and went back to the cornfield. The whole move took less than twenty seconds and she never saw a thing.

The clothes fit surprisingly well. They were damp, but they would do. I left my cap, T-shirt and shorts in the field. They'd be found when the corn was harvested, but that would be a while. By then it wouldn't matter. This had to be over by then.

I had to hitch a ride. It was risky, but I found a place where I could hide in some trees until I saw a truck coming. I stepped to the side of the road and put out my thumb; hitchhikers weren't that uncommon nowadays and I hoped truckers might not have heard that the police were looking for a kid like me.

The first truck flew past with a blast of his air horn, but another was right behind it. That driver slowed to check me out and then I heard the hiss of brakes as he eased the semi to the shoulder. The name on the trailer said CONSOLIDATED FOODS.

"Hop in, kid." He was a black guy in his thirties with a big, friendly smile. "Where you headed?" he asked as we pulled back onto the highway.

"Up north on 24 about halfway to Minturn," I replied noncommittally. "I'm going to see my grandparents. Where are you going?"

"I'm on my weekly run from Aspen to Vail. I handle all the restaurants in the resort areas. You know, food and stuff. I'm Bill. What's your name?"

I hesitated a second and hoped he didn't notice. "Travis. Travis Coates." Travis was a character in *Old Yeller*, my favorite book when I was growing up. It would be an easy name for me to remember.

"Your folks live in Leadville?"

"Yeah, just outside of town near where you picked me up. Where do you live?"

He laughed. "Any more it seems like I live in this truck. I'm pulling double shifts, trying to make some extra World points so my girlfriend and I can get married. We live far enough outside Vail that it's not a tourist area. Man, the rent in these ski areas can be crazy during the season."

We didn't have far to go and I had already decided where I'd get out. It was a couple of miles past the turnoff to my house, but it was safer that way. I looked out the window and began wondering how I'd ever find my parents.

"Travis?"

"Travis?"

Dammit! That's my name!

"I'm sorry. I guess I was daydreaming."

"They're looking for a boy your age, you know. I heard it on the radio."

I gulped. "Really? For what?"

"They're not saying, but they're offering five thousand World points to whoever turns him in. Man, that'd get me a long way toward that wedding we're planning. Know what I mean? Sometimes you can get a little piece of luck just dropped right into your lap."

"Yup," I replied with an attempt at a laugh. "That's a lot of points. I bet he's a murderer or something."

"Maybe he's just a kid who's on the run and has something to hide. You never know these days."

I didn't say anything, but I was getting more scared by the minute. What if he wouldn't let me out? What if he took me to the EP office in the next town?

When we passed the turnoff, I was glad there wasn't a black Suburban sitting there. I'd half expected it, and just because I didn't see one didn't mean they weren't at the house. After a couple of minutes I said, "You can drop me here. They live just down there." I pointed to a dirt road that led to a house a mile away.

"I can take you up to the house," Bill said. "Let's make sure they're home."

"Thanks, but there's no need. They're always home and they're expecting me." I said all that in a breathless rush.

For a second he kept going. I held my breath, praying he'd start slowing down. Just as I was thinking how hard it would be to open the door and roll out while the truck was moving, he pulled over, stopping on the shoulder with a squeal.

Bill looked me in the eyes and patted my shoulder. "I'm giving you a break, kid. You seem like a nice guy. Good luck."

"Thank you, sir," I replied with evident relief. "Please don't ..."

He gave me one last big smile. "Get outta here. Go do what you gotta do. I've got half a dozen restaurants up the road waiting for me. I never saw you."

CHAPTER THIRTEEN

As soon as the truck was out of sight, I started walking back, staying in the trees as much as I could. If Bill had already heard about the reward for me, others would have too. A kid walking alone on the road could be the one the cops wanted, and there was enough reward to make me radioactive.

Once I turned off Highway 24, it was a mile to our property line and two more to the house. I stopped at our fence to look around. I didn't see any vehicles, but I knew they'd be there somewhere. I skirted the motion detectors in the trees just ahead so they wouldn't go off. Instead I went to the tree line that ringed our pasture and stayed hidden as I approached the house.

I heard them before I saw them. I picked up the now-familiar crackle of a radio. They were parked behind the house – three Suburbans and a van with the words CRIME SCENE INVESTIGATOR running down its side. A couple of men stood around smoking cigarettes under a tree. I could hear banging and thuds coming from inside. Someone was going through the place room by room, and it sounded like they were tearing the walls apart.

Were they looking for me? Had my parents told them?

I wouldn't accept that. Unless they tortured them – *but in today's civilized world the cops didn't torture prisoners, did they?* – my parents wouldn't have voluntarily given me up. But what if they'd used truth serum? I'd read novels about hostages being injected with thiopental to make them talk. Did the World Union do stuff like that? I had no idea.

If they weren't looking for me, then what were they doing here? And where were my parents? Already dead? Maybe. The old days when you had a trial, an appeal, another appeal and four or five stays of execution were long gone. The government was very efficient at rapid euthanization once you were found guilty. One or two days – that's all it took.

I wouldn't accept that either. I wouldn't stop looking until I had proof one way or the other.

I watched the EPs for hours. They brought furniture and clothes out of the house and tossed them into our backyard. They pulled Dad's tractor and most of the equipment out of the barn. They didn't see the hidden space where Dad had put the guns and ammo; it didn't matter anyway because thanks to me it was empty now.

Pretty soon a man with a stock trailer showed up and took away six cows and Dad's horse that I'd left grazing in the pasture next to the house. I had put them there on purpose; it would be very unusual not to find livestock at a ranch, so I left a few. Mom's horse and mine, twenty-six cows and forty pigs were corralled far away, and our chickens were safely in the fort.

Speaking of which, my biggest fear this very minute was that they'd send a party to search the rest of the ranch. If the EPs found the fort, it could be the end. Even though I lived underground in the warren of rooms and tunnels, the solar panels were a dead giveaway that there was activity somewhere. A patrolman hell-bent on finding me could absolutely do it if he got this far. If they found my stuff, I'd be on my own with nothing at all. If I was there too, it would be over for me. If Mom and Dad didn't turn up soon, I had to leave the ranch, but I hadn't given any thought to where I'd go next.

Gray clouds began rolling in off the mountains and the wind picked up. Even the long-sleeved shirt I'd stolen wasn't enough to keep me warm. I shivered as the temperature quickly dropped.

"Rain's a-comin'," one of the officers shouted to the others. "Let's wrap it up for today."

Fifteen minutes later they were gone. I gave it a little more time for safety's sake; then I ran to the house just as the skies opened up with an enormous crack of bolt lightning and a rolling rumble of thunder that reminded me of what my mother used to say. That was the sound of the gods bowling. That thought made me sad. I missed my parents even though I tried not to dwell on it. I needed to focus.

It rained furiously as I walked through the ruin that had been our home, tears streaming down my face. They'd torn the kitchen cabinets off the walls and dumped everything from the drawers and cabinets onto the floor. They'd pulled the stuffing out of the chairs and ripped sheetrock off the walls. The floorboards in the living room had been pried up and tossed aside.

Just for kicks I went down to the hole. There was no question they'd gone into the root cellar, but I pulled aside the shelf and saw that the area behind it was undisturbed. They'd missed it, and that was good. Finding it would have raised questions about why someone had a secret hiding place under their house.

I checked the phone to be sure the wireless cameras were transmitting properly. Everything was fine. I could be up at the fort and still know when the EP came back. I began to gather more things I might need. Earlier I had left everything in the kitchen drawers so it would look normal, like my parents had just gone to town, which actually was true. Now that the kitchen floor was littered with knives, pots, pans and utensils, I gathered a lot of things up. The patrolmen would never miss them since they'd tossed everything in a pile as they searched for ... something.

I couldn't get the questions out of my mind. What was it? What *were* they actually looking for? What the hell was going on? Why the need for all this damage? My dad and mother were simple ranchers. Weren't they? Sure, they harbored an Outcast, but the wanton destruction laid out before me didn't jibe with someone searching for a fugitive. Whatever was happening, it was becoming more and more likely that my parents weren't coming back. What did the

Enforcement Patrol think they were hiding? And *were* they hiding something?

Were there secrets in this house even I didn't know about?

CHAPTER FOURTEEN

I needed a vehicle. If I was going to make this work long-term, I had to be able to get back and forth to town without arousing suspicion. A kid riding a horse or driving an ATV on the highway was not the solution.

That night I walked to town. The twenty-mile trip took nearly six hours and I was tired, but things had gone smoothly. I was in good physical shape from working at the ranch and I didn't plan to walk back, so this was the only way. I left around 8:45, as soon after sunset as I thought it was safe. I stopped for a rest once and drank lots of water from the bottles I carried in my backpack. When I was near Leadville I started watching the houses along the road until I found what I needed. An ancient pickup was sitting in a field near an abandoned house. I took a screwdriver out of my pack and in thirty seconds I had removed its license tags. Fifteen minutes later I was in town.

By 2:30 I had scouted out four car lots. The first three had nice used cars and lots of lighting. I was looking for just the opposite. And soon I saw it. Danny's Cars. Buy here, finance here. Bad credit or no credit? No problem!

The clock on the bank building several blocks away chimed three times as I sat cross-legged and motionless in the bushes across the street from Danny's dimly lit lot. When I decided it was safe, I walked over. There were maybe two dozen cars and trucks sitting on an unfenced gravel lot. I looked around until I found the vehicle I wanted, an ancient Chevy Trailblazer sitting at the back of the lot. It was dusty and dirty and had a dent in the rear bumper. It was perfect. I walked to a wooden shack that said "Office." I hoped Danny cared as little about security as he did about appearance.

The door was locked, as I'd expected. There were four windows, one of which was open just a crack. It slid up with a groan and I ducked into the shadows to wait. Everything remained quiet, so I climbed through and found a wooden board affixed to a wall. It was loaded with keys and it took me only a couple of minutes to locate the right set. I went back through the window and lowered it.

The Trailblazer's battery was low, but I only had twenty miles to drive. Charging up in town would actually be harder and take longer than stealing the car, and I wanted to get out of town fast. I could recharge at the ranch. Our bank of solar panels kept all our stuff running without a problem.

I kept the lights off as I backed out of the lot and pulled onto the street. I drove a couple of blocks to make sure the SUV would run; then I turned off the ignition, got out and swapped its plates for the ones I'd taken from the old truck. That might or might not buy me a little time once Danny figured out one of his precious autos was missing. At least the plates on it now weren't those of a stolen car.

The Chevy coughed and sputtered now and then. That could be a big problem, or it could simply be that the Trailblazer hadn't been off the lot in a while. Things sounded better the longer I drove. Before sunup my new ride was safely tucked into a grove of trees half a mile from the fort, the old plates were at the bottom of a pond and I was sound asleep.

In my underground bedroom I slept through the first dings. Around ten another one jolted me awake. I looked at the outside cameras and saw three SUVs at the house. The camera in Dad's office showed two men carrying out his tablet device and monitor.

Seeing his tablet reminded me of something I'd totally forgotten about. What he had stored might give me a clue as to what was going on. The tablet itself was useless to the cops because for many years there had been no long-term storage on tablet devices. A tablet would retain anything you were working on, but when it was inactive for a while, everything went away. It was all still there in the Galaxy, so all you had to do was recall your last session, but the device itself had no retention capability.

When the World Union nationalized Microsoft in 2054, they commissioned its engineers to create a new, massive storage and sharing entity called the Galaxy. Years ago there was the cloud, but after the Twenty-Minute War, the world lost a lot of infrastructure. It didn't take long before things began to grow exponentially again, like they always do in technology.

The Galaxy was unfathomably large – over a billion domegemegrottebytes – and it was all free since the government owned it. Surprisingly in a time when chips kept track of people worldwide, the World Union had insisted on more privacy and security for individual and corporate users of the Galaxy. In my present situation this was a very good thing.

Like most people my age – Outcasts or not – I'm totally techie. My dad taught me about technology, gave me all the passwords and made sure I understood everything he'd installed here at the ranch.

I picked up my tablet – actually Dad's old one since I can't register a device – and instructed it to take me to the Galaxy. I linked to Dad's personal account in Galaxy, entered his password and backed it up to mine. Then I deleted his account. Now even if they hacked in, there was nothing to access.

I began to feel the same light-headed dizziness that had hit me now and then for the past three days. I had to admit that I was totally overwhelmed. In seventy-two hours I'd gone from the normal routine of daily life to a crazy hodgepodge of conflicts, questions, doubts and fears. I was a car thief, my parents were missing and possibly dead, people were tearing the hell out of my house looking for God knew what, and I was even more of a fugitive now than before when I was just an Outcast. Frankly I didn't know what my situation was, because I still didn't know what was happening or why.

What I needed was fresh air and some time to think at the place Dad and I always went to clear our heads. I saddled Dixie and we rode to Fremont Pass. Up here at eleven thousand feet the wind was strong and it was crisp and cool. Billowy white clouds seemed so close I could touch them. I was maybe six the first time Dad brought me up here – the top of the world, he always called it – and from that moment I had loved this place as much as he did. But now he was gone and I felt totally alone. Right now, for the first time since all this started, I wanted to pray.

Was there a God? I always thought so; we weren't a religious family and obviously I'd never been inside a church, but when you were with your best friend – a fine horse named Dixie – looking out over a sight like the one that lay before me, you had to believe in a higher being. If he was out there somewhere, I sure hoped he'd give me a hand. I bowed my head and asked for answers, for guidance, for protection for my parents and me, and for help to understand what to do next.

I opened my eyes and considered where everything stood in my life. Dad had prepared me well. I was as self-sufficient as any Eagle Scout could be. I was comfortable in the wild, I could cook, build stuff, work on cars and farm equipment, slaughter a cow or a pig, and I was an excellent marksman. *Thanks, Dad,* I thought, praying to God I could tell him that face-to-face once this was over.

I took in the beauty stretching in every direction. On one side there was the old Climax Mine, a large molybdenum mine that was abandoned in the 2060s. I saw the river meandering through lush green valleys and I looked at our ranch two thousand feet below. There was movement; I pulled out my binoculars and watched the men getting into the Suburbans. It was only one p.m. Maybe they were all finished. I hoped so. What they did there made me physically sick to my stomach. I saw the vehicles pull away from the house and head down the road.

I turned and focused the glasses on the place where the fort stood. It was completely hidden within a vast forest of pine and cedar, and even though I knew exactly where to look, I couldn't see anything. I was more worried about the solar panels. I couldn't see them either, and that was perfect.

Dad had installed them high in the treetops, and he'd camouflaged them so they wouldn't reflect. Both my hideout and its source of power were well hidden.

I noticed movement again – people were running away from the house. I swung the field glasses back around and saw that the SUVs hadn't left at all – the men just moved them a few hundred feet down the road. Now there were more men running out of the barn and suddenly two huge fireballs belched flames into the sky. Within seconds the smoke was fifty feet high, then a hundred as the wind grabbed it, hurling it up and up.

Dixie stood patiently as I sat astride her and heaved everything in my stomach. I watched the house I lived in, not just mine but my parents' home and my grandparents' too, going up in flames. It was a place I loved, a home full of laughter, family and hope, where I had spent every night of my seventeen years. I sat transfixed, unable to look away as flames engulfed the structures that my ancestors had built with their own hands in the 1800s.

I thought about crying, but then, like having a cloak drawn over me, I became immersed in a completely different feeling. The heavy, nasty black clouds of smoke were like a signal to me, a beacon that opened my eyes and my mind to bitter, harsh reality. There was a lot I still didn't understand, but there was one thing I damned sure did. This was war – a battle between good and evil just like Armageddon. Nate Dax against the establishment.

I said one last thing to God. *Please forgive me. They have to pay for this, so please forgive me for what I'm going to do to them.*

When Dixie and I went down the mountain, I returned to a different place than the one I had left a few hours earlier. Nothing would be the same, ever again. I wasn't even the same person. I was a driven man with a mission that would not fail.

CHAPTER FIFTEEN

Two deputies from the Enforcement Patrol stood in front of Sheriff Vargas's desk. He wasn't sheriff now, of course. The Enforcement Patrol had integrated all local law enforcement a few years ago, but everyone in Leadville still called Lenny by his old title.

"How'd everything go?"

"Not really that great. We searched the place and didn't find much. All we got was the guy's tablet and monitor and some files off his desk. Then we torched the house and the barn."

"You're sure you didn't miss anything?"

"We got the only things that might matter. There really wasn't much."

The next morning Sheriff Lenny Vargas loaded a box into his SUV and went to Denver. The hundred-mile drive took nearly two hours and he listened to country music while he spit tobacco out the window every few minutes, staining the side of the Suburban with streaks of brown.

He also had plenty of time to reflect. He couldn't figure out why they had arrested Dan and Melanie Dax. They didn't look or act like people who would do the things they'd been charged with, so it had to be something else. It didn't usually pay to question orders that came down from his superiors, and he had done exactly what he was supposed to this time. Still, he wondered. Maybe he'd ask when he got to headquarters.

Once he got to Denver, he pulled into a multistory garage that was the district headquarters of the Enforcement Patrol. He showed his badge to an officer holding an automatic rifle, who examined it closely.

"Park right over there, Captain Vargas." He pointed, twisting his mouth in disgust at the tobacco streaks down the side of the EP vehicle. "Go through those double doors to the security desk and check in. You have your access card – right? You'll need it to get around the building."

Vargas held the red card up for the man to see, then clipped it to his belt. He carried the box to a set of glass doors, swiped his card and walked inside. He put the box through a scanner, went through another one himself and took an elevator to the third-floor office of his direct superior, John Wheeler.

"Good morning, Sheriff," Major Wheeler said with a smug grin as he noticed Vargas's usual bulging cheek crammed with nasty tobacco. "Sorry, it's captain now, isn't it? Old habits are hard to break."

Wheeler was needling him again. Lenny had been Wheeler's boss back in Leadville fifteen years ago. They hadn't liked each other then and it was much worse now that the tables were turned. Lenny always thought he should have had Wheeler's job instead of this smart-ass kid ten years younger than he was. The guy had politicked his way into the rank of major and got transferred to Denver while the sheriff had become a captain and remained stuck in dead-end Leadville.

"Right, Johnny," Vargas answered, gloating as he saw the younger man wince. Wheeler hated that nickname, so now that was the name Lenny always used. "But you can still call me Sheriff. Everyone back in town calls me that."

"I doubt if they're smart enough to know any better," he muttered under his breath. He glared at Vargas. "I'm busy, so let's get this over with. I'm sure you're busy too, making sure your residents don't run red lights or speed in a school zone."

Vargas ignored the barb. He actually wanted this meeting over as much as his former lackey did. He pulled the tablet, monitor and files out of the box and set them on Wheeler's desk. Then he walked around to the side, pulled out his boss's trash can and spit a gob of tobacco into it with a loud twang.

"What the hell are you doing, Lenny? You have a nasty, disgusting habit that marks you as a total redneck. That's no skin off my back as long as you do your job. But by God, the next time you spit that crap into my wastebasket, I'll write your ass up. You got it?" He was shaking with anger.

The sheriff nodded, sat back in his chair and folded his arms over his ample chest. He'd gotten the rise he wanted. "Got it, Johnny. My bad."

Wheeler looked at the things sitting on his desk. "This is it? You searched an entire house and this is all you have?"

If you think you can do it better, you should have gone out there and done it yourself, you little pissant. But no, that would mean getting your hands dirty and scuffing your shined shoes.

"There wasn't anything except exactly what you'd expect in a house on a ranch. I could have brought you the lady's underwear, I guess ..."

"Knock it off! You know what I'm talking about." He stopped a moment, then said halfway to himself, "Maybe I should send a team from here to be sure."

"You could do that, only the house and barn aren't there anymore. My men burned them to the ground after they finished searching. Like you told me to."

"*Like I told you to?* What in hell did I ever say that made you think I wanted that?"

"You told me what we were looking for, said to tear the place apart until we found it, and don't leave stuff around for the public to find."

You couldn't miss the look of pure fury on the major's face. He wanted to fire this moron right now, but he held back. Doing something impulsive would mean another conduct hearing, another investigation and probably a demotion. The last one hadn't gone so well – he was still on probation from it. His uncontrollable temper had begun to show up on his performance evaluations. He couldn't afford another run-in with his superiors.

He responded in short, clipped sentences, struggling to maintain his composure. "Great. I actually planned to send in our crack evidence team from here once you'd finished. Instead your men – your team of specialized, highly trained *investigators* – went through the house, found this tablet, which we both know is worthless to us, a couple of files and nothing else, and then you burned the house down. You made certain my people here, who actually know what they're doing, wouldn't have anything left to find. I'll never know if you did a good job or not because you destroyed everything. Is that pretty much it, *Sheriff?"*

"Why did we arrest the Dax couple in the first place? I can't believe they'd –"

That was it. Wheeler exploded. "Dammit, get out! You've done enough! You've botched this thing completely. Who cares what you believe? You work for me, and you'll do what I say! I guarantee you there was more to find at their house, but thanks to your great detective work, we'll never know. Go home, Lenny. Get out of my office. I'll take it from here."

Fuming, Wheeler walked across the room and held the door open as his old boss said, "Nice to see you too," and walked out. He slammed it so hard the frame shook. He walked back to his desk, sat down and made a decision. He wasn't going to let that idiot screw up this investigation any longer. Tomorrow he'd make some changes.

The Dax couple would talk if John Wheeler persuaded them to talk. And he knew how to be persuasive.

CHAPTER SIXTEEN

The easiest way for me to do surveillance on the Enforcement Patrol in Leadville would have been to buy a wireless Wi-Fi camera. I could have installed it in minutes on a building across the street. There was a perfect place to put it, and I could have watched their movements from the ranch. But that wouldn't work for me since I couldn't buy anything. World points – our currency – are stored on a person's chip and they're automatically deducted at the point of sale. I've never had points – even if I'd had them, I couldn't go to a store, and there was no ranch house left where I could have a package delivered.

So I did the only other thing I could think of. It was risky, but I didn't have a choice. I spent four nights hiding in City Park half a block from the sheriff's office. I watched from dusk until dawn, taking notes about everything that happened. Now I knew when the shifts changed, how many officers there were at any certain time, and who didn't lock his Suburban. Through the open windows I could hear their radio transmissions, so I found out how many men patrolled the county roads, their routes and when they returned. If my parents were in a cell in there, I had to know everything so I could get them out.

Doing nighttime surveillance had been simple compared to what was next. The darkness had been my friend, but now I had to spend a few days observing without making myself conspicuous. On the surface it sounded easy – someone passing me on the street would never know I'm unchipped unless they had a wand, and only the EPs routinely carried those. But if I even came close to a recharging station or an ATM, a reader would go off. I had to be aware of my surroundings every minute.

It was a huge risk being out in the open. Nobody knew me; it would take only one busybody to wonder who the strange kid was and alert the cops. It was dangerous, but what else could I do? Number one on my list was figuring out if my parents were alive and where they were. And that meant learning everything I could about the EP.

Leadville is mostly about tourism. It's an old silver mining town founded in 1877 by Horace Tabor, a flamboyant man who went on to become a US Senator, divorced his wife and married Baby Doe McCourt. He died penniless, but on his deathbed told his much younger wife that his Matchless Mine would be her salvation when silver prices rebounded. She lived in near poverty up at the mine for the rest of her life, waiting for a miracle that never happened.

Having tourists all over town was great. I blended in with people going to the ice cream shop or taking carriage tours. Some stopped for a drink in one of the saloons that were rebuilt to look like they did in the 1880s, and others took walking tours complete with tales of whores, murderers and scam artists who sold mining shares to unsuspecting Easterners looking for a fast buck.

On the morning of the second day observing, I was sitting on a bench in the shade in front of the Baby Doe Bookstore. The sheriff's office was half a block down and across the street. I'd tried to make myself look different from the boy they were looking for. I had a couple weeks' growth of facial hair, I was wearing sunglasses, and I slouched so I wouldn't look six feet tall. Even with that I stayed away from the café where I'd talked to the guy the other night. If he recognized me, he'd call the cops before I knew what was happening.

I had my journal and a pen and I jotted notes – just another tourist putting his thoughts on paper. Something caught my eye; there was movement in an upstairs window across the street. It was open and some frilly curtains were pulled back just a little. Was someone peeking out? I glanced away, and when I looked back, there was nothing. It must have been the wind. I got up and strolled nonchalantly down the block. I spun around, looked up and saw a face this time – a girl's face that was looking straight at me. We locked eyes for a second and then she was gone.

Damn! With my chest heaving, I tried to walk casually back to where the Chevy was hidden in some trees at the edge of town. I sat behind the wheel, hyperventilating. My heart was pounding and my head was filled with possibilities, all bad. Someone had noticed me! I'd been careless. What was I thinking? I was an Outcast – there was no place for me in the naked light of day.

Come on, Nate! Get real. If you get caught, who's going to save your mom and dad?

Just then something moved on my left. She was there – standing next to the truck. I jumped like a scared puppy and it made her laugh. All I wanted to do was run – to drive the damned truck away as fast as possible and hide forever – but I'd created this monster and now I had to deal with it. I opened the door.

"Sorry if I startled you." Her voice was pleasant and so was her face. She was really, really pretty – beautiful, I guess you'd say – but I had to get away from her as fast as I could.

"Uh, yeah, I guess I didn't see you there." I was usually pretty quick on my feet, but I stammered around this time, fumbling to say something. I'd never been this close to a girl before. I thought how nice she smelled as I tried to come up with something to say.

She took the pressure off me, thank goodness. "I saw you in town."

"You did? How'd you find me out here?"

"I followed you, silly. How else? Do you live in Leadville?"

Every neuron in my brain was shooting danger signals, but all of a sudden I didn't want to run anymore. I wanted to find out who she was. I stepped out of the SUV and saw that she was about my age. She was wearing some kind of lacy white shirt, jean shorts and tennis shoes. She had blond hair and deep blue eyes. I stared at her longer than I should have, I guess.

"See anything you like?" she said with a twirl and a teasing laugh that sounded like music.

"I'm ... I'm sorry. I don't usually ... uh, usually I don't ..."

"That's okay." She stuck out her hand. "I'm Allie. Allie Cooper."

I took her hand. It was soft and warm. She squeezed a little and I let go like it was on fire or something.

"Nate. Nate ... uh, Jackson." She laughed again at my apparent shyness, not realizing how hard this was for me.

She's laughing at me, but it's not a bad thing. She's really not laughing at me, it's like she's laughing with me, like we're friends. It's nice.

"I saw you yesterday in town, Nate Jackson. You were sitting there writing in your book all day long. Then you were there again this morning. That surprised me. What are you writing about?"

She was shooting questions so fast that I struggled to answer.

"Just a project for school. We, uh ... we have to write about what kind of place Leadville was in the 1880s."

She nodded. That made sense to her. "I figure you're – what – a senior?"

"I'm a junior, actually." And I was. I should have had one more year of home-schooling to complete high school. I wondered for a moment if that was ever going to happen – if I would ever see my mother again. "How about you?"

"Sophomore. I go to Lake County High School in town. Do you live here? I haven't seen you before and it's a pretty small place!"

I didn't know any school names. I'd only been to Leadville twice and never anywhere else. I decided to choose another town.

"I'm ... uh, from Denver."

"Wow! So am I! Well, not now, but my mom and I lived there before we moved here."

Crap! That's no good. How could I have randomly chosen the very place she used to live? I didn't know what I was going to do next, but fortunately she rescued me once again.

"It's so different in a city. The high schools there are so big compared to here," she said with a smile. I smiled back, thinking how her eyes sparkled. "I went to South and I didn't know anyone from the other schools. I've never seen you before – I'm pretty sure I'd remember." That made me feel warm deep inside. "So did you go to Lincoln? No, I bet you were a Cherry Creek guy!"

Thank God she'd tossed out a name. "Actually it was Lincoln, but I was only there a semester. We lived in Houston before that." *That should be far enough away to be safe.*

"Are you out of school this week?" she asked. "It's spring break here."

I was thankful for the change of subject. "Yeah, in Denver too." That was a lucky break, so to speak.

"So are you staying with people in town?"

She was really firing the questions. I knew I should be careful, but I'd never experienced these feelings before. I wanted to stay here and talk to her, I wanted to walk her back to town and hold her hand, but I knew that was never going to happen. I was in the most dangerous place I'd been in my entire life, and I couldn't fall under the spell of this enticing, bewitching female who looked, acted, smelled like ... something wonderful.

"I'm staying with my grandparents up north off Highway 24, but I'm going back tomorrow. It's been good to talk to you, Allie, really good. But I have to go now."

"Nice to talk to you too. Our apartment's on the second floor over Max's Hardware, where you saw me looking out my bedroom window. If you come back, I hope you'll look me up."

"I will," I lied, watching her turn and walk away.

I knew I'd never see her again. I couldn't risk it. I felt a lump rising in my throat. I wanted to be like everyone else, to talk to her, sit and have a Coke with her, find out more about her. Maybe even kiss her.

BILL THOMPSON

But that wasn't possible. Just those few minutes with Allie had opened my eyes to something. I had a sick feeling in the pit of my stomach. My entire being yearned for someone else – someone just for me.

For the very first time, I realized what it really meant to be an Outcast and how it would always be.

I was all alone.

CHAPTER SEVENTEEN

Allie, her mom Mabry and her stepdad sat at the kitchen table, finishing dinner. He had gotten off work at seven and was home five minutes later. One of the advantages of living in a very small town was that nothing was far from anywhere else.

Tonight's meal was fried chicken and cream gravy, a dish that had become a favorite in the nine months since her mother remarried and moved from Denver to be with her husband. Allie thought Leadville was okay, but it was incredibly different from city life and she was often bored.

Yesterday she had been idly looking out her bedroom window when she noticed a cute boy sitting across the street. She watched him through the sheer curtains, deciding he must be a tourist since she'd never seen him before. She checked back on him now and then and saw him sit there all day long, writing things in some kind of journal.

This morning he was back so she impulsively decided to open the sheers and let him see her. When he finally looked up, she drew back and then peeked out. He'd moved; now he was half a block away, staring intently at her. He looked scared, she thought. But he looked really nice too. She wanted to know who he was.

She ran down the stairs and luckily ended up on the same side street he was walking down, just a couple of blocks ahead of her. He was moving fast; she stayed behind him until he came to an old SUV parked in some trees. She made another impetuous decision to stop him before he drove away. But he didn't leave. He just sat there behind the wheel for a couple of minutes. She waited and watched and then she made her move. She walked up and stood by the driver's window until he noticed her.

Tonight during dinner, her mother watched as Allie hummed, whistled and smiled. She was an easygoing child who'd been a pleasure for a single parent to raise, and Mabry was glad her daughter seemed so happy right now.

"You look like you just won the lottery," her stepdad commented. He was a gruff man, but he had accepted Allie because she was part of the deal when he married her mother. Now the sixteen-year-old was a permanent addition to his little second-floor home above the hardware store.

"I met a boy today," she said with a mischievous smile.

"Really? I figured by now you knew every boy in Leadville."

"Nate's not from here. He's from Denver."

With a sly grin and a wink, her mom said, "Nate, huh? Nice name. Is he cute?"

Allie blushed, averted her eyes and nodded. "But there's nothing to it. He's leaving tomorrow to go home."

"Where'd you meet him?" her stepfather asked. He was concerned about strangers. You just never knew with all those tourists passing through town. "Was he here with his family?"

"I saw him on the street and we started talking. He looked like someone I might enjoy getting to know. He's been staying at his grandparents' house out on Highway 24."

"Did you get his number? I'll run it for you if you did. You gotta be careful these days ..."

"I didn't get it." She could have kicked herself for not giving him hers either, but at least he knew where she lived. All she really knew was that he had an old truck, but she didn't tell her stepfather that. "No, I didn't get anything. We just talked for a minute, you know? It all happened really fast and then it was over."

"You look like you're not quite over it, honey," her mother noted with a smile. "I haven't seen you dancing around the house like this for ages!"

"Mom, stop it! I just liked him, that's all." She hummed again as she carried dishes to the sink.

"Honey, I have to go back to the office for a few minutes," her stepfather said, pushing back from the table. "There's a report that has to go to Denver tonight. Won't be long."

He took his gun belt off the hall tree where it always hung when he was home, strapped it around his waist and opened the door. "Back shortly."

Mabry walked over, gave him a hug and kiss and said the words she repeated each time he left. "Stay safe and come back home, Lenny."

The sheriff of Lake County went downstairs, stepped out and walked to his office. He wondered about this boy his stepdaughter had met. Sure, it was good to see her happy, but kids – girls especially – could get in trouble if they weren't careful. Maybe the boy would reappear in her life sometime. If he did, Lenny would check him out.

He sat at his desk and wrote the daily report about the ongoing investigation. It was becoming clear that Daniel and Melanie Dax had been harboring a fugitive – an Outcast, by the look of things – at their ranch. There might be a lot more going on up there in the mountains where they lived – he planned to send men to search the whole place.

There was something more to all this. The higher-ups at headquarters in Denver were taking an unusual interest in the couple, so there was obviously something more here than harboring an Outcast. Lenny was determined to learn what they were up to and where the Outcast was hiding. This was personal; he wasn't going to let his boss – that little jackass John Wheeler – see him fail. It was time to turn up the heat. Once he did, one of the prisoners would start singing like the proverbial canary. He would learn everything soon. Tomorrow morning – that was when he'd tighten down the screws.

He hit send and his report went to headquarters. He stood, stretched and said good night to the duty officer, who was playing the latest VR game on his tablet. The man was so engrossed in the action he simply grunted a response. Vargas walked down the sidewalk and was back in the upstairs apartment in minutes.

I was sitting across the street in the dark when Sheriff Vargas walked out of his office. I'd gone home after meeting Allie but decided it was a good idea to come back and observe the Enforcement Patrol office some more. If my parents were still in Leadville, that was where they were.

There was more, even though I kept telling myself there wasn't. I really had come back to watch the office, but there was something else I was watching for, something that made me shiver with anticipation. I wanted to see Allie in the window again. I'd stay in hiding, but I wanted more than anything in the world to look at her face again.

I crouched behind some old fifty-five-gallon barrels in an empty lot across from the EP office and down fifty feet or so. It was dark enough now that I was safe. There were lights inside the old sheriff's office, and to my right I could see Allie's room was lit up through the curtains.

What is she doing? I let myself wonder. Was she watching a movie on her tablet or combing her blond hair or taking a shower ... oh man, I had to quit thinking about this stuff. Just as I had begun to fantasize, I was jolted back to reality. I heard the jingle of the EP office door as the sheriff stepped out. I recognized him immediately. Lenny Vargas was the top law enforcement guy in this area, and his picture was on a weekly email update the county sent all its citizens. I'd seen it a hundred times on Dad's tablet.

Sheriff Vargas strolled along the sidewalk and stopped at a door just below Allie's window. What was he doing? In a second a shaft of light appeared and I knew. He'd used a key to open the door that was the ground-floor entrance to where Allie lived upstairs. I saw him walk into a narrow hallway and close the door. In a moment his shadow appeared upstairs behind curtains too, but in a different room – the room next to Allie's.

This was crazy! What was he doing there? Allie had said she and her mom moved here from Denver. Why did Vargas have a key to their place? Her last name was Cooper, but that really didn't mean anything. The sheriff could be her stepfather or her mom's boyfriend or something else entirely. My mind was reeling – I'd just met this fascinating girl, and now it looked like she was all mixed up with the people who might be holding my parents.

Just then I felt a prickle on my neck. I sensed that someone was behind me. I tensed up, preparing to swing my fist when I heard that now-familiar, wonderful, melodic voice.

"Are you spying on me, Nate Jackson?" she said with a laugh. "I saw you when you first came up and hid here."

I stood up, glad she was here because I was going to find out what was going on. Just as I started to say something, she pulled me deep into the darkness, put her arms around my neck and kissed me deeply. I wanted to be careful, cautious, and wary of this girl whom I didn't know at all, a person whose house was occupied at this very moment by a man who was legally required to send me to be euthanized if he found me – a man who might hold my parents' lives in his hands or who might already have executed them too.

The part of my brain that wanted to be careful disappeared in the craziness of what was happening. I tumbled headfirst like Alice down the rabbit hole. I soared into a place I'd never been before – a colorful, magical place full of excitement and whirling thoughts that spun through my mind. It was the Fourth of July and Christmas and every wonderful part of my life all rolled into one. It was a sensational experience I didn't understand and something that I wanted to hold in my heart forever.

I kissed her back. Over and over and over. I held the first girl I'd ever kissed as tightly as I could and hoped she'd never go away. Whoever she was – whatever was happening – everything would be all right. It just had to be.

As crazy as all this was, it felt good – really good. What to do next became clear. I had to trust her. I had to put my faith – and my fate – into the hands of a stranger. For once in my life, I needed a friend. But not just anyone. I needed – no, I *wanted* Allie Cooper.

CHAPTER EIGHTEEN

I had intended to ask her a million questions, to find out who she was, why she'd come back into my life, what was going on – but instead we held each other for a long, long time that could have lasted forever if it had been up to me. I knew she had questions of her own, but there would be time for that. I knew now that I would see Allie Cooper again, and I think she felt the same way.

"I have to go back," she said at last. "I can't be gone long. They'll wonder where I am."

I wanted to ask who *they* were, but I couldn't waste the time now. She was about to leave, and all I wanted to know was when we would be together again. And to hold her just a little longer.

"I have to see you tomorrow."

Although she hadn't said anything, she knew now that I had lied about going back to Denver. There hadn't been many words tonight at all. Mostly it was kisses.

"Meet me at the place where you parked your truck this afternoon." We set a time and she turned her face up to mine. We held each other in a locked embrace, kissing again and again until she pushed back, patted my cheek with a smile, stuck a piece of paper in my hand and left. I watched her unlock the door and go up the stairs. In a moment I saw her pull back the sheers and wave. After that she was gone. But she'd given me her phone number.

I allowed myself to cry all the way home. Everything bad had pervaded my mind for so long, and I sobbed gut-wrenching tears of anguish. I was terrified for my parents and I promised to find them. I would make the bastards who burned our place pay. Until tonight I thought that everything I loved ... and *everything* I might have learned to love ... was beyond my reach. Until now – until Allie ... but there really was no Allie.

Come on, you dumb bastard! This isn't going to work and you can't even let it start.

Most of my tears were because of her. Part of me – a huge part where the hole in my heart was – wanted to think about the future, even after I'd been with her for less than an hour in my whole life. But there was no future. She was a girl, a regular, normal girl who had no idea who and what I was. And she was somehow involved with the man who was my sworn enemy. I knew there had to be a good answer for that, but Sheriff Vargas wasn't the problem here. *I was.* It was stupid to think I could ever have a relationship like chipped people. I had no business allowing myself to fantasize like that. I. Wasn't. Normal. I didn't fit in with the world. I didn't deserve Allie Cooper, and I couldn't have her.

Physically, no one could have been better prepared for life alone than I was. I didn't need World points or stores to spend them in. I had already started planning how I'd live by bartering – even by stealing if necessary. The ethics of it didn't bother me a bit. It was me against the establishment.

The idea of spending the rest of my life in hiding was challenging, but I could do it if I had to. But before anything else, I had to know about my parents. With the exception of a night or two, I'd never been separated from my dad and mom in seventeen years. The thought of life without them, of never even knowing what happened, was excruciating. I couldn't let that happen. Despite the risk to me personally, I vowed to keep digging until I knew where they were and I rescued them. What did personal risk even matter anymore? I was dead. I'd never lived and I never really would.

I fell asleep fruitlessly trying to push Allie Cooper out of my head. At two o'clock in the morning I sat straight up in bed, jolted awake from the most vivid dream I'd ever had. It wasn't about her – it was about Dad. My father had been here in my room. Really here. He sat on the end of my bed and spoke to me.

Remember, Nate. Remember where the most important things are hidden. You know this. I told you.

Where are you, Dad?

He smiled and shook his head. *Remember, Nate.*

And he was gone.

I grabbed my tablet and looked at the feed from the cameras I'd installed down by the highway at the entrance to our place. Then I checked the ones in the trees where the house and barn used to be. The light from a nearly full moon in a cloudless sky illuminated everything with a ghostly glow. It was quiet and still.

I dressed, grabbed my toolbox and some work gloves, and walked toward the woods where I'd parked the ATV. Dixie whinnied when she saw me and I waved to her. I climbed aboard the four-wheeler and drove down to the ruins of the barn.

Although I'd forgotten, the dream made me recall what my dad meant. The most important things were hidden in the floorboards below the barn. He'd drilled that into my head when I was a kid, although he never said specifically what the important things were. I'd already taken some stuff. Right after Mom and Dad disappeared, I took the weapons and ammunition from their hiding place, but I'd totally forgotten about another secret chamber. I could only hope that the towering heap of incinerated boards that had been our barn hadn't destroyed it, or that the Enforcement Patrol hadn't found it before they torched the place.

By midmorning I had cleared a lot of rubble. The recent rains had extinguished all traces of the fire itself, and I worked toward the middle where the weapons cache had been. Hopefully the other place was somewhere nearby. I'd never actually seen it; I hoped it looked like the first one – a simple trapdoor in the floor that was almost invisible and was usually covered by hay.

I stopped around noon and drove up to the fort, ate some beef jerky and a tomato and lettuce salad for lunch, and then I went back to the barn to keep looking. Suddenly I heard a notification on Dad's phone.

I couldn't have told you one thing about what had been happening in the world since my parents disappeared. My mind was completely occupied with learning what had happened and finding them. But the message jolted me back to reality.

There was an email from the World Union headquarters. Dad got them all the time – every citizen did. The Population Control Council had concluded their biannual meeting at the World Union headquarters in Tel Aviv. They'd reviewed the world population numbers and found that there were one million eight hundred and ninety-two thousand more people than the eleven billion maximum allowed by law. So they'd conducted a drawing.

Over three million people held the number they had drawn, enough to cover the overage and then some. Everyone with the number would be required to report to a Euthanization Camp two weeks from today. Once they were removed, the population would be back under eleven billion and things would continue until the next adjustment period six months from now.

I finished reading without giving it much thought. This happened twice a year, and as brutal and heartless as it was, it was also routine after all these years. Before clicking out of it, I glanced back and did a double take. I'd missed the most important part! I looked in horror at the screen, wanting the message to say something else and feeling sickness growing in the pit of my stomach. The lottery number hadn't registered with me when I first read the story. The numbers usually made no difference since I was an Outcast and didn't have one anyway. Only two numbers mattered. Two numbers meant everything to me.

They'd drawn one of them: three hundred and sixty-three. That was a number I had memorized as a little boy.

That was my mother's number.

CHAPTER NINETEEN

I shrieked and wailed. I sobbed and moaned, beating my fists against the rock I was sitting on until they were bleeding. I cursed God, blaming him for what was happening on his watch.

You made everything, God. You made this whole awful, horrible world. Why the hell are you letting the government do these things to people? You're supposed to love us, not want to kill us. What kind of God are you? What kind of crazy God would do this?

After a while I cried myself out. Exhausted and emotionally drained, I lay back on the grass, steps away from the ruins of the house Mom, Dad and I had lived in. Even though I didn't completely feel like doing it, I apologized to God for blaming him. Maybe there was a reason, I rationalized. Maybe a good thing could come from the horrific lottery that happened every six months. Maybe I would find my mother before they took her to Denver. I had to, even though I didn't have any idea where she actually was.

I had to get things under control and get moving. I was suddenly on a completely new and very short timetable. I'd been anxious to find my parents, but now I had to redouble my efforts. At most I had two weeks before they would kill her. That was if the authorities waited until the last day to send her to a camp. It could actually happen anytime. There was no time to waste.

Dad and Mom had always talked about what they'd do if one of their numbers was drawn. They weren't going to obey. They were going to run or hide or do something else if it ever happened. The people with chips really couldn't get away, of course, because they could be tracked by the government. That never seemed to discourage my parents, though. They seemed pretty comfortable that things would work out. Although they never gave me specifics, I always knew that if anyone could figure out a way to beat the lottery, my dad would do it.

But things now were as horrible as they could get. It was obvious my parents were in custody for some unknown reason. Why else had a team of officers destroyed our house? If they were in jail, then my mother would absolutely be euthanized in two weeks. Wherever she was, they would simply transfer her from jail to the euthanization facility. The only thing that might delay it would be if they thought she knew something and they weren't finished interrogating her. If interrogation was even what was going on here. I had no idea.

The cops who'd torched the house had left our farm equipment there. It all looked old and rusty-looking on purpose, even though Dad kept it in perfect working order. I hooked a snow blade to the tractor and in ten minutes I had the debris pushed to one side. Now the barn floor was clear. The floorboards were thick and sturdy, and though they were seared in places, they hadn't burned through. If there was something hidden beneath them, it should still be there – unless the officers had already found it.

I drove the tractor back, unhitched the blade and returned to the barn. It had been easy to find the concealed space where the rifles had been hidden since I knew where to look. The hinged door blended in perfectly with the rest of the floor; if you didn't know it was there, it would be impossible to see. I pulled it open and saw the empty space where the guns had been. The officers hadn't seen it. I hoped that Dad hadn't been forced to tell them there was stuff hidden here. If he didn't, they might not think of a secret cache.

After trying for twenty minutes to find the second trapdoor, I set up a grid and walked it inch by inch, staring at the floorboards. Finally I saw it, barely visible in the floor where the horse stalls had been.

THE OUTCASTS

I pried up the door with a claw hammer. Inside was a metal box a foot long, two feet wide and two feet tall. It had a handle on top of a hinged lid that was secured with a padlock. I tried to get it out, but it was heavier than I expected. I knelt down, gripped the handle with both hands and gave it a pull. The thing must have weighed fifty pounds and it was hard to maneuver in the tight space, but finally I got it out.

I lugged it over and set it on the back of the ATV. Suddenly there was a ding from the motion detectors. Someone had turned off the highway and was coming toward our gate. I had to go.

CHAPTER TWENTY

I raced to the fort, parked the ATV in the trees and ran inside. From the safety of the tunnel I watched the cameras. Two men stood beside a white-and-blue pickup with a gold emblem on the driver's door – the World Union logo. I'd never seen a truck like that before. I zoomed in to get a look at the words on its side.

Criminal Investigation Division.

More criminal investigators, this time from the World Union? This was getting more and more weird.

They dug around the rubble of the house for a while, but then they noticed the cleared-off space where the barn debris had been. I watched them walk to the barn – I was glad I'd moved the tractor back, but my heart jumped as I realized I'd made a mistake. The second trapdoor was standing wide open and my hammer was next to it.

The cops' frenzied excitement was unmistakable. Why wouldn't it be? They were talking and gesturing animatedly. After they'd torched the barn, someone had cleared off the debris and opened a trapdoor in the floor. They had to be wondering what was up. I wished I could hear what they were saying.

One of the officers ran back to the pickup and got a toolbox. He put on rubber gloves and took out a plastic bag, gingerly picked up the hammer by its head and dropped it in the baggie. They were collecting evidence.

They also found the other hiding place – the one where the guns and ammo had been stored. They pried it open and felt around inside. I knew there was nothing to find, but I watched them take out a long stick with a pad on the end. They swabbed down both spaces, then dropped the pad into another bag. They'd find residue from the ammunition, which in itself was evidence of a crime. But possessing weapons wasn't what this was about. It might be part of it, but there was a much bigger mystery here.

I had no idea what to think. Why were the cops so interested in the ranch? Were they looking for the metal box that sat on the table in front of me right at this moment? I had visions of my dad – or worse, my mom – tied to a chair in an interrogation room with a man promising horrible things if she didn't talk. But I wasn't sure Mom even knew the box existed. I had never heard my folks talk about it to each other. I didn't think my dad would break down and tell the authorities anything. He would protect me. He wouldn't do anything on purpose to put me in danger ... unless they were using Mom to get to him. What if they were torturing her right now?

My God, I'll kill the sons of bitches!

Anger roared through my body. My head throbbed and I could feel the blood pulsing in my temples as I clenched my fists. Then I forced myself to be calm. I slammed the door on the terrible thoughts. Dad would want me to focus, to concentrate on figuring this out instead of getting mired down in what-ifs.

I returned to watching the officers. *Good luck on matching my fingerprints, bastards.* However readable they might be, they were in no database anywhere. But even with that, there was another problem. My prints on the hammer matched the ones the cops had lifted from Dad's Jeep that night back in Leadville. The Enforcement Patrolmen were looking for me – they'd put out an APB even though they didn't know who I was – and my prints in the Jeep matched ones right here at the ranch. They wouldn't know who I was, but there would be no question an Outcast was here somewhere.

Harboring an Outcast was a crime, no question, but that wasn't why the government had arrested my parents, ripped apart our house and burned it down. That didn't make sense. They were looking for something. They either knew for sure something was here, or they suspected it was. I looked at the old metal box again. Was this what they were looking for? Was the box why they'd burned everything? Once they were gone and I could see what was inside, I hoped I'd find out.

They spent an hour going over every square inch of the barn floor with a sophisticated sonar cavity detector. They walked a grid just like I had done. I had wondered if Dad had more hiding places he hadn't mentioned, but there were only the two and I'd emptied them.

Next they searched the only building they hadn't torched – an old shed that was leaning to one side and hadn't been painted in years. It was where Dad stored shovels, rakes and larger tools. Those were up at the fort now, thanks to my all-night move earlier this week. At last they put their things back in the truck and drove away.

CHAPTER TWENTY-ONE

I didn't know if the rusty old box was heavy simply because it was made of metal or because of whatever was inside it. It was time to find out, and I shook nervously, excited at the thought of what Dad had hidden for me to find.

This wasn't going to be simple; I could see where the hasp had been welded onto the box long ago. It was solid and the padlock was heavy-duty and strong. I put the end of a crowbar under the hasp and gave it some pressure, but nothing budged. I wasn't going to get in that way, so I attacked the padlock instead.

In an effort to learn what I was up against, I went online and found the exact lock. It was a good one and it had cost my dad a lot – over two hundred World points. The description said it was made of hardened steel with a high resistance to cutting, grinding or drilling. I wasn't going to get in that way either. Disappointed but determined, I turned the box around and took a look at the two hinges on the back that joined the lid to the box itself. They were caked with rust, but they were solidly connected. Each half of a hinge had three screws with heads that looked like they took a huge Allen wrench.

Along with almost all of our tools, I had brought Dad's welding torch up here from the barn after my parents disappeared, but I was afraid to use it on this job. Whatever was inside the box could be destroyed if the outside got too hot. I searched online again and learned that propane was the way to go. A little heat wouldn't affect steel, but it would free up rusty bolts. I had a torch and several canisters of propane, plus there was a five-hundred-gallon tank hidden in the woods down by the house. Even though almost everything ran on solar now, even in 2094 there was always a use for propane around a ranch.

In a few minutes I was sitting outside in what my dad said had been the fort's old parade grounds, a large open area surrounded by an ancient pole fence. Two hundred years ago this place had been bustling with activity, but now that the fort was engulfed by towering trees, it was quiet and shady, much cooler than in the pasture a hundred yards away. The box was next to me.

I'd never used a propane torch, but I'd watched Dad, so I knew how it worked. I fired it up and held the flame close to a screw. I applied heat for a minute or two and then I crammed the biggest Phillips screwdriver I had into the screw head and twisted it. I alternated those steps for twenty minutes, and at last the screw began to move. Being careful not to strip it, I gingerly turned the screw until it dropped out. One down, five to go.

Two hours later I took out the last screw. I pulled the hinges back and lifted the heavy lid. I looked inside with anticipation. Completely out of patience now, I couldn't wait to find out what Dad had painstakingly put into a heavily secured strongbox and hidden beneath the floor of our barn. What I saw in the box wasn't what I had expected, but then again what *had* I expected? People didn't have precious valuables to hide anymore, since gold and silver couldn't buy anything. I guessed they hid important stuff – things they didn't want other people to know about. Now I had to go through the box, figure out what all this stuff meant and why Dad had considered these particular things so important.

Now the box lay open in front of me. As I started to remove the thing on top, I became aware of a "whop-whop-whop" sound coming from somewhere in the distance. I was so excited about the box that the noise didn't register for a second, but it got louder and louder and suddenly I knew something was wrong.

There was a helicopter approaching from the west, heading straight for the fort. Even though nothing was visible from the air, I couldn't take a chance. I had to move the box and close the hatch that led down into the tunnels. If the chopper passed over low enough, a spotter might see something through the dense foliage.

I ran and shut the trapdoor. Now no one would notice anything was under the grassy field. I tried to move the box, but it was a struggle since I'd unscrewed the lid that had the handle. I tugged and pushed, raising puffs of dust and creating a distinct trail as I moved the heavy container to safety under a collapsing wooden balcony.

Suddenly I remembered Dixie! She was in the corral out in the open. I ran out, opened the gate, grabbed a rope and shooed her toward the fort. I left her tied to a tree, totally out of sight.

The sound from the blades was much louder now. There was no time left – I swept away the track marks from the box with my shoes as best I could and then sped back to where I'd put the box. Just before I slid underneath the overhanging balcony, I saw a massive black copter through the trees. It was more than a hundred yards out and moving away towards the north. They hadn't been close enough to see anything, and now the sound was growing fainter and fainter. They weren't looking for me or the fort. Not this time, at least.

There was no doubt the chopper belonged to the Enforcement Patrol. Decades ago the EP had received thousands of utility helicopters deemed surplus after the former United States government's military was disbanded and the World Union became the planet's peacekeepers.

Although I'd skirted the problem this time, I knew my luck wouldn't last forever. The fort was a landmark they could easily find out about simply by going to the historical society. Everyone thought it was nothing but a ruin, but it would still be on the maps for sure. I couldn't stay here any longer. It simply wasn't safe – if the EP came here, it would be the end for me.

I unpacked the box, sorting things by type but not looking closely at anything for now. Finally I had four piles: file folders, some stuffed with papers, newspaper clippings and articles printed from the Internet; two old-fashioned USB thumb drives people hadn't used in years; an Apple tablet that was probably five or six years old but looked brand new; and a Smith and Wesson .38 Special handgun with two hundred rounds of ammunition. The gun had to be ancient – they'd been outlawed since 2044 – but it was well oiled and appeared to have been cleaned recently.

Sitting on the floor with all these things around me, my mind filled with crazy thoughts. What was this about? Did Dad go to the barn, pull out the box and clean the pistol every so often, keeping it ready for something? Did he add to this stash of stuff every now and then, putting things in here that he might need for later? Or had he hidden all these things away for another reason?

Up to now I had thought there were no secrets Dad kept from me, but this box appeared to be full of them. Until I went through everything, I wouldn't know what all this was, and even then I still might not understand why he'd done it.

Along with everything else that was happening, all day long I had fought with myself. First I rationalized that it was better not to see Allie again; then I told myself I had to do it. I literally ached for her, experiencing feelings so strong and so unusual I couldn't identify them, but I knew this couldn't go on. Every meeting with her would be more dangerous than the last, and I couldn't risk involving her in my life. One more time, I told my heart. Just one more time.

I believed the things my dad put in that box were keys to understanding my future, with or without my parents. As important as it was to learn what they were, it would be an overwhelming job and take a lot of focused time. Tomorrow morning I would tackle that project. Tomorrow I would take one piece of the puzzle at a time and see where it fit. For now, I would go to Allie.

At four o'clock I eased the truck into the grove of trees where I'd first met her. And there she was, waiting, smiling.

I ran to hold her and kiss her lips. I felt her arms move up and around my neck. I threw caution, fear and uncertainty aside. This time I'd never let her go.

My hands went up and down her back as we kissed. She moved closer into me, our bodies melding like one.

Suddenly there was a ding from my back pocket – an email popup on Dad's phone.

Damn. Bad timing!

Feeling my sudden tension, she pulled back. "Maybe we should slow down a little," she murmured in a tone that sounded like she didn't mean it.

I was loving the rush of sensations coursing up and down my body. The last thing I wanted to do now was slow down.

"I just need to see what this is. It could be something important. Hold on for a second. I'll be right back."

It was another email from the World Union. This time the subject line read "Courtesy notification from PCC." I opened the mail, read it and stood transfixed, looking at the screen but seeing nothing. I felt a whirling sensation and the phone fell from my hand, landing hard on the ground.

Tears began to run down my cheeks as I pounded my fists against the hard metal of the truck. "I'm going to kill them! I swear I'm going to kill them! They're going to die for this. All of them."

She bent down and picked up the phone. The email was still open.

"May I read it?" she asked gently.

I nodded. *Why not?*

"Dear Friend or Relative of Melanie Dax," it began. "In accordance with the System of Laws, the Population Control Council wishes to advise you that your friend or relative was humanely euthanized today ..."

"Who's Melanie Dax?" Allie asked sympathetically. "She must have been someone really close to you."

I looked at her quizzically for a second; then I remembered I'd said my last name was Jackson. She'd probably never heard the name Dax before.

Wiping away the tears, I said, "I need to explain." But then I stopped. Something changed – it was like a thick curtain was lifted from my brain, allowing me to see clearly for the first time. Everything came together in a terrible, awful wave of understanding that ripped out what had barely begun in my heart.

The facts were clear. The sheriff had a key to Allie's house and this girl I barely knew had sucked me into a fantasy world. That wasn't entirely true – I had eagerly wanted it all to happen and she had no idea who I was. Whatever she wanted with me, it wasn't good. It was dangerous, and I wouldn't let her get close to me any longer.

From now on it would be just me, and I was ready. If my parents had suffered, then others would suffer. Starting now I my life would be driven by two things – anger and revenge. There would be no more room in my heart for love or tears. There would be only answers, suffering, justice and death.

My mind burned with savage determination. I had no doubt Vargas and his men had arrested my parents. A fleeting thought of the sheriff tied to a table crossed my mind. I'd read a lot about torture techniques in the wars long ago and I already had ideas for Lenny Vargas. He would talk. Oh yes, he would talk, and once he had told me everything, he would die.

For a moment – last night and today – I had thought maybe I didn't have to alone anymore. But I'd been wrong.

My jaw was clenched and my fists were in balls as I returned to reality. I looked into that face that had been so wonderful just moments ago. She put her hand on my arm and whispered, "Are you all right?"

I jerked my arm away, and then I decided to ask. I had nothing to lose at this point. "Why does Lenny Vargas have a key to your apartment?"

She looked startled. "Because ... because it's *his* apartment. Mom and I moved in when they got married ..."

Sheriff Vargas is her stepfather.

"Nate, what is it? Whatever's going on, I'm sorry. I want to help ..."

Allie Cooper wasn't a solution. She was a problem. She was part of all this.

"What makes you think *you* can help?" I spat in clipped, even words that felt like bile when they left my mouth. "My name's not Nate Jackson. It's Dax. Nate Dax. Melanie Dax was my mother and the government killed her.

Go home and tell that to your stepfather. *He* killed her and I'm going to make him pay."

She stood open-mouthed, staring at me. A tear trickled down her cheek. "Nate, I'm so sorry. But Lenny didn't kill her. You know that."

"He's part of the system just the same as if he injected her himself. He started it and he's first on my list. Now go, Allie. Get out of here and get out of my life."

I walked to the truck and drove away. In the rearview mirror I could see her standing there sobbing. I told myself I didn't care. I didn't need anyone now.

CHAPTER TWENTY-TWO

There are dozens, maybe even hundreds of caves that dot the mountainsides above our ranch. Today I sat in one of them that had become my new home for a while, sifting through the file folders Dad had hidden in the metal box.

I had moved all the stuff from the fort I thought I'd need, even though there was no telling how briefly I might be here. Time was running out – I knew the EP would find the fort soon. They'd know immediately that I'd been living there when they saw furniture, the electrical hookups and all the other stuff Dad had installed. But it didn't matter now.

The cave was three or four miles from our property. I had explored it lots of times as a kid, and the other day I came up here again to see if it would work. The Chevy bounced along on unpaved ruts, winding up the mountain until the road ran out. The entrance lay about a thousand feet above where I had parked the SUV and it was almost completely obscured by undergrowth, just as I had remembered.

I installed some of the camouflaged solar panels from the fort in a nearby tree and ran wiring to a room hidden deep inside the cave. Now I had a light and electrical outlets. I had brought up the nonperishable food, but I had to leave the freezer loaded with meat.

Thoughts of Allie crept into my mind, but I forced them out. I was lucky that she hadn't turned me over to her stepfather. I'd be dead by now if she had.

I turned back to the stack of files sitting on the wooden table in front of me and opened the top one. I presumed Dad was responsible for gathering all this stuff since he'd hidden it under the barn floor. There were magazine and newspaper clippings, articles he had downloaded and printed, and pages torn from books. Some were decades old, but others were from last month. He must have added things often. I skimmed a few articles just to get an idea of what all this was. It would take days to go through everything, and until I figured out its significance, I wasn't going to spend valuable time on it.

It didn't take long to see the common theme. All this stuff was about something called the Resistance, a dedicated movement that had arisen after the CHIP Act of 2049. It was a group of people who chose to be Outcasts rather than accepting the loss of privacy and individualism that came with a chip. I'd never heard about the Resistance and I didn't know there were people out there who had lost everything – jobs, money, security, even their lives – to fight against something they believed was fundamentally wrong with our country.

Dad had been an Outcast until he met Mom and got chipped so she'd marry him. Even after twenty-something years with a chip, he had followed the Resistance movement and saved articles about its activities. It was obvious why he'd hidden them. It was a felony offense to possess subversive literature, and this cache of documents would land its owner in jail. It was a crazy world when you could be arrested just for reading articles about the Outcasts, but that was the law. Yet for some reason my father had been willing to risk imprisonment to keep them.

Looking at all these things my father considered important enough to hide, I wondered what they had to do with my parents' disappearance and the torching of our house and barn. The cops were looking for something, but would they have gone to such lengths simply to catch a rebel sympathizer? It didn't add up so far, but there were other things in the box that might provide answers.

I pulled out a baggie that held two small storage devices – thumb drives, I think they were called back in the dark ages of computer technology. I looked at the little connectors that would have plugged into some kind of port and wondered how I could access them. Everyone today had a tablet, and as far as I knew, the only computers with ports were in museums. I'd only seen pictures of these little devices; I'd never actually held one. Each had only 256 gigs of data – a tiny amount – and I had no idea what was on them. For now, I set them aside.

Next I took out the pistol and two boxes of ammunition. There wasn't much to figure out about them. I think they were part of Dad's plan to protect our family.

The only thing left was an Apple CQX49 tablet that looked new but was at least five years old. It was a big and clunky predecessor to Apple's sleek, powerful tablets today. It was so old it had a power cord and I plugged it in to charge the battery. Two hours later I went back to it, only to find it required a password that I didn't have.

Once I had plugged in the tablet, there was nothing left to go through except the stack of maybe twenty file folders. I gave each one a quick glance and saw that Dad had arranged the material by category – the World Union, the Enforcement Patrol, the CHIP Act, the Twenty-Minute War and so forth. By the time I got to the last file – the one on the bottom – I had decided to move on to other things until the tablet was charged up and I could check it out. The last folder turned out to be the important one.

Written in red ink on the outside were the words FOR NATE.

There were only a few papers in this folder and I cautiously looked at the first one, wondering what my dad had put in this box. He had to have known I'd probably never see it unless something had gone terribly wrong.

CHAPTER TWENTY-THREE

"You interested in helping me out at the office after school? I have some work you could do," Lenny Vargas mentioned one night at dinner.

Allie looked up from her homework. "What kind of work would it be? I don't know anything about law enforcement."

"It's not like that," her stepfather explained. "The clerk who does our data entry has to go part-time because her mother's sick. I could use an extra hand a couple of hours a day after school and half a day on Saturday. I know you can use a tablet – I watch your fingers fly over the keyboard – and this would simply be entering data into our Galaxy account. Investigation reports, processing records for people who are arrested – that kind of stuff. It's boring, but it'll earn you some World points." It sounded good to Allie and she said yes.

Almost every afternoon from three to five she sat at a desk in front of a business tablet that was networked to the Enforcement Patrol's Galaxy account. She uploaded reports from the officers' tablets and found the work more interesting than she'd expected. Although there wasn't much crime these days, the men patrolling the county dealt with everything from loose livestock to runaway teenagers to bar fights on the weekends. She enjoyed reading their accounts.

Across the room was a steel door that led into the county jail. It was open most of the time and she could see a long hallway with cells on either side. Curious, Allie asked her stepfather, "How many people are locked up back there?"

"Let me look at the daily report." He picked up a spreadsheet and counted names. "Eight right now. There'll be more by Sunday morning – the drunk tank is home to a few regulars on Saturday nights. During the week, it's mostly the ones waiting for transfer to EP headquarters in Denver."

"What did they do?"

He ran his finger down a column on the sheet. "Domestic abuse, DWI second offense, DWI first offense – that guy will be here in our jail for a year – and stuff like that. Pretty ordinary except for one. We have a guy back there who's been here awhile but hasn't been charged with anything yet. It looks like he's going to transfer to Denver and be charged with treason."

Allie gave him a confused look.

"You know, plotting to overthrow the government or something like that. That one I don't understand. I planned to start his interrogation, but Denver overruled me. It's my boss's case now, not mine. He won't be here much longer. They're transferring him in a few days."

On her break, she sipped a Coke and gazed idly at the desktop screen, suddenly seeing something she hadn't noticed before. There was a folder called "Cross-Reference Information–Lake County Residential/Business." Wondering what it contained, she opened it and saw a few Excel files, one of which was called "Cellphone Numbers–Lake County."

That gave her an idea. She clicked on the file and was prompted to enter a password. She tried the one she'd been assigned for her data entry duties, but it didn't work. She rummaged through her desk drawers, hoping but not really expecting to find passwords someone had carelessly jotted down. There was nothing.

If this database contained all cellphones in the county by user name, maybe she could find Nate Dax's phone number. *What would I do if I had it?* Allie thought. *Would I call him?* She knew she would.

Her stepfather's office was behind her. She heard him call out, "How's it going out there?"

"Great," she replied without turning around. "Just finishing my break." Over the next couple of days she tried several more times to access the file. Nothing worked.

On Saturday she worked eight till noon. Lenny had told her it would be quiet; there was a limited shift on weekend days. He wasn't there himself – he and her mom had left yesterday afternoon to go fishing in the mountains, as they often did in the summer. There were two men on duty – a patrolman manning the radio and the jailer, who was back in the cell block, chatting with the inmates and serving their breakfast trays.

While she entered data, the other cop sat at his desk across the room, watched TV on his tablet, and monitored routine radio transmissions. He had a baby face and pimples. He had to be twenty-one to work here, but she thought he looked like he was her age, around sixteen.

The jailer left shortly after the inmates had eaten. Half an hour later Allie glanced at the young officer, who was leaning way back in his chair with his eyes closed. The steel door to the cell block was standing open and she could hear the muted sounds of a TV and people talking back there.

She tiptoed into her stepfather's office and looked around on his desk until she found the spreadsheet that listed the current inmate population. Today there were only six names – two must have been released in the last day or so. She was looking for a person who might not be in Leadville. But he was, and she found him. Nate had been telling the truth.

Dax, Daniel John, DOB 03MAR2052, age 42, CHIP ID 295-52-2881. Charge date: Pending. Charges: Pending. Treason, subversive activity, conspiracy to overthrow the World Union. Transfer DEN 29OCT2094.

Nate's father was in a cell a hundred feet from where she sat! He hadn't been charged yet, and it appeared he was being transferred to Denver tomorrow.

She had to tell Nate about his father and she needed that password. She tiptoed into Vargas's office, sat behind his desk and opened one drawer after another, not even sure what she was looking for. The bottom one held hanging file folders with name tabs. She found one that might work – "EP Password Procedure" – and pulled out the contents. There was a six-page manual with the World Union logo and behind that a couple of sheets of paper that were folded in half. The manual explained the importance of password protection and regular changes and reminded users that it was a violation of policy to write down passwords. It also had a long list of information that officers were required to password-protect. She glanced down the list and saw "Cross-Reference Information, Residential/Business." That was the file she wanted to access, but there was nothing to help her.

"What are you doing?"

Startled, Allie looked up and saw the young cop standing in the doorway. She let the papers in her hand slip to the floor. "Uh ... I was looking for a pencil with an eraser," she said. "Do you know where I can find one?"

He turned for a second and glanced at the desk where she worked. "There's one on your desk next to your tablet. What are you doing in the sheriff's office?"

She slowly closed the drawer and used her foot to push the papers that were on the floor under her stepfather's desk. With a nervous smile she stood, walked to the doorway and slid past the officer, who was partially blocking the doorway.

"I told you what I was doing. I needed another pencil and I was looking for one. No big deal." She hoped her voice sounded breezy and unconcerned.

She spent the next thirty minutes entering data and hoping to God her stepfather didn't for some reason come back early. If he walked in right now, he'd find papers lying under his desk. She had to get in there and put them back.

The cop spoke to her from across the room in a voice that was barely loud enough to hear.

"I should tell the sheriff what you did."

She figured he'd do this and had decided what she'd do. She swung her chair around aggressively.

"You know his wife, Mabry? That's my mom. You know that, right? We live in his house, for God's sake. I wasn't doing anything and he wouldn't care anyway. You want to tell him? Go right ahead and make yourself look like a tattletale." She turned and went back to work, hoping he didn't notice her trembling hands.

Allie was gambling that this guy, the newest, youngest cop on the force, didn't have the cojones to rat her out. He was low on the totem pole – he was assigned to weekend duty when everyone else was off, and she gambled that he was still unsure where things stood with his boss – the former sheriff of Lake County and an EP captain. He didn't say anything in response, so she went back to work.

At 11:30 he walked over and said, "Look. I don't care what you were doing in there. Makes no difference to me. I'm sorry I said anything. Can you cover for me while I run out and get a hamburger? I'll come back here to eat, so it shouldn't take more than ten minutes."

"What do I have to do?"

"There hasn't been anything on the radio except routine traffic all morning. Just keep an ear out. If someone radios headquarters, you just use the mike and say, 'Headquarters. Over.' I'll hear you on my handheld radio and run back to handle it. No big deal, just like your going through the sheriff's desk was no big deal. Know what I mean?" he said with a smile.

Yes, I know. Quid pro quo. He helps me out; I help him out. Sure, why not? I need him out of here anyway.

"Okay. I'll cover until you get back."

He clipped a radio to his belt, put on his hat and walked out. As soon as the door closed, Allie ran to Lenny's office, put the manual back in the folder and opened the two handwritten pages. They were covered with rows of letters and numbers, just like she'd hoped to find. These were probably Lenny's passwords – she just needed time to see if one worked. She quickly copied the pages, stuck the originals back in the folder and refiled it in his drawer. She had just come out of his office when the radio crackled to life.

"Headquarters, come in. Sandy, are you there?"

Damn. She ran to the desk and clicked the mike. "Headquarters here. Sandy's gone out for a minute. This is Allie. Can I help? Over."

"This is unit six, going code seven at Crescent Diner. Over."

"Okay, I'll tell Sandy."

"Six out."

The door burst open and Sandy flew in, his lunch in his hand. "I heard the call. I can take over now."

"It's all good," she said. "He said unit six was code seven. I guess that means he's taking a lunch break too."

Sandy looked frazzled. "Yes, that's what it means. That's fine. I'm just hoping your stepfather didn't have his radio on. I'm not supposed to leave my post until the shift is over."

"Was that call a big deal?"

"No, but that's not the point. Something big could have happened. I shouldn't have left ..."

She smiled and said, "Don't worry about it. If it comes up, I'll tell Lenny exactly what happened and that I offered to watch things for ten minutes. I'll put it all on me and he won't think a thing about it."

She paused, deliberating whether to take the next step she was considering. Then she went for it.

"Okay, Sandy. Now how about you do a little favor for me? Something I could get in trouble for too, but with your help, no one will ever find out."

Five minutes later she and the young officer walked down a hallway with barred cells on either side. There were men in some, and a couple began to whistle as they walked toward the back.

Sandy had warned her the guys might act up since females weren't usually allowed into the men's section of the cell block. "Just keep walking to the last cell on the left and look straight ahead," he advised, just as the radio back in the office began to crackle.

"Crap!" he sputtered. "I shouldn't leave you back here ..." He glanced back and Allie assured him she'd be fine for a couple of minutes. Actually this was perfect; she wanted to talk to Daniel Dax alone. The officer ran back to his desk and she walked to the last cell.

A handsome man wearing jeans and a T-shirt with the word INMATE on the front rose from his bunk and walked to the front of his cell. There was no question he was Nate's dad. The resemblance was remarkable.

She whispered, "Mr. Dax, I'm Allie Cooper. I'm a friend of Nate's. I just have a second."

"How did you get in here? Is Nate okay?"

"I work here. Nate's just fine. They're moving you to Denver tomorrow, so I had to talk to you now. I have to reach Nate. Do you know how –"

He interrupted frantically. "You have to tell him something for me. Tell him to go through the box; it's critically important. Memorize this number." He called out the ten digits twice and she repeated them back. "That's our house phone. Unless something's gone wrong, he should have it. Is Nate okay? And where's my wife? Do you know what they've done with her?"

"Nate's fine, but I don't know about your wife," she lied, almost out of time. "I have to go. Don't tell anyone I was here." She ran out of the cell block just as the young cop turned the corner to come get her.

"What was that all about?" he asked.

"There was a guy I thought I knew," she answered noncommittally, "but I was wrong."

She wanted to call Nate, but she couldn't leave until her shift was finished an hour from now. Carefully watching the cop, she entered one of Lenny's passwords after another until she found the one that opened the cross-reference information file. It was a huge spreadsheet that listed every one of Lake County's eight thousand two hundred and four residents along with street and email addresses and phone numbers.

She scrolled down to the Ds and found one entry for Dax. The name was Daniel John Dax, born in 1952, living at a rural county address off Highway 24 north of Leadville. It was the same man with whom she'd just spoken.

The number he'd given her was there, along with two others. Dan Dax had said this was the house phone. The other two must have belonged to Nate's parents. *But why didn't Nate have a phone too? Everyone his age did.*

Then she noticed something she'd missed the first time. *The single entry for Dax was Nate's father. There was a reason his mother, Melanie, wasn't there. She'd been euthanized. But why wasn't Nate listed? He'd lied to her once about his last name. Was he lying to her again? If so, why was he doing it?*

At noon her shift was over at last. She shut down the tablet, quickly gathered her things and left. She rushed to the apartment and called the number Nate's father had given her. Whatever Nate was hiding from her, she wanted to help him. The call went straight to voicemail and she heard a computer-generated message, then a beep.

"I want to be sure this call gets to the right person. If you recognize my voice, call me back. I have urgent information from a relative of yours."

Meanwhile an employee of the Enforcement Patrol sat at her desk in the Denver headquarters building. Her responsibility was to monitor security on the EP's network across the Northwest Americas region. At 11:13 a.m. there was a breach in the Leadville office. Someone attempted to access the EP database, entering several incorrect passwords. Then the password of Captain Leonard Vargas, the commander of the Leadville unit, was entered correctly. The person reviewed only one file – the cross-reference records. Nothing would have been noted if the only unusual activity was a few incorrect password attempts. That happened often with so many EP passwords and strict change requirements. The problem with Captain Vargas's access was that he wasn't supposed to be in the office. When he'd signed out as off duty for the weekend, his card had automatically gone to inactive status.

This particular kind of breach happened now and then. People occasionally gave passwords to others who needed access. It was a breach of security that might result in a reprimand, but this one was relatively minor. It might even have been Vargas himself, who came back into the office and forgot to log in. It was a minor infraction, nothing to be concerned about.

If the breach had involved classified records, it would have immediately been reported to a senior security officer. Since the particular file was a routine one – a compilation of county residents and businesses – the matter was logged onto a spreadsheet that would be sent along at the end of the day.

CHAPTER TWENTY-FOUR

Son, if you're reading this, then you're in danger. I'm sorry if it's because of something I did, but in my heart I know that's really the only reason you could be holding this piece of paper. Now all I can do is give you some information that may be helpful to you going forward.

There are resources available to you and I'll show you how to use them. But always be careful. Without a chip you can't go where other people go. Do exactly what I tell you and you'll get to where you need to be.

So you'll know, I update this information as often as it needs to be. The last sheet in this folder is always the most current one. And don't forget our trusty old password. It'll come in handy. Good luck, Nate. We love you.

That was it. I flipped to the last page and looked at the date. It was written only a week before he and Mom disappeared. I began to read his letter through my tears.

Your mother and I love you so much, Nate. We love you more than anything and we did the best we knew how in raising you, even as an Outcast. With what I've given you here, hopefully you'll understand how important the lives of you and others like you really are in our world today and how you can help make things right again.

Things are coming to a head. The EP is getting closer and closer to discovering what your mother and I have worked on for years. Once they do, they'll make their move.

I've tried to prepare you for life without us, because eventually – for one reason or another – I figure everything will catch up with us. Since you are reading this, I know now it's happened, but you're going to be fine. All those camping trips, all those fishing lessons, all those days helping me fix things – there was a reason for every bit of it. You're an intelligent young man and you're ready for what lies ahead. I hope you can help the others who are trying to make our world better.

You've been a blessing and a joy to us for seventeen years, and you're going to make an impact on this crazy world. I believe that with all my heart. God bless you, son, and God give you the wisdom and strength to face the enemies all around you.

Love,

Dad

P.S. The most important things are written on the back of the folder.

On the back of the file there were lines filled with letters and numbers, but by now I was crying so hard I could hardly see them. Most were gibberish, but a couple looked like phone numbers, and there were some words thrown in here and there. Some of the letters were written backwards – I knew exactly what that meant.

As the tears flowed, I reread some of his words, grasping for their meaning.

Hopefully you'll understand how you can help make things right again.

The EP is close to discovering what your mother and I have worked on for years.

All those camping trips and fixing things – there was a reason for every bit of it.

What had he and my mom been working on and planning for me all this time? Who were the others who were trying to make the world better? And what did his very last sentence mean?

God give you the wisdom and strength to face the enemies all around you.

Who were the enemies all around me? I was an Outcast, sure, but his words sounded much more ominous than that.

I wiped my eyes and turned to the back of the folder again. There was no more time for crying. I had to learn what he had left for me.

In the letter Dad had said to remember the trusty old password. I did, of course. We'd used it for secret codes since I was a kid. There were backwards letters here and there on the sheet; when I got to them, I'd need Dad's secret word.

The first line was a ten-digit telephone number that was easily recognizable because the first three numbers – 303 – were an area code for this part of NWA. Next to it Dad had written *PASSWORD: Name of your first dog plus your birthdate numbers all added together.*

I thought I understood. My first dog – one of only two we ever had – was named Samson, and my birth date – November 10, 2076 – was 11-10-76 in numerals. Those numbers added together totaled sixteen.

I stared at the phone number, somehow reluctant to call it. Whose number was this? What was I going to find out when I called? At last I gave in. What did I have to lose by following the instructions my father had left for me? Why put it off any longer? I entered the numbers and initiated the call. A man answered and said only one word.

"Password."

I stumbled for a second. "Samson sixteen." I hoped I'd understood Dad's instructions and that was the correct answer.

There was a pause and I heard the click of a keyboard in the background. The man's next words were much more cordial.

"Hi, Nate. We've been waiting to hear from you."

The warm, friendly voice and clear instructions gave me comfort and reassurance for the first time since this nightmare had begun. I listened for a long time, took notes and asked questions. I heard news about my father for the first time in weeks – information that could only have come from someone inside the Enforcement Patrol itself. These people – the Resistance, they called themselves – were structured and prepared. Obviously I wasn't the first Outcast they'd dealt with, and I felt a sense of calm that I was following Dad's instructions. At last I had plans for a future.

"Do you have safe transportation?" he asked me. "We can send someone for you if we need to."

I told him about the Trailblazer and the stolen plates. He praised me for my ingenuity and asked for the tag number. "I'll run the tag while we talk to be sure there's no problem," he explained. Minutes later he advised me the SUV's tag was fine and told me time was critical. I needed to get out of Lake County as quickly as possible and I agreed to go to Denver tomorrow.

While I was on that call there was another, this one from a number I didn't recognize and let go to voicemail. The area code was the same as mine, but that didn't say much. The phone could be registered anywhere in a huge chunk of what was once southeastern Colorado.

When I was finished, I played back the message. "I want to be sure this call gets to the right person. If you recognize my voice, call me back. I have urgent information from a relative of yours."

Of course I knew that voice. But I thought I was finished with her. She was dangerous.

How did Allie get my number, and what information did she have?

As risky as it was, I had to find out.

CHAPTER TWENTY-FIVE

In June, hikers came across scattered bones in a remote ravine below Johnson's Pass. Thinking at first it might be the remains of an animal, they changed their minds when they found a human skull, hair still matted to its surface. They called the Enforcement Patrol in Leadville, and that afternoon Sheriff Vargas and two officers clambered two thousand feet down the muddy slope of the mountain. The ground was still saturated with moisture from the melting snow and it was slow going, plus the fact Lenny wasn't getting any younger or any skinnier. He slipped a few times, slid on his butt part of the way and reached the bottom long after the two younger men.

When they ran his chip, the cops learned who the man was and when he had died. He was a drifter named Samuel Unger who had no family. His chip had deactivated in April 2089. The EP had received the usual automatic notification but did not investigate. The pass was still closed then and the ravine was packed with snow. The cops assumed Unger was wandering up there for some reason, got into trouble and died from exposure. It happened now and then in the harsh winters. For five years the body had lain in the ravine, covered by snow in the winter and by heavy brush in the warmer months. Animals had scattered the bones everywhere.

After all those years the authorities finally knew how Samuel Unger died. "Looks like blunt force trauma to me," one of the cops said as the sheriff wheezed from his struggle to get down to where the bones lay. "Someone bashed in the right side of his head." Careful not to touch it, he pointed to a patch of matted hair still clinging to a place where the skull was crushed.

A few minutes later Lenny and one officer went back up the mountain. The sheriff took his time and stopped to rest now and then while his younger subordinate scampered up in no time. The third man would stay to secure the area until experts from Denver arrived. Investigating homicides wasn't part of the local EP office's duties. Crime scene investigators from headquarters would come, make an official ruling and take the remains to be disposed of. In this case it would be a pauper's grave. In five years no one had filed a missing person's report on Samuel Unger and the likelihood of finding anyone who cared was remote.

CHAPTER TWENTY-SIX

"Nate! Oh God, it's so good to hear from you. Are you okay?"

"What is it, Allie?" I answered curtly, my heart beating wildly as I heard her voice again. "What information do you have?"

"It's from your father. He's in the Leadville jail and I have a message from him."

My heart jumped. At last I had news about Dad! But could I trust her?

"I don't believe you. How could you have seen my father if he's in jail?"

"You have to believe me, Nate! I have a message from him! I've been working for my stepdad part-time at the EP office and I saw the prisoner report. Saturday when it was quiet I went into the cell block and talked to him. He made me memorize your phone number. He said for me to tell you it's critical that you go through the box. Do you know what he's talking about?"

Of course I knew what she was talking about. I wanted to believe she was on my side, but she could be the enemy. As long as I didn't know, I couldn't jeopardize myself or Dad.

"What else did he say?"

"He asked where your mother was, Nate. He wanted to know what they'd done with his wife and I didn't tell him." She began to cry. "I should have, but there just wasn't time. I was so afraid of getting caught ..."

"Don't worry about it," I answered. "It wasn't your place to tell him."

"Your father's accused of really serious stuff – conspiracy and treason. My stepdad says that headquarters has taken over his case and they're moving him there tomorrow."

"Is there anything in the records about my mom?"

"Nothing. I didn't see anything that showed when she left the Leadville jail or where she went afterwards. There's just nothing about her at all, at least in the records here. I'm so sorry about her."

Now I was crying too. God, how I wanted to believe she was sincerely trying to help me.

"I think about her all the time, Allie. She was the nicest, kindest person and she didn't deserve any of this. She didn't deserve to be arrested and put in jail, dammit, or to be killed by a government that draws lottery numbers to decide who dies. No one deserves that. I have to fight them. Do you understand that? I know you're on the other side and you've probably told your stepfather all about me –"

"I didn't tell him anything! I'm not on the other side; I'm trying to help you, even if you don't believe me. But, Nate, I saw something today that I don't understand. I accessed the list of Lake County residents from my computer at the office. Your father's name is there. Your mother's not listed – we both know why – but your name isn't there either. I really want to help you and be a friend, but I don't know what to believe. What's really going on, Nate? Who are you?"

I hesitated a moment before saying, "Thank you for calling me." I paused again, eager to tell her more. A big part of me wanted to confide in her and tell her everything. I desperately needed someone to talk to. But I couldn't. I couldn't trust anyone, especially Sheriff Vargas's stepdaughter. So I ended it there.

"Thank you, Allie. I'll be in touch."

"Just remember, I'll do whatever I can. Anything –"

I hung up before she was finished. I had to keep myself from getting sucked in.

Her words aren't real, I told myself. *She's not real. Don't get caught up in what she's saying. I barely know her. She's not my friend.*

THE OUTCASTS

The sun was setting as I began to sort out the stuff that constituted my entire life. They were just things – clothes, schoolbooks, papers, notes from Mom and Dad, that kind of meaningless stuff – but they were everything I had. I put what I was taking to Denver in the SUV and the rest I tossed into a pile outside the cave. At daybreak I doused the remnants of my childhood with gasoline and set them on fire, staying close until they burned completely to ashes. That fire consumed a part of my soul along with everything else it destroyed.

CHAPTER TWENTY-SEVEN

I sifted through the ashes to make sure there was nothing that would lead the EP to me, and then I threw water on the smoldering pile. It was six on Sunday morning and it was time to go. I stood beside the fully loaded Chevy Trailblazer and ran down the checklist one last time. The man from the Resistance had asked about what I owned, and he told me what things I should bring to Denver. I had loaded everything from the metal box, Dad's weapons and ammo, all of the nonperishable food and a lot of clothes. The man said the Resistance could use our things to help others. He also sent detailed directions to my tablet and assured me even though I'd never been in a city, I'd be fine if I followed the instructions.

As I drove through our gate, I stopped and got out for a last look back. I doubted I'd ever see the ranch again, this place I'd called home for seventeen years and had rarely left. Now I was about to take the longest trip of my life – one hundred miles to Denver. Not only was it the furthest I'd been from home, it was a passage from the innocence of family, comfort, security and love into a world where, according to Dad, enemies were all around me.

The man I'd spoken with had cautioned me about the trip. He assured me once I got to Denver I'd be safe because they would handle everything from there. I already knew the stolen Chevy was fine; its tag wasn't on the EP's watch list. The Resistance man's biggest concern was that officers would come to the ranch before I could get away or that there would be a routine traffic stop before I got to Interstate 70.

"They know an Outcast's been at the ranch and they'll definitely be coming for you," he pointed out. "There's no telling how quickly they'll react, so you have to get on the road fast." That was why I had worked all night.

I turned south on the main road because I had to drive into Leadville to get to the interstate. Less than a minute later two Enforcement Patrol Suburbans, blue and red lights flashing and sirens wailing, flew past me, going north. Trembling, I kept driving but watched them in the rearview mirror. They turned onto the road that led to just one place – the Dax homestead. I took a deep breath, realizing I had evaded arrest by a matter of seconds.

Nervous as hell, I stayed well below the speed limit through Leadville and turned north onto Highway 91. About five miles out of town there were two more black Suburbans sitting on the shoulder of the highway. One cop looked at me when I passed and my heart jumped, but I kept driving and they stayed where they were. At Copper Mountain I saw the freeway entrance and began to merge into three lanes crammed with the most traffic I'd ever seen. I stayed all the way to the right as dozens of enormous semitrailer trucks flew past me.

The sheer numbers of cars and trucks on this road amazed me, plus the fact that everyone seemed to be in a huge hurry. I kept my speed low as I tried to get accustomed to all this, but people kept honking and passing me, flashing dirty looks or worse. As one guy whizzed past, he pointed to a road sign that said "Minimum speed 40 mph." I glanced at my speedometer; I wasn't even doing thirty. I increased my speed, afraid now I'd get pulled over for driving too slowly. Although that seemed to help the other drivers' attitudes, every single vehicle on the road still passed me.

A little before nine I came down out of the mountains. The bright sun was almost blinding as I saw Denver sprawled in the valley below me. I'd never seen a place so enormous. It was packed with houses and buildings and stretched eastward as far as I could see. Keeping an eye out, I found the exit for Wadsworth Boulevard and pulled over to stretch my legs and recheck my instructions. I kept driving and saw the sign for Broomfield. Soon I turned onto a quiet, tree-lined, dead-end road. There were only a few houses – all large and old and set back behind trees. I drove to the last one on the right and turned into the driveway. Hidden behind a row of tall shrubs there was a two-story red brick house. Smoke was drifting gently from a tall chimney. The place looked friendly and warm. I wondered whose house it was.

Following my instructions, I drove around back to a detached three-car garage with one of its doors open. A man around Dad's age was inside. He gave me a smile and waved me in, closing the door behind me.

"You must be Nate." He stuck out his hand as I got out. "Any trouble getting here? Did my instructions work for you?"

"Yes, sir. I've never been out of Leadville before. I was a little nervous, but it all worked out."

He grinned. "Glad to hear it. This metro traffic can be a little daunting, but you're in good hands now. I'm Jim Gordon, by the way. Call me Jim. Here, let me help you with your stuff. This place will be home for a while."

We unloaded the packed Chevy, putting the things for the Resistance on one side of the garage. He said I should take my own stuff and leave the rest for some guys to pick up tomorrow. "Be sure to bring everything that was in your dad's box," he added. "That stuff needs to go downtown with us this afternoon." It surprised me for a second when he mentioned the metal box, but I figured there were no more secrets now.

He helped me carry my things into the house and led me to a second-floor bedroom full of light. There were two twin beds – this would be my room for a while, Jim said, and I'd be sharing it with a guy named Ben whom I'd meet this evening. The room was a refreshing change from the cave and the dank tunnels underneath the fort where I'd been living for years.

Jim pointed out a bathroom in the hall and said this upstairs one was guys only. He explained that including me, there were six residents here – two females and three males, plus Jim. There were three bedrooms upstairs. One was his, one was a single, and Ben and I would share the third. The girls slept in a downstairs bedroom with its own full bath.

"We'll be leaving at one. You have several hours. Would you like to relax, maybe take a shower or a nap? If you're asleep, I'll wake you when it's time for lunch."

A shower sounded like the greatest thing imaginable. I'd only had a sponge bath since I moved to the cave over a week ago and I wondered if Jim had suggested a shower because I smelled. I stripped and stood for ten minutes under the hottest stream of water I could stand.

Afterwards I put my clothes in the drawers and closet and suddenly I felt incredibly tired. It was 9:30 in the morning, but I hadn't slept all night and my body ached from nervous tension from my narrow escape and first experience at interstate driving. I put on a sweatshirt and shorts, crawled under the cool sheets and was out in minutes.

It seemed as though I'd been asleep for a few seconds when I heard a knock at my door. "Nate? Are you awake?"

I glanced at my watch and saw I'd slept for over two hours. I jumped out of bed, opened the bedroom door and immediately caught the intoxicating smell of food. Suddenly I realized I was starving – I hadn't had a hot meal in weeks – and my stomach began growling.

"Fifteen minutes till lunch," Jim advised. "Then we'll head downtown."

I asked him what I should wear and he told me the clothes I had on were fine. Everything was casual, especially with today being Sunday, he added.

When I got to the kitchen, Jim was at a table in a breakfast nook, looking at his tablet. A really cute girl introduced herself as Maeve and ladled out a big bowl of vegetable soup with a side of cornbread. It looked heavenly and smelled even better. She brought Jim a bowl, fixed hers and we sat down to eat. Jim explained that there were three other residents who were out working, so today it was just the three of us for lunch.

"Are you an Outcast?" Maeve asked as I dove into my first hot meal in days. I said yes and she said she was too. "I've been here a year. Everyone who stays here helps out. I do the shopping and cooking. They'll assign you chores and things. It sounds like work, but it's all good." I liked her attitude and her friendliness. But behind her warm smile there was something else. She was really sad inside – I could sense it from the moment I met her.

"How can you go shopping if you're an Outcast?" I asked.

"Oh, I've got a generic chip. I can go anywhere I want and Cassie goes with me when I buy stuff. She's my roommate – Cassandra Cox. She's chipped."

Maeve has a generic chip? I asked what that was and Jim explained to Maeve, "He just got here. He hasn't been told about that yet." To me he said, "You'll learn about chipping soon."

None of it made sense. All my life I'd heard either you were an Outcast or you were chipped. There was no in between. What was a generic chip? I'd never heard of one.

"Where are you from?" I asked as she walked to the stove to refill my bowl.

"Oklahoma City originally, but my folks moved to Las Vegas to help with the Resistance. But I don't want to talk about it right now."

She took a bite of soup and I saw her dab her eyes with a napkin. "I'm sorry ..."

"Do you mind if I give him your background?" Jim asked.

She shook her head. "That's fine."

"Maeve's mother and father were leaders of the Resistance, like your father," he explained. "There's a cell in Vegas, even bigger than the one we have here. Just like yours, her folks were chipped people. Those are the ones who can help us the most. They move freely in society without arousing any suspicion. Have you ever heard of the Underground Railroad back in the Civil War?"

I nodded. I'd learned about it in American history. It was a way for slaves to escape from the South to freedom in the North.

"Maeve's parents helped create a modern-day Underground Railroad to move Outcasts from dangerous situations to safe houses like ours, where they could be protected and integrated into society. There's a lot you don't know yet, but I can tell you this. Her mom and dad were heroes to the Resistance movement. So was her brother, Carlton."

He's talking about them in the past tense. Has she lost three members of her family?

She whispered, "But they got caught."

"I'm so sorry," I said, dreading where this story would end up. I felt a tear in my eye as I thought of my folks.

"Nate understands what you're going through better than most," Jim said, patting my arm. "His mom was euthanized by the PCC and his father is in prison." He looked at me and finished Maeve's story. "Her brother was killed a year ago. If that wasn't enough for one person to bear, her parents were given up by a mole inside the Resistance."

She suddenly let out a raging scream. "Seven weeks ago! They were arrested for treason, sentenced and euthanized within twenty-four hours. Seven weeks ago! Now do you understand why I'm here? I hate the government! I hate what they've done to people. I'll fight them until I die!"

We finished lunch in awkward silence. Afterwards everyone cleared dishes, and then Maeve shooed us out of the kitchen, saying she'd finish up so we could go to the office. She gave me a big smile and said, "I'm glad you're here. It's about time there was someone else my age."

She's really nice, I thought to myself as I got ready to leave. *She's been through a lot, just like I have. Maybe ...*

No. There was no room for anyone else in my world. It was complicated enough already.

CHAPTER TWENTY-EIGHT

We took Interstate 25 downtown. In the rear seat was a suitcase Jim had given me that held everything from Dad's metal box.

He told me the end of Maeve's parents' story. She and Cassie had moved to Denver a year ago, not long after her brother died. Her parents continued fighting the World Union in Philadelphia, and they wanted their daughter somewhere far away where she'd be safe. She was a huge help running the safe house, Jim continued. She'd only learned about her parents' arrests and deaths after she'd tried several times to contact them, then called a relative. It had been a horrific experience.

In a way, her story was my story too. She'd left her parents one day, fully expecting to see them again. My parents had gone to town one day, fully expecting to come home. Now both of hers were gone, and my mom was too. Maybe Dad was next, but by God I would do whatever I could to save him. I hoped the people I'd meet today would give me a way to do that.

I really wanted to change the subject for now. This was hard to talk about.

"Can I ask you a question?"

"Fire away, kid. Anything you want to know, just ask."

"Are you an Outcast?" He hadn't talked about himself during lunch and I wondered.

Jim laughed. "My old girlfriends would tell you yes, I'm as outcast as you get, but in the World Union sense of the word, no. I have a chip. I bet I know your next question," he continued with a smile. "Why am I here, risking my life when I could be existing like a billion other so-called normal people?"

"Yeah, I guess that's what I want to know." In reality, I had no idea what this was about. I had simply followed my father's instructions and now I was hooked up with something called the Resistance. I didn't really even know what they were resisting or why it was such a big deal.

"Most of us believe what the World Union is doing is wrong, but there are lots of different reasons people have chosen to resist. For me, it's pretty simple. It sounds old-fashioned after all these years, but I'm a throwback to the days before population control. Even though protection of our planet is a noble aspiration, achieving that goal by killing people every six months is barbaric. In a technological world like ours, there have to be better ways to save the planet. Those of us who have chips are valuable to the cause because we have free movement within society."

I didn't say anything. His answer gave me a dozen more questions, but I wasn't sure if I should ask them.

Jim broke the silence. "Your dad has been a huge help to the Resistance for years," he said quietly. "But you didn't know anything about that, did you?"

I shook my head in astonishment at what I was hearing. I'd been through all that stuff in the box, so I knew he was interested in the Resistance, but I had no idea that he was actively working with them.

"But he almost never left the ranch. How could he have been so involved?"

"You may not have been aware of it, but he was with us a lot. Did you know he was gone one or two nights every week?"

"Sure. He was on some kind of neighborhood committee. He went to meetings at night to meet with other ranchers and talk about things we all needed." I paused, suddenly realizing that he hadn't been doing that at all. I was beginning to understand a little of this.

"He wasn't really on a committee, was he?"

"No. He was with us. Your parents kept his work secret to protect you. He talked about your safety all the time.

He would come here to Denver and work with us, sometimes all night long. Other times we'd meet somewhere halfway. And about your mother – I'm so sorry, Nate. What happened to her is exactly why so many of us are part of this. I should have said something about your mom before I started raving about population control. That was really insensitive of me and I apologize. Sometimes I let my fervor get ahead of my brain."

I choked back a sob and changed the subject. "Do you know where Dad is now?"

"I'm going to defer that one to my boss. You're going to meet him in a little while and he knows a lot more than I do."

In a few minutes we turned a corner and Jim pointed to a four-story glass building with the name SECURITY BRIDGE CORPORATION on its top. "Home sweet home," he said as we went down a ramp into a garage where dozens of cars were parked. He found an empty spot and pointed to an elevator. "Grab your stuff and let's go upstairs."

"What does this company do?" I asked, wondering why so many cars were in the garage on a Sunday afternoon.

"We do high-tech information monitoring and security services for corporations and the government. Very hush-hush stuff."

The company does work for the government! I started to ask about it, but just then the elevator door opened into a large waiting room on the second floor. It was filled with couches, chairs and tables. The company must have a lot of visitors, I thought, but today it was empty. Jim waved at a security guard sitting behind a reception desk and said, "Having a quiet Sunday, Mike?"

The guard gave a thumbs-up. "At least the Broncos are playing. Keeps me out of trouble."

Jim walked to the desk and I saw the guard hand him something that he stuck in his pocket. He returned, using an access card to open a door into a narrow hallway.

I was walking behind him, but suddenly I stopped. There was a portal ahead, blocking the entire hall. There was no way around it. I'd never been through one – since I was a kid I'd been conditioned to stay clear of them. For an Outcast, a portal meant one thing only – danger.

"Uh, Jim." I hesitated, pointing at the detection device.

He laughed. "Come on. Don't worry."

I approached the machine cautiously and he asked, "Is this your first time to go through one of these?"

I nodded and he said, "Just follow me. You'll be fine – you have to learn about these contraptions and now's as good a time as any. At least you're among friends instead of out there on the street somewhere."

Jim walked through the device and nothing happened. When I passed through, a buzzer sounded and a red light on top of the portal began to blink.

He reached in his pocket and pulled out the thing the guard had given him. It was a big yellow smiley-face button. "Stick it on your shirt. You'll need to wear it all the time."

"Will this keep the buzzer from sounding? Is this what Maeve called a generic chip?" I hadn't seen one of these buttons on her, but maybe I'd missed it.

"No. They're a little more sophisticated than this. Chipping comes later. Outcasts who are in the building get a button so our staff can identify them easier. There's no reason to be afraid – there's no place on Earth where you're among more friends than here. It's mostly a reminder for when someone takes you outside. No one wants to make a mistake in public. Now come on. There's someone who's waiting to see you."

He had mentioned that I was going to meet his boss. But what if ... my adrenalin began flowing as I wondered if somehow my father might be here too!

We walked through a large room filled with cubicles. Dozens of men and women wearing headsets were talking, creating an undercurrent of low rumbling babble.

"Tech support people," Jim explained. "They're assisting call-in customers."

We went across the room and walked down a carpeted hallway with large offices on both sides. Jim ushered me into one of them, closing the door behind us. In the middle of the expansive room was a huge desk filled with papers and manuals. There was a sitting area with armchairs and a coffee table, and dozens of plaques and photos were hanging on a wall. Each picture included a tall, handsome black man in a social setting with one or more politicians, sports figures or celebrities. Many were autographed.

Jim walked to a panel on the opposite wall, put his index finger on a tiny pad I hadn't noticed, and the panel swung open silently. We went through and it closed behind us. Suddenly we weren't in a busy corporation's offices anymore; we were walking down another hallway – this one long and dark, with closed doors on both sides. At the end we came to a brightly lit room with sunshine pouring through huge windows. Jim stuck his head inside, rapped on the door and said, "I have someone you need to meet."

It wasn't my dad. It was the tallest, blackest, friendliest-looking giant of a man I had ever seen – the same man who was in the pictures in that office.

"Carlos," Jim said, "meet Nathan Dax. Nate, this is Carlos Fine. He's president of Security Bridge and head of the Resistance in Denver."

Carlos came from around his desk and put his arms around me in a bear hug. "Man, I'm glad to see you," he gushed, pushing me backwards and looking me over. "Chip off the old block, isn't he, Jim? Sit down, sit down. You want a Coke or something?"

"No, sir, thanks."

He took an armchair next to mine and leaned in when we talked, making me feel that everything I said was important to him. "You don't need to call me sir. I'm just Carlos. We've wondered about you ever since your mom and dad ..." He paused for a second, thinking. "I need to tell you about them before we do anything else. Jim, give us a few minutes, will you?"

Jim pulled the door shut behind him as Carlos looked me in the eyes and began to talk.

"Your mother was a wonderful woman," he began as I felt a lump in my throat and fought back tears. "I met her several times up at your ranch ..."

"How? I've never seen you before. How could you have come to the ranch and I didn't know it?"

"Because you spent the nights at the fort for the past two years. You weren't aware of what was going on at the house. Most of the time your dad would come here for meetings, but sometimes I went to Leadville. Melanie never came with him because he kept her away from us on purpose. If he was caught, he didn't want her being taken too and leaving you alone. Sadly, what he feared was exactly what happened. They took them both. When I learned they were in the Lake County jail, I figured they'd have to let her go because they couldn't connect her with anything your dad was involved in. But then her lottery number was drawn and that changed everything."

I struggled to put on a brave front, but when I began crying, he pushed a box of tissues in my direction. "I'll never see her again. She and Dad left that morning to go to town like always, and now she's gone. Just like that. The bastards ..." I put my head in my hands and sobbed like a child. "The bastards just killed her."

Carlos sat back and let me get it out. It was the first time I'd opened up to anyone except Allie, and I hadn't said much to her in the short time we'd been together. He explored my feelings, asked how I was doing on my own, wondered if I was willing to help other people in my situation, and seemed to genuinely care about what I was going through.

"Thousands of people like me take risks every day in hopes your mother and others like her didn't die in vain," he said at last. "The murders of innocent citizens around the world have to stop, and I'll work until I die for justice and equality for everyone. We all will – all of the people who dedicate ourselves to the Resistance."

I told Carlos I had secretly hoped my father would be here waiting for me.

"I can't imagine anything that would have been better. Actually, your father's incarcerated at the Enforcement Patrol headquarters building three miles from here. They brought him from Leadville less than two hours ago."

I must have gotten to the safe house in Broomfield around the same time they were transporting Dad to EP headquarters here. That was a bizarre coincidence. I thought for a second about what might have happened if I'd known. Maybe I could have wrecked their SUV and freed my father. Stupid, right? But I'd have tried. I would have died trying.

"How do you know so much? How do you know my father was transferred two hours ago?"

"You're going to learn a lot about us while you're here," he answered. "I never confide in anyone I just met, but I'm making an exception because of your dad. He's the most trustworthy man I ever met and I'm treating you just as I'd treat him. You're no stranger to secrecy – you've been hiding for seventeen years – but the things you're going to learn here are so critical that people would lose their lives if information got out.

"To answer your question, Security Bridge Corporation – the company I founded – is an information services provider. The name explains part of what we do – providing security bridges that encrypt and protect highly sensitive information. But we also perform background checks, do intensive training and maintain web-hosting services for our clients. We install servers that network the Galaxy for the world's largest corporations. Most importantly, we're a contractor to the World Union. We maintain the information networks for the Enforcement Patrol's worldwide operations."

He sat back and let me absorb that information.

"So let me get this straight," I said, hardly able to believe this. "You have access to the EP's computers?"

"A lot of data but not everything. It took me years of patience and effort to get my company accepted as a contractor. Security Bridge is one of the most respected companies in its field and the World Union trusts our work implicitly. No one has any idea I've been a leader in the Resistance movement for all this time, and thanks to the company's government contracts, we can access almost all of the World Union's Galaxy accounts."

"How do you keep your employees from telling someone? Does everyone who works here know what you're doing?"

"Absolutely not. Did you see the tech guys out there in the bull pen when you came through? We provide twenty-four seven support for thousands of clients, and like most everyone else here, they have no idea Security Bridge is a front for what's going on behind the scenes. The office you came through – my office – is the only way to access this part of the building. The cubicles in the open areas are specially placed so that our workers can see windows and each other but not the traffic areas where visitors come and go. If someone's coming to this building on Resistance business, we know about it and we get them through the office and back here before the employees know anyone's around.

"There are almost six hundred employees in this building and several thousand more in places where we have major clients – Geneva, Tel Aviv, Mexico City and the other hubs of government. None of those employees knows anything about our efforts. Others – the ones who do know – work behind the scenes back here in the part of the building we outfitted for the Resistance. The chipped ones are on the payroll of Security Bridge. The ones who can't get paid – the Outcasts – are very good at making ends meet in whatever ways are required. You'll learn about all that, not that you don't already know." He smiled. "I hope that gives you a little idea of what's going on. You're privy to top-secret information just by sitting here in my secret office that the world has no idea even exists."

I had to bring up the questions that had been weighing on me since he began to talk. "So why did they burn our house and barn? They weren't looking for an Outcast, right? What's really going on?"

"They were looking for evidence tying your parents to the Resistance. Specifically, I think they were looking for that box your dad hid. Speaking of which, did you bring the contents?"

I nodded and opened the briefcase next to me. Carlos laid everything out in neat stacks on a coffee table and said we'd go through it as soon as he finished giving me the background I needed.

Over the next hour I learned about my dad's decades-long involvement with the movement. His dedication and intense passion for a cause he believed in made him a role model for the others, Carlos told me, and he said he was proud to be associated with a true patriot like Daniel Dax. He had donated supplies, given his time and talents, and worked tirelessly for freedom. It made me proud to listen to those words, even though at this very minute he was in a cell because of what he had done.

"The World Union doesn't think he's a patriot," I replied angrily. "They arrested him and Mom. What's going to happen to him?"

His face turned serious. "This may be hard to hear, but you need to know it. I'm going to be completely honest with you. The World Union has been known to use interrogation techniques that are barbaric, and we hear they've brought in a specialist from Mexico City for Dan's case. Your dad doesn't know about Melanie's death. I think they intend to use her as bait and get him to confess if they promise to release her."

"We have to get Dad out! You have access to the EP's database. Do you know exactly where he is? Can you send someone to rescue him?"

"Slow down a second, Nate. We do have access to some information inside the EP. Not everything, but enough to get an idea of what's going on. Believe me, I wish it were as simple as sending in a rescue squad. Of everyone who's in custody, I want your father out the most. The Enforcement Patrol knows he works with the Resistance, but I think they'd be blown away if they knew what he actually could give them. He knows every single thing we're doing here. He's been my top advisor for years. The information he has could take us down and put all of us in prison, or worse. I know

Dan; in normal circumstances he would die before he'd reveal anything. He's as dedicated and committed as any soldier on earth. It's your mother's situation that has me a little worried. If your father thinks he can help her, he will. In your dad's mind, she comes first. As she should."

"But my mother's dead." I looked at Carlos's face, but I could read nothing. "She *is* dead, right?"

He stared at me without saying a word.

CHAPTER TWENTY-NINE

It seemed like forever before Carlos spoke.

"Everything in the World Union's database indicates your mother was euthanized. The standard notification email was released" – I knew that, I had read it – "and her chip was deactivated like all the others they killed in that round. So to answer your question, yes. I believe your mother died at the Euthanization Center here in Denver eleven days ago."

"But you hesitated ..."

"Because I wanted to get my thoughts together. Losing your mother is a terrible thing. I know that because it happened to me a long time ago. My mom died the same way as yours. That event caused me to dedicate my life, my strength and my resources to this battle.

"I'm sorry, Nate. I'm sorry we live in a stupid world where the government has a lottery to see whose loved ones are going to die. My life's committed to righting the wrongs and I want to let you in on a little secret. Your dad and I have had many conversations about you and I've followed your life since you were a kid."

He must have seen the look of surprise on my face. He continued, "It's true. I helped develop the list of homeschool subjects you'd learn based on what would be most important for you later on. Do you think every Outcast kid gets so much training and education about American history and politics? You have no way to know, but the answer is no. And look at the survival techniques Dan taught you so you could manage on your own if you had to. All that was planned and look how it's paid off already. Your parents hoped you would join the Resistance someday, and right now I'm praying it happens. I need you – we all need you.

But there's time for that down the line. For now we have to focus on your father. We're working on a plan."

"A plan for rescuing Dad? But you said he's in a jail cell at EP headquarters. And you said it wasn't as simple as sending in a team."

"We have to take things more slowly than we'd like. It's not a rescue plan yet. We have to let him know your mother was euthanized as quickly as possible. As awful as that news will be, he can be assured nothing he does will harm Melanie. The World Union interrogators have a lot of nasty things they can use. They have drugs to make prisoners talk, for instance, but that tactic's not going to work on your father. I'll keep you in the loop as my guys are working on your dad's situation. For now, I'd like to see what clues he left in the old metal box."

"What do you mean the drugs won't work on Dad?"

"I'm sorry I said that, Nate. You just have to trust me. The less you know about some things, the better off you are."

Carlos called in a nerdy-looking guy who looked to be in his early twenties, told me he was the best hacker in the universe, and gave him the ancient USB thumb drives and the Apple tablet. "I know I don't need to tell you I need this sooner rather than later," he told the pimply-faced kid.

"Like everything else you give me, boss? No prob. You got it, dude."

"I'm not a dude, dude. Now get out of here and get to work," Carlos said with a laugh as we turned to the file Dad had left for me. We read his letter together – I almost had it memorized by now – and he looked over the hodgepodge of letters and numbers on the back of the folder.

"Good for your dad, putting our number first on the list," he said. "He knows we're your best resource."

"What's all this other stuff?" I asked. "Do you think they're all passwords?"

"Knowing your dad, I'll bet you're right." He asked if he could turn his technician loose on Dad's list. That was fine with me; we had to know what Dad had left for me, and cracking his codes seemed to be the way.

THE OUTCASTS

It was almost 5:30 and Carlos said, "I think we'd better wrap up for today. Who's in charge of the kitchen out where you're staying – Maeve?"

I nodded.

"Then I'm damned sure not going to make you late. She can be a crazy woman when people aren't on time!" His infectious laugh had me smiling too, even after all the heavy things we'd gone over this afternoon.

He asked if there was anything I needed, and I was glad he did. In all the frenzy of activity, I'd totally forgotten about my horse Dixie. She was in the corral by the fort. There were cattle in the back pasture too. They'd have to be moved soon because winter was coming.

Carlos promised to take care of everything at the ranch, especially Dixie. "There are people who'll give her a good home until you can come get her," he promised as he walked me out to the lobby. "See you tomorrow, Nate," he said, giving me a bear hug and turning me over to Jim for the trip back to the house. "I'm proud to know you and I'm glad you're here with us. Remember this – anything you and I talk about is just between us. Agreed?"

I nodded, glad too that I was here. I not only felt like I was among friends, I was buoyed by the possibility that the Resistance might somehow rescue my father.

CHAPTER THIRTY

When Jim and I got to the safe house, all the others were home. I walked into the kitchen and Maeve started the introductions. There was Cassie Cox, who had blue eyes and blond hair and was really tall. I met my roommate, Ben Creel, a black guy who was built like a football player. When I shook his hand, I thought he was going to crush mine. I winced and he laughed, apologizing.

"He has that effect on everyone," Maeve said with a smile. "Just doesn't know his own strength. Only I can defeat him!" She socked him lightly on the arm and he recoiled as if she'd thrown a knockout punch. The camaraderie between these people felt really comfortable.

"And they saved the best introduction for last," the other guy said, standing up with a flourish. He was short and thin, wore thick glasses with out-of-style black frames and had a cowlick sticking up. "Aristotle Smithins Hightower the fourth at your service," he announced in a pronounced British accent as he bowed deeply. "My friends – that includes you now, Nate – call me Smitty."

"Anybody ready for a beer?" Maeve asked. "Uh-oh, I'm forgetting that we have a new resident. ID check! How old are you, Nate?"

"I'm seventeen, but I don't drink anyway, so none for me."

"I certainly drink," Smitty responded with a theatrical sigh. "After the day I've had, I believe I'll have one." The others joined him.

"Smitty's got the most interesting job of all of us," Cassie said in a pleasant voice. "He works for –"

Smitty exploded. "Don't tell him! After dinner we'll make him guess! He'll never figure it out!"

149

The six of us sat around the dining table – Jim and the five of us – and I learned more about them as we ate another simple but delicious meal. Maeve was twenty-two, Cassie twenty-five and the guys were in their early thirties. Cassie and Maeve had been here the longest – just over a year. This wasn't a permanent housing solution, I was told. It was a transitional residence until permanent digs could be arranged.

"Why don't you all tell Nate about yourselves?" Jim suggested. "Cassie, you start. And we'll want to hear Nate's story too."

I watched the girl begin talking. She was so pretty, so tall and graceful, but she was painfully shy. She lowered her eyes and clasped her hands in her lap as she began. "There's not much to tell about me. I'm chipped and I'm from Philadelphia. My mom and dad are surgeons. I work downtown for the World Union Republic Bank. I'm in World points tech support, helping people whose chips malfunction and won't issue them points to buy stuff. That's about it for me."

The confusion must have shown on my face because Ben picked up on it. "I don't think Nate understands ..." he said. "Maybe you can explain why a chipped person lives in a Resistance safe house."

"Mom and Dad are undercover supporters of the Resistance because of population control. Doctors take an oath, you know – the Hippocratic Oath. One part of it says they can't play at being God. They decided a long time ago that euthanizing citizens simply because there are too many of us was playing God and it wasn't right. After ... after my boyfriend was murdered by the EP, I told my parents I had to go away. I needed to breathe, to get a new start. Maeve was moving to Denver to work for the Resistance. She was my best friend and I decided to come west with her."

Her boyfriend was murdered by the EP! More shock and confusion in my mind.

"Cassie's story becomes intertwined with Maeve's at this point," Jim explained. "Can one of you tell Nate the rest?"

"I'll try," Cassie answered. "I'm here because I believe in the Resistance like my parents. My boyfriend ... the Enforcement Patrol ..." She dabbed at her eyes with a napkin. "I guess I can't do it after all. I'm not as strong as you are, Maeve. You tell him."

"It's okay, baby," Maeve whispered, squeezing her hand. "I'm not strong either. I fell apart today at lunch telling Nate about my folks." She took a deep breath. "Cassie's boyfriend was my older brother, Carlton. He was in college in Philly, where we all lived. He became interested in the Resistance and talked a lot to Cassie's mom and dad about it. They encouraged him because, as Jim said earlier, chipped people can help the movement way more than Outcasts.

"Somebody at the university ratted him out and the EP showed up to arrest him at the busiest time of the day, when afternoon classes were dismissed and kids were everywhere. They wanted to make a point, I think. Cassie and I were walking toward him, meeting him like we did every day after class. We saw the whole thing." She began to cry, but her voice got stronger as she continued.

"They ordered him to put his hands up, but he refused. He struggled and an officer hit him twice with a Taser. They didn't know he had a heart murmur. Only Cassie and I knew that. I tried to tell the cop, but he hit Carlton anyway. He died right there on the sidewalk. Everyone around was afraid to get involved. The EP yelled at us to back away, but we wouldn't. They threatened to arrest us, the bastards, but we didn't move. We held him ..."

I wasn't surprised when she broke down. Hers was a heart-wrenching story, especially coming so soon after what had happened to her parents. "He wasn't doing anything to hurt anybody. He had a damned heart murmur, just like I do, and they killed him. They killed my brother, just like they murdered my parents!"

The girls ran out of the room.

After a few moments of silence, Jim said, "Chipped or Outcast, each of us has a story or we wouldn't be part of the Resistance. Some are more horrible than others. Those two have tough stories – especially Maeve, who lost her entire family – but every one is painful to hear."

In a few minutes the girls came back to the table and sat quietly as we finished dinner without further discussion. Afterwards Maeve set a carton of vanilla ice cream on the table, brought out a steaming-hot apple pie, sliced and served it. I'd been smelling the incredible aroma since I got home earlier. This wonderful pie also broke my heart. I hadn't had dessert since Mom left, and now I was flooded with memories of what a great cook she had been. I kept my emotions in check in front of my new friends, but now I understood them better. Each one had something inside that ate at them just like I did.

After the dishes were cleared and done, Jim went to his room to catch up on work. Everyone else ended up in the living room. Most evenings they watched movies, they told me, but tonight we continued the conversation from earlier.

Maeve started by saying, "I want to tell you something else, something you'll learn yourself if you stay here for a while. I was all alone in the world until I found this safe house. Now I have friends, security and my life has a purpose. I thought I'd never have any of that, especially after losing my entire family. You'll find it too, Nate. You're among friends here, friends who can help you."

I thanked her and Smitty interjected, "Enough sad for now. Guess what I do. Betcha a hundred World points you'll never guess."

"I'll give it a try, but first you have to tell me if you're an Outcast."

"Fair enough," he responded. "Obviously if I'm an Outcast, that'd eliminate a lot of jobs I might be doing. So the answer is no. Ben here is the only castoff among us," he added jokingly. I liked Smitty already – his personality made me feel relaxed.

"Ben's not the only one anymore," I admitted. "I'm an Outcast too." Ben gave me a high five, joking that the "chippers," as he called them, in this house were a little too snooty for his taste. Now I knew that Maeve, Ben and I were Outcasts, although she had a generic chip.

Back to Smitty's guessing game, I didn't know much about what kind of jobs people held since I'd led a sheltered life on the ranch. "I bet you work for the Resistance downtown at headquarters," I answered at last.

Everyone smiled. "Good guess," Smitty replied, "but how about just the opposite? I work at Enforcement Patrol headquarters. Told ya you'd never guess it! You owe me a hundred World points. Oh yeah, you're an Outcast. You can't pay me, can you? Pretty sneaky how you got out of that one!"

He works for the EP! That *was* a shock! Was he the Resistance mole? I doubted it; he was open about working there, but he was also living here in a safe house. That made no sense to me. There had to be lots more to his story, but I was beginning to feel the effects of only two hours' sleep in over forty hours. I couldn't last much longer and hoped we could put off the rest until tomorrow. Unfortunately for me, they asked about my story next.

I gave them a brief version of my life so far. I didn't mention that I killed that guy five years ago, but I explained that the EP had arrested my parents and burned our house. Mom's lottery number had been drawn and she was euthanized a few weeks ago. My dad had left a cryptic message that led to the Resistance, and here I was. They asked a lot of questions and I tried to answer them. Yes, I said, my dad was once an Outcast too and he was part of the Resistance, although I only learned that last part when I got to Denver. He was in jail for subversive activity, but they hadn't charged him with anything.

"I know my dad was involved with the Resistance and they think he's a traitor, but arresting Mom too ... I just don't get it. And now – now she's gone. I have to focus now on rescuing my father."

"The EP thinks all Outcasts are traitors," Ben said sympathetically. "I'm sorry about your parents, Nate. This is why we're all here. You found the right place, coming here and meeting Carlos," he continued, becoming more fervent by the minute. "We all are here to fight the World Union. Our government – our leaders – are a bunch of heartless, greedy, selfish bastards who don't care anything about the common people."

"Why don't you say how you really feel?" Maeve responded. She looked at me and said, "We're all passionate about the cause. I'm sorry too about your loss – and mine, and Cassie's, and everyone's. Tonight's conversation has been hard on all of us. Let's lighten it up before we turn in. And by the way, don't worry about your new roommate. Poor Ben just gets a little lonely now and then and needs some tender loving care, don't you, baby?"

"Not from you, crazy woman!" he said in mock horror. "The day I need your TLC will be my worst day ever."

"You know I'm the love of your life. But it'll be our little secret."

Everyone laughed at their good-natured sparring, including me. They were obviously close friends and I thought about how much I'd missed by being an only child in an isolated environment. I knew Dad and Mom did it for a reason, but as bad as things were in my life right now, I couldn't imagine a more welcoming situation than this one.

"Nate already heard my story at lunch," Maeve told the group. "Ben, I guess you're up. Try to limit the BS and make it at least partially truthful."

He countered, "You could only wish your life was half as interesting as mine."

She stuck out her tongue at him. I yawned loudly and Maeve said, "See? You've already bored Nate to death and you haven't even started yet!"

"This has to be the last one for me," I said, admitting I was dog-tired."Go ahead, Ben. I can't wait another minute for your exciting life story!"

"You'll be glad you heard it," he began as the others booed. "You'd better hang on for dear life. It doesn't get any better than this! My father and my uncle had a very unusual occupation. You think it was hard guessing what Smitty did? How about this? My dad and his brother were pirates!"

Everyone looked at me to see the reaction. This time my face was full of astonishment and disbelief. I shook my head, certain I was being played in some kind of joke.

Smitty laughed out loud and said, "Like Maeve said, Ben's full of BS most of the time. But this story really is true and I think it's fascinating."

Ben put on a major frown. "Are you finished interrupting, and may I continue?"

"By all means," Smitty responded with a magnanimous hand gesture.

Ben was born and chipped in Vero Beach, in the Northeast America sector. His parents divorced when he was four and his mom moved away to pursue a career, leaving Ben to be raised by his dad and uncle, who were commercial fishermen. The brothers moved into one house, sharing expenses and the responsibilities of raising a child. At some point while he was in high school, Ben's dad and uncle shifted the scope of their fishing venture, branching out into a more lucrative enterprise – hijacking cargo ships that constantly moved along the East Coast from Charleston and points south to and from the Caribbean.

They ignored the massive container ships whose decks were ten stories above the water. No small-time pirate could pierce the security and sheer magnitude of those vessels. But there were hundreds of smaller boats, including the ones Ben's relatives liked best – tramp steamers. They'd pick the older, slower, smaller ones that were usually less than three hundred feet long, and they'd always pick boats heading northbound, since those were returning from Caribbean ports fully loaded and usually with a crew of only two or three.

The two men would pick up one or two more hands and use one ploy or another to lure an unsuspecting freighter to stop. Sometimes it was a fisherman whose boat had run out of gas and who was now lost in the dark. Another time it was a forty-two-foot pleasure craft with loud college boys on board, drinking and ignoring the shipping lanes they were drifting aimlessly in. Whatever it took, once the cargo boat stopped, the pirates would board, disarm the crew and tie them up. Another boat would be situated close by and it would pull alongside where as much cargo as could be offloaded in a reasonably short time would end up on the new boat.

The pirates would leave, knowing the crew would free themselves soon and were in no real danger. Meanwhile Ben's dad and uncle would end up with a load of rum, sugar or petroleum oil. Occasionally they hit the jackpot, finding a stash of cocaine, marijuana or even gold hidden inside bags or crates of ordinary cargo.

I interrupted. "But with the World point system, they couldn't sell that stuff, could they?"

"They didn't have a little pirate shop down on the beach, if that's what you're asking," he replied affably as the others laughed. "They bartered what they stole to get things they could either use themselves or trade to someone else. My dad and uncle didn't use drugs, but one time they traded twenty bricks of cocaine they'd discovered inside a container of bananas for a fifty-four-foot sport fishing boat.

"Things finally caught up with them one night. They got wind of a shipment of rum coming from Jamaica on an old tramp steamer named the *Jessie B*. The captain was a drunk and he had only one mate on board. This would be the simplest job ever. But it was a setup. When they intercepted the boat, floodlights came on all over the place and they saw World Union Coast Guardsmen everywhere. The first time I knew something was wrong was when they didn't come home the next morning."

Ben had visited his dad right after the arrest, when he was still in the Vero Beach jail. "Get out of town and get rid of your chip," his father had advised. "If they think you're involved, they'll come for you."

"I stayed around until their sentencing a few days later. They each got twenty years for smuggling, and when they were taken off to the World Union penitentiary at Fort Knox, I took Dad's advice. I packed his truck with everything I could carry, started west, and the cops never came after me."

"But you were chipped, right? How'd you end up being an Outcast?"

"That's another story entirely," he said as the others groaned.

"I'm tired and we need to get Nate off to bed too," Cassie said. "I've heard Ben's story, every version of it, a hundred times." She stood and so did Maeve.

I was exhausted. This had been a long, hard day of revelations. I stifled a huge yawn. Ben promised to give me part two of his saga another day, and Smitty chimed in that his story was far more interesting than Ben's and it too was yet to come. I barely washed my face I was so tired, and I crawled into my new, soft, comfortable bed. I was encouraged and happy to be among friends who could possibly help rescue my dad. He wasn't the only one who needed rescuing, I thought to myself as I drifted off to sleep.

I needed it too.

CHAPTER THIRTY-ONE

As his son spent that Sunday afternoon learning about his father's work with the Resistance, Dan Dax sat in a straight-backed metal chair with his hands cuffed behind him. A leather strap held his torso secure and he stared at the men who sat in front of him at an old wooden table. They were in a windowless basement room made of concrete block walls with peeling gray paint and a steel door that had bars in a small window. The door was scratched and nicked. This room had seen plenty of use.

Major Wheeler had taken Lenny Vargas off the Dax investigation after Vargas and his men burned the house and barn, destroying whatever evidence might have been there to find. Then Wheeler had separated the couple, bringing Dan's wife to Denver weeks ago, not long before her lottery number was drawn. All along he had planned to interrogate Daniel Dax himself. This was a high-profile case, one that could earn him a promotion if it were handled right. But Wheeler never got the chance.

Before he could transfer Nate's father to Denver, orders had come down from the World Union district office in Mexico City. Federal agents were taking over the case and Wheeler was instructed to back off. He protested, insisting the prisoner be moved to Denver, where the jail was more secure, but the feds ignored him. That was nothing new – they never took advice from the EP. The World Union officers considered EP officers to be hillbillies. The federal agents were, in fact, better trained in every respect, but they were also slower to make things happen. As a result, Daniel Dax had sat in Leadville without being charged for three weeks longer than Wheeler had wanted.

This morning the prisoner had ridden in an EP Suburban from Leadville to the headquarters building in Denver, unaware that his son, Nate, had taken this same road an hour or so earlier. During the ride, Dan tried to get the officers in the front seat to tell him where his wife was, but they followed the strict orders they'd been given and said nothing. He was taken to a solitary confinement cell, given lunch, and then a guard had brought him here to the bowels of the building.

He looked at the two men sitting in front of him. One wore the uniform of the Enforcement Patrol with the insignia of a major. The other was dressed in a black suit and tie with a white shirt. In the lapel of his jacket was a World Union pin, and a blue access card was clipped to his jacket pocket. He was clearly a federal agent.

They brought out the big guns, Dan thought to himself.

"Who are you guys, the Gestapo?" he sneered. "This looks like a Nazi interrogation chamber. Where's my wife? You have no right ..."

Wheeler squirmed in his chair, itching to respond to this traitor. He wanted to tell him that he'd never see his wife again. He wanted to break this defiant man's spirit and make him talk. But he couldn't. The man in the suit would be asking the questions today. Heston Abbott, a trained interrogator from district headquarters, would run the show. The major was here only because the EP wanted one of its own people there during federal interrogations. Wheeler had no role today. He'd been told to sit and keep his mouth shut.

"I have *every* right, Mr. Dax," the man in the suit responded calmly. "Do you understand the seriousness of the crimes you've committed? You're a terrorist, plain and simple. I know it and you know it." He paused. "Where are my manners? I haven't introduced myself. I'm Heston Abbott and I've come all the way from Mexico City just to talk to you. I'm a specialist at interrogation and I'm very good at what I do. This can go well if you cooperate completely. I might even get some of your pending charges reduced so you don't face the death penalty. If, however, you *don't* cooperate, things will be – shall we say, *unpleasant* – for you. It makes me no difference. My job is simply to learn what you know. So what do you say?"

"I say go to hell. Where's my wife? What have you bastards done with her?"

"She's as comfortable as she can be, stuck in a jail cell. She's already told us everything she knows and her release is dependent on your cooperation. There are things you kept from her, aren't there? Those are the things you're going to tell me. Are you going to make this difficult –"

Dan interrupted with a shout. "What the hell are you talking about? It sounds like you're threatening me! You can't torture citizens! This is the twenty-first century; I have rights and I demand to see an attorney."

"How familiar are you with the laws governing citizens who commit treason against the World Union? That'll be just one of many charges against you. For now you haven't been charged, and under the law you have no right to an attorney until you are charged with a crime."

"We've been locked up for weeks without charges. That's illegal in itself."

The man smiled and replied, "I have a feeling you're going to be upset about a lot more things before this is over. You're a dirty, low-life traitor to your nation and there is no punishment too harsh for people like you. You were an Outcast once, Mr. Dax. You were a scumbag, but the government gave you a chance to be chipped – to become normal like everyone else. But no, you took the chip and kept on betraying your country and your neighbors. They should have euthanized you way back then. It would have saved everyone a lot of hassle."

Abbott reached for a briefcase on the floor, put it on the table and opened it. He slowly put on a pair of rubber gloves and took out a round wooden stick an inch in diameter and two feet long. He stood and walked to where Dan Dax sat and said, "I think people like you are the most despicable pieces of dung on earth. I'm ready to get this over with and get you out of my sight. Listen to me; I'm only going to say this once. We can do this the easy way or the hard way. I'm going to ask questions and you're going to answer them. Do you understand?"

The prisoner said nothing.

The federal agent raised the stick above his head and brought it down hard on the fleshy part of Dan's right thigh. He screamed and writhed as agonizing pain shot through the muscles of his leg.

"I merely asked if you understood, Mr. Dax. Now I'll ask you again. When I ask questions, you are going to answer them. Do you understand?"

Dan sat in silence.

"All right then. Have it your way. Let's get started so we can get this over with. I'm taking Major Wheeler to lunch at one of my favorite restaurants and I'd hate for you to make us late."

John Wheeler considered himself a loyal servant of the state who was strong and forceful, an officer who would go to any length to extract information, especially from a prisoner who had betrayed the very country Wheeler loved. But this was different. He would never have believed what was happening except he was seeing it with his own eyes. Was any of this lawful? These tactics weren't taught at the Academy. Surely this man couldn't be doing them unless they were legal, but in today's civilized world Wheeler was astounded that they must have been.

For a while he had sat in shock, unwilling to watch but somehow unable to turn away. At one particularly violent point he vomited and the man in the suit snarled, "You're a disgrace to your uniform. There are towels in my briefcase. Take them out and clean up your mess. Then get out of here if you can't handle a simple interrogation." He turned back to the prisoner and continued as the major knelt on the concrete floor and wiped up what he had done.

Sixty minutes after it had begun, Abbott opened the door and called for two guards to take the prisoner back to his cell. As they hoisted him from the chair, a guard supporting him under each arm, the interrogator said, "I'll see you tomorrow, Mr. Dax. Until then, please work on refreshing your memory. I'm afraid you didn't do so well today. Oh, and to answer your earlier question, your wife's dead, I'm afraid. They drew her lottery number. Saved the state the cost of a trial, so that's a plus."

The prisoner slowly raised his head and glared at his interrogator with a look of pure hatred in his eyes. His voice was weak but determined. "You'd better be lying, you son of a bitch. If you've killed her, I'll see you in hell!"

Abbott smiled broadly but said nothing in response.

When Dax was gone, the agent removed the rubber gloves, took a pack of wipes from his case, carefully washed his hands, and then packed away the tools he'd used. Humming a tune, he closed the lid and turned to Wheeler. As nonchalantly as if he'd just finished a game of cards, he said, "I don't know about you, but I've worked up an appetite. Shall we go to lunch?"

The major shook his head. He didn't want to spend another minute with this monster. He had sweated through his clothes and his face was ashen. The very mention of lunch had made the bile begin to rise in his throat again. He walked out of the room, knowing he was expected back here tomorrow. He wasn't sure he could do it.

CHAPTER THIRTY-TWO

I tossed and turned all night, trying to come up with a way I could help in the rescue effort. I felt so helpless, knowing my father was locked in a jail cell and being subjected to whatever interrogation techniques the World Union was allowed to use. The mere idea that he was accused of being a traitor would be enough to incite some people to lash out at him. He wasn't, of course. I knew what my dad was. He was a good man, honest and brave, but like Carlos, I knew he would do anything to save my mother. We had to get him out before he was forced to do something that would hurt the people he had helped all these years.

After breakfast Jim brought me back downtown and now I waited in Carlos's secret office while he finished a meeting in another room.

"Is there any way you guys can break into the EP headquarters?" I asked once he arrived.

"The place is a fortress and they have very sophisticated security. I was up half the night thinking about this."

I nodded my head and pointed to myself to indicate I hadn't had much sleep either. "What's the security like over there?" I asked.

"It's arranged in levels, like a security clearance. The highest is black access – only a few people have black cards and they can go anywhere in Enforcement Patrol or World Union buildings worldwide. This would be the EP director and his top staff, World Union big brass and the like. Next comes blue. Those cards are issued mostly to federal people who have direct involvement with the Enforcement Patrol, which as you know reports to the World Union. Hardly any high-level regional officials in the EP have blue cards. They carry green ones, which gets them everywhere in EP buildings but not very far in the World Union areas. A man could get inside the district building in Mexico City with a green card, but he'd have to be accompanied by someone else after that."

My mind suddenly began churning. "So if I was an officer in one of the EP's local offices, I'd have a green card?"

He grinned and said, "Hold your horses. I can see the wheels turning already, but you're not quite there yet. If you were employed here in Denver at EP headquarters, you'd probably have a green card. The heads of local law enforcement, like your guy in Leadville who used to be the sheriff, have red cards. Those are mostly held by officers who move prisoners. Red cards allow access to prisons and jails throughout the region to facilitate transfers."

"And that's it?" I was fidgeting, eager to tell Carlos about the plan I had developed.

"Almost. There's a white card too. It's the lowest level and lets employees into World Union and Enforcement Patrol building lobbies, but that's as far as they can go. Every federal or EP employee has at least a white card."

He sat back and looked at me, a smile back on his face. "Okay, mister know-it-all. You look like you're about to burst. What are you thinking?"

I explained it to him.

He sat in silence and thought about it, and then he said, "Very interesting, Nate. And it might work. Let's run through it again from the top."

Fifteen minutes later we had laid out a plan – *my* plan – which we both knew was a long shot. There were several things that could go wrong, any one of which would be disastrous. But the plan actually might work; plus it was all we had. The biggest obstacle was the very first part of the plan. None of it could happen without this one piece of the puzzle.

"You're putting yourself in real danger if I let you do this," Carlos advised. "You'll be putting the Resistance at risk too if you get caught. But your father is in more danger than you can even imagine, so I'm prepared to shoulder responsibility for whatever happens. Are you sure you want to do this?"

"For Dad, you bet I am. He'd have done it for me."

"You're right about that. Okay, let's rehearse the whole thing again. And, Nate, not a word of this to anyone – understood? This is ours to win or lose. No one else's."

An hour later he said I was ready.

CHAPTER THIRTY-THREE

"Hi! I can't talk right now. Leave me a message and I'll call you back!"

I listened to her bright voice, felt a tiny buzz in my heart and immediately quashed the thought. I couldn't let my emotions run away this time. Carlos had cautioned me to keep this strictly business. This would be like acting in a play – reading a script full of lies and made-up feelings. It was what I had to do for the plan to work, and I knew it would screw things up completely if I let the old feelings come out again. It wasn't going to be easy, starting things back up with her when it was all a ploy this time. Now I was going to use Allie to achieve a goal. She was simply a pawn in a game. That was all there was to it.

"Hey, it's me. Please call me when you can. I have a question for you."

At exactly three p.m. my phone rang. She must have just gotten out of school.

"Hi, Allie," I said, making my voice sound upbeat. It was easier to do than when I'd practiced it.

"Nate, I'm so glad to hear from you. I wanted to call, especially after ... well, you know, after the officers went out to your place yesterday. I ... uh, I checked the intake sheet at the jail to ... you know ..."

"I guess you noticed I wasn't there," I joked, putting an end to her awkward attempt to say she was concerned. "I was lucky I wasn't at the ranch when they came." I wanted to ask her what was going on, but now wasn't the time. Today I had to stick to the script.

"Allie, I owe you an apology."

"No, you don't. I can only imagine how awful you felt when I told you about your father being in jail. I don't blame you for anything."

"You've been such a huge help already, and I'm sorry I hung up on you last time. You were only trying to give me information and I acted like a jerk."

"I want to see you," she said softly. "You're not at the ranch or they'd have found you. I'm not going to ask you where you are. I'm just asking you this: will you meet me?"

This was going perfectly. I had to go to Leadville to see her – she didn't have a car and I had no idea if she even knew how to drive. I didn't relish the idea of driving again, but there was no way around it.

"I want to see you too." The words – the lie – it *was* a lie, dammit – flowed easily, almost as though I meant them. Carlos said it was important to sound sincere. "I need your help. I'll meet you in our usual place tomorrow. Can you come right after school?"

"I can be there at four. I can't wait to see you, Nate."

"Me too. See you tomorrow."

I looked across the desk at Carlos, who had listened in on the entire conversation. He raised his hand, gave me a high five and said, "So far, so good. Now we have to get you chipped."

I guessed I was about to find out what a generic chip was.

Carlos took me to a strip mall in a part of town that had seen better days. We drove past an adult bookstore, a flea market in an old Walmart building and a shop that repaired data tablets. He pulled into a parking slot in front of a grimy storefront window painted with huge red letters that said Abel Veterinary Hospital. Low-Cost Spay/Neuter Program. An oval neon sign flashed the word *Open*.

"We're going to a veterinarian?"

"You got something against veterinarians?" he jested as he held the office door for me.

There was nobody in the dingy waiting room. Carlos and the receptionist chatted like old friends while I sat down and checked my mail. Shortly he said, "Okay, we're ready to go back."

We walked through a narrow hallway that smelled of antiseptic. There were little examining rooms on both sides and we went into the last one, where a man in a white lab coat was waiting for us.

"Good morning," he said to me. "I'm Dr. Abel."

"Hi, Doc," Carlos said, shaking his hand. "This is Nate. He needs a chip."

Ten minutes later the painless procedure was finished and we were back in the car. The doctor had used something that looked like a syringe to insert a tiny pod the size of a grain of rice under the skin in my left upper arm. I noticed that Carlos didn't pay him anything. I thought that was strange at first, but then I decided it made sense. How would you deduct World points to buy something that's illegal?

We sat in the parking lot while he loaded a program on his tablet. "Put your arm right here," he said, pointing to the screen. I held it close and he pressed a couple of buttons. "That's all there is to it," he said in seconds. "You're activated."

He looked at the screen again, jotted a note and handed it to me. There was a name – Robert Cane – and a ten-digit number. "According to your chip, that's your name and ID," he explained. "You need to memorize them. If the EP ever wands you, that's the name that will come up. If you can calmly recite your name and ID number, you should be fine in ninety-nine percent of situations. But if you get in trouble for some reason – if they take you to the station for a complete chip check – then you have a problem. But we're not going to let that happen," he assured me.

Carlos said my appearance was sufficiently different from the World Union's APB that no one would suspect I was the one they were looking for. Then he pronounced me ready for a test run. "Let's try out your chip together so you can get used to it. I don't want you to be uncomfortable when you go in and out of places." Since I'd never been in any "places," I thought that was a great plan.

On the way back Carlos explained about generic chips. He wouldn't say how they got them, only that the Resistance had real chips, the ones used by World Union. The only difference was that these could only be programmed with two things – a name and ID number.

Only the government issued lottery numbers and World points. Without the latter a generically chipped person still couldn't buy or sell things, but he could move freely about without setting off alarms. The fake name and ID number would pass a cursory EP inspection but nothing more. You couldn't hold a job, for instance, because your information wouldn't appear in the World Union's database. Carlos assured me if I did nothing to call attention to myself, I could go just about anywhere.

We parked in the underground garage and walked up a ramp to street level. "Let's get a Coke," he suggested, pointing to a McDonald's on the corner. What a normal-sounding suggestion ... to a normal person, that is. I'd never "gotten a Coke" in my life.

Inside the restaurant it was noisier and more crowded than I'd imagined, and he cautioned me to stop looking around so much. I was fascinated; this place was crazy with activity – there was even a three-story indoor playground that little kids were scrambling all over. The tables were incredibly close together and the noise level was unbelievable. We sat twelve inches away from a group of rowdy teenagers looking at their tablets and talking at the same time. Carlos said they were playing games. In our few minutes at McDonald's I mastered the unfamiliar concept of how to talk in a room where fifty other people were conversing at the same time.

Back on the sidewalk he said, "You passed! Next test. Let's try a scanning machine." This was scary because I'd been warned my entire life not to get near one. We walked to a convenience store. I stood outside as Carlos explained we'd go through the machine just after we entered.

He walked casually through the metal detection device and up to the counter. I put my foot out in front of me and tried to look casual too. I passed through the metal tunnel.

Nothing happened.

It was an exhilarating feeling being normal - being just like everyone else for the first time in seventeen years.

I stood with Carlos while he bought two bars of candy. He handed me one and said, "Ready to go?" I nodded and walked back through the device like I'd been doing it for years.

We went to a couple more stores, going through the detectors until I could move without looking like I was nervous. It didn't take long and I enjoyed every second of it. Back at the office we talked about what was going to happen tomorrow. I was dreading the round-trip drive to Leadville, and Carlos made my day when he told me Jim was going with me and would be the driver. "You can drop him somewhere when you get to town," he said. "Once you've finished with Allie, you'll pick him up again."

Carlos also asked me not to discuss my mission in Leadville with Jim. There was a role for Jim in the plan, he added, but everyone now was on a strict need-to-know basis because of the plan's need for absolute secrecy.

I dropped Jim at the public library and at ten minutes to four I parked the Trailblazer in the grove of trees that had become our secret meeting place. I watched her come around the corner. She was dressed in a school uniform – white cotton shirt, khaki skirt and black tennis shoes. She looked
...

She looked like a person that was part of the plan to rescue my father. That was all she looked like.

Allie rushed up to me, pushed me back against the side of the Chevy and gave me an enormous, long kiss. I did my best to feign mutual interest in all this, kissing back with as much intensity as I could muster. I must have done pretty well because she seemed to like it and we did it for a while.

But it was all part of the plan. She had to believe that nothing had changed on my side.

She pulled away at last. "Oh God, I'm glad to see you. Where are you staying? Are you okay?" Her voice was a little breathless.

"I'm in Denver. I'm staying with a friend. Yes, I'm okay. Are you?"

"I'm fine. I still work at the Enforcement Patrol office every afternoon. I told Lenny I couldn't come in today because I had debate practice until five. And I've tried to find out anything I could about your dad. I look at the stuff that comes in from Denver every day, but since they moved him, there's been no word."

She asked me if I was going to school. "Not now," I answered truthfully. "Right now I'm working on a plan to rescue my father." This was where the conversation was going to get tricky. If I said too much – or not enough – I could blow everything.

"Can I do anything to help you? I told you all along I'll do whatever you want."

"Why, Allie? Why would you be willing to help me? Anything I do is going to probably be against the law – the law administered by your own stepfather. There's no telling what he'd do to me, and what about you? You're his wife's daughter. He might have to resign his position with the EP."

She looked at me tenderly and guilt began sweeping through me as I listened to her answer. "Because some of what the government does is wrong. I may not be very old, but I'm old enough to know what's right and what isn't. You're an Outcast. I know that – I knew it that day I couldn't find your name on the list of county residents. And you're right. Lenny would go ballistic if he even knew I was seeing you. The EP's looking for you. They don't know your name and they don't have a good description of you, but it's you, isn't it? It's you they're looking for."

I nodded. This revelation wasn't part of the plan, but I didn't see what it could hurt at this point. She was either going to turn me in or learn a lot more soon.

"You're an Outcast and they'll kill you if they find you. What's right about that? What's right about our government killing someone just because they refuse to do what everyone else does? I asked Lenny about your father and mother. He told me they're subversives, terrorists and revolutionaries. He says they plotted to overthrow the World

174

Union. I saw your father in jail. He's no terrorist. Do you remember the only things he said to me? He asked where your mother was and he asked me to tell you to look in some box. Call it a gut feeling, but I knew immediately he wasn't a criminal. There was something about him that told me he's a good man, like my real dad is."

I'd never heard a word about her biological father. Then again, we hadn't said a lot of words in the few times we'd been together. *And Dad* is *a good man*, I thought to myself. I had to make this happen. For him.

Lenny Vargas put down the binoculars. Although he couldn't hear them, he'd seen enough. Whoever the kid was, Allie was all into him. That had been evident from the moment she saw him. She was too young to get this involved with a boy. Plus she was sneaking around, keeping this thing a secret from Mabry and him.

For the last couple of days, he'd known something was going on and he watched and waited to find out who was involved. When he had gone back to work Monday morning after the camping weekend, there was an email from the security division at EP headquarters in Denver. While he was logged out over the weekend, someone had used his password to access the Lake County register of residents and businesses. The email had been copied to Major Wheeler, Lenny's supervisor. He'd get some kind of reprimand and that would be that. The file itself wasn't a big deal – it was password-protected but not classified.

In order to settle the matter quickly and simply, he responded to the email, advising the security officer and Wheeler that he had stopped by the office to look up an address and had simply forgotten he was logged out. That would end the discussion, although Wheeler would probably give him grief about it. No big deal.

Next he shredded the list of passwords he had jotted down. That had been stupid of him, but the older he got, the more often he forgot the damned things that changed every few weeks.

He wondered why Allie wanted to see the list. She was the culprit, of course. He was certain of that. No one had ever before used his passwords and suddenly, the first Saturday she worked at the office, the one day he and Mabry were gone camping, someone used his password to access a file. It disappointed him – she had to have gone through his desk drawers to find the password list – but he said nothing to her about it. He chose to wait and see what was going on.

This morning he'd had a feeling she was lying about having to miss work because of debate practice. She was bubbly, upbeat and humming around the house again, just like the other day when she told them she'd met a boy. He'd been a cop too long to miss the little signs.

He called the school, confirmed there was no practice and tailed his stepdaughter to her covert meeting place. Sure enough, she met a boy there – a boy she knew well enough to kiss. Lenny wished he could have gotten the plate number off the kid's truck, but it was parked in some trees.

Who was he? How long had they been seeing each other, and why didn't they meet someplace in town? He would find out who that kid was, and he'd be sorry if he was doing anything – anything at all – to Lenny's stepdaughter. He'd also find out why Allie was being so secretive. It just wasn't like her.

The sheriff went back to his office, determined to get to the bottom of this.

CHAPTER THIRTY-FOUR

Now came the scary part – letting Allie in on the plan. She sat in the passenger seat of the SUV as I explained that I had to help my father. Yes, he was a traitor in the eyes of the World Union because he believed in fairness for everyone and the right to choose your own destiny. Yes, he hated the lottery and the whole euthanization process. And yes, he chose to fight against the government – *his* government. Was all that wrong? Did that make him a terrorist, an evil person who should be tortured and murdered according to the law?

"Tortured?" she interjected, a note of alarm in her voice. "What are you saying? He's in jail in Denver. They don't torture people."

"You're wrong. I can't tell you how I know it, but I know for certain they will torture my father – maybe they already have – if he doesn't tell them everything he knows, including giving up his own son, me. You don't know what kind of man he is, but I can tell you they won't break him. There's only one thing they can get. If he doesn't know Mom was euthanized, he'll barter information in exchange for her life. It's useless since she's already gone, but he doesn't know that. I have to get him out. I hope you can understand."

She was agreeing with everything I said, nodding her head over and over. When I finished, she asked, "You said you needed my help. What can I do?"

I took her hands in mine. "Can I trust you? Will you promise not to betray me? Even if you can't or won't do what I ask, will you keep everything secret so your stepfather and the others can't use it against my dad?"

"Of course I will. I'm proud of what you're trying to do, and deep inside, I believe the same way. What do you want from me?"

"Lenny has an access card, right?"

"Sure. It's hooked to his belt most of the time. It gets him in and out of places. I have one too, since I'm an employee now."

"Yours is white – right?"

She nodded, wondering how I knew what color hers was.

"What color is Lenny's card?"

"Red."

Perfect.

"I need to borrow his for twenty-four hours. Is there ever a time he doesn't have it on him?"

"Sure, almost every weekend when he and Mom go camping or fishing. He leaves it in a drawer in their bedroom. But I can just loan you mine. It'd be a lot easier. What are you going to do with it, anyway?"

"That's all you need to know," I answered truthfully. "If Lenny gets suspicious, I don't want you to be dragged into this. It'll be bad enough if he catches me. I don't want him to catch you too."

We agreed on what we would do next. It was almost five and Allie had to get home. She leaned over and we kissed again. "I'm so glad you asked me to help," she said as she jumped out. "I'll be in touch as soon as things are ready."

I watched her walk away, stopping at the corner to give me a glance, a smile and a wave.

Jim was where he said he'd be, waiting in front of a boarded-up gas station. Seeing it reminded me of Dad. He had told me about them, how there used to be lots of stations when he was a kid. By federal law, vehicles ran on solar now, but many people still had old ones, especially in rural areas like Leadville. Mostly they were farm or hunting trucks. So there was still a gas station in most towns even though they didn't do much business anymore.

On the trip back Jim never asked what I'd done this afternoon. He brought up all kinds of things – sports, cars, those kinds of topics – but he soon realized my sheltered life had kept me insulated from things other guys talked about. We settled on fishing and swapped tall tales about the biggest fish we'd ever caught and where the best lakes were. Dad and I had loved to fish. It made me nostalgic thinking about it. I hoped we could do it again someday.

Ben and Smitty weren't at the house when I got back and Maeve said they were both working late. That news was frankly a relief to me; this had been a tense day filled with lies and subterfuge and I just wanted to eat, get in bed, play a couple of games on my tablet and turn in early. I expected to hear their life stories tomorrow. I never thought things would start happening so quickly that we wouldn't all be back together again for almost a week.

CHAPTER THIRTY-FIVE

"Good morning, Mr. Dax," Heston Abbott said to his prisoner secured once more in the same chair in the same basement room. "I trust you had a good couple of days. You certainly look better than you did when I left you Sunday. You were a little – shall we say, under the weather – then." He smirked.

"I thought you were coming back yesterday," Dan Dax shot back, his face a mask of fury. All day long he'd steeled himself for the interrogation, but nothing happened. He had also asked two different guards to find out if his wife was a prisoner here too, promising them cigarettes or whisky he would get from the outside when he was able. One turned him down flat, sneering that of all the prisoners, Dan was the least likely one to be getting out. The other guard said he'd ask around. He returned hours later and advised she wasn't on the inmate roster.

"Yes, I did tell you I'd be back yesterday, didn't I? Change of plans, I'm afraid. You're not the only traitor in my den of thieves," he said with a cruel laugh. "There are others I had to deal with too. And as satisfying as the questioning is, I need a break now and then. But here we are. I hope you're ready to give me some information."

Major John Wheeler wasn't there. Expecting that Abbott would resume the barbaric interrogation on Monday, he had called in sick. This morning when he came to work, he learned to his shock that the questioning would resume in an hour. Wheeler quickly filled his schedule with fictitious, seemingly important meetings, telling the World Union man he should have been informed about the change in plans.

Abbott had known Wheeler wouldn't show up. He'd observed how weak he was during the last session, and he was glad that today there wouldn't be an EP observer. It would make things easier, just Abbott's word against a traitor's as to what happened.

As cruel as he was, the interrogator fervently believed his work was important to the World Union and he was proud to be doing it. He also believed an EP officer of Wheeler's rank should be proud too. His behavior was just another sign of how much more professional federal agents were than these locals. He'd do just fine without anyone from the Enforcement Patrol butting in today.

He opened the briefcase, pulled on his gloves, laid out a few things and said, "Are you ready to begin?"

Two hours later the session ended. Abbott carefully put away everything, then called for guards with a gurney. When they arrived, they were appalled to see the prisoner's condition. He was unconscious on the floor, his body badly bruised.

"Mr. Dax slipped out of his restraints somehow and fell down. Take him to the infirmary."

CHAPTER THIRTY-SIX

As Jim and I were returning from Leadville around dark, the nerdy technician sat at Carlos's desk with Dad's USB thumb drives and the Apple tablet in front of him. He gave his boss a progress report, starting with the tablet, which he said had been simple to crack. The only things loaded on it were videos – seventeen years' worth of memories of Daniel and Melanie Dax's only child, Nathan. There were birthday parties, Christmas dinners, learning to ride a horse, swimming in a pond, shooting a rifle ... all the typical things families memorialize. The sad difference with these, the tech commented, was that there were never any presents and there were no outsiders – no friends or relatives – ever.

"Makes sense," Carlos commented. "He's an Outcast. They couldn't have anything around the house that made it look like a kid lived there, and his existence was a secret. They couldn't afford to have friends. How sad, though."

"It must have been hard for him."

"Not if he didn't know what it was like for other people."

They understood why the tablet had been encrypted and hidden in the metal box. These were memories that could be shared only by Nate Dax and his parents. Carlos set it aside to show Nate tomorrow morning and asked, "What about the thumb drives?"

"I couldn't break the code. We've run all the letter-and-number combinations he put on the file folder, but there was nothing that worked on the drives. Some of the letters are written backwards – so far I can't figure out what that means. All I can think of is this – in the letter to Nate, his dad said to remember the trusty old password. Have you asked him about that?"

"No," Carlos admitted. "I read those words too but never thought about them again." He picked up his phone. "Let me see if I can get hold of Nate. They should be on the road back to Denver by now."

I explained that the secret password started with the word REPUBLICAN. Each letter of that word was a number from one to ten, left to right. The letter R was one and N was zero. When they were written backwards, you substituted a numeral.

The hacker went back to work. By noon the next day he knew what was on the thumb drives. They were heavily encrypted; all he could see was a list of folder titles. He needed at least one more password in order to open them.

CHAPTER THIRTY-SEVEN

"How was debate practice? Are you going for a career in politics?" Lenny asked as they sat around the dinner table an hour after she'd left Nate.

"It was good," she answered smoothly. "There are only six of us, but my teacher says I'm catching on faster than most of the others."

"Tell me how it all works. Do you have to take different sides on an issue and compete against another team member?"

"Why are you suddenly so interested in her debate class?" Allie's mom laughed. "You haven't cared much about her schoolwork before."

Allie perked up. Mom was right. Something was going on here. She had to be careful; she hadn't actually had a debate practice yet and didn't really know how they were done.

"I ... yeah, we take opposite sides. It's just like having an argument with another person. You stand up for what you believe in –"

"Who's your debate coach?"

What is he doing? Her mind began spinning, frantically trying to keep the lies going.

"It's Mr. Venner."

"Bob Venner? I know him. I see him every Wednesday at Rotary Club."

Rotary Club? Wednesday? That's tomorrow!

"Well, he wasn't there today. Miss Browning filled in for him."

Irritated, Allie's mother stepped in. "Lenny, what's going on? Why are you asking her all these questions? It's like you're interrogating her."

185

He put down his fork and looked her in the eyes. "Where were you this afternoon from after school until you got home, Allie?"

She began to cry. "I told you I was at debate practice. Why are you doing this to me?"

"Lenny, if you have something to say, say it," Mabry screamed. "If you don't, get off her back and stop using your police tactics on my daughter!"

He stared at Allie for a few more seconds and went back to his dinner without another word.

Allie tried to eat a few more bites, but suddenly she was about to vomit. She jumped from her chair, ran out of the kitchen and barely made it to the bathroom. Afterwards she put on her pajamas and got into bed. Her mother came in to say goodnight.

"I'm sorry, honey. I don't know what he was thinking. Sometimes living with a cop can be difficult. He must have had a bad day at the office and he took it out on you."

That night in bed she asked her husband what in hell that was about.

His answer was curt. "She's not herself these days. Sometimes when people act like she's acting, they're hiding something."

"Leave her alone. She's a teenage girl with all the baggage that comes with it. She has enough stress with school and activities. She doesn't need any hassle at home."

Lenny didn't respond.

The next morning at breakfast Allie learned Lenny and her mom were heading up to the White River National Park to camp out and fish for the weekend. "Want to join us?" her mom offered, bringing just the trace of a scowl to her husband's face. He liked having his new wife alone on camping trips, but after the confrontation last night he kept his thoughts to himself.

Allie answered immediately. "Sure, if it's okay. I know you all like to get off in time to set up camp before dark. I could leave right after school. If we left at three, would that be enough time?"

"Yeah," Lenny muttered. "With daylight savings it's light until after eight. It won't take more than a couple of hours to get up there. We can set up camp and be finished with dinner before dark."

Once she was off to school, the sheriff hooked his gun belt around his waist, clipped the red access card to his belt and walked over to the sink, where his wife was soaking dishes.

"Thanks for letting her join us," Mabry said, giving him a peck on the cheek. "I know it's more fun with the two of us, but we have plenty more weekends for alone time before winter. Besides, she's never been interested in coming before. I was surprised she agreed."

Yeah, me too, he thought to himself. *It took her no time at all to decide. Wonder what's going on.*

When her parents were going off for the weekend, Friday morning breakfasts became more frenzied than other days. Allie ate eggs and toast as her mother made sandwiches for the campout. Lenny had driven the Suburban over to their storage unit to load it with chairs, a tent, fishing gear and the other supplies they always took. She left for school with a promise to come home as soon as the bell rang. They'd be waiting for her, car loaded and ready to go.

She ran home, changed clothes quickly and ran downstairs to join her folks, who were waiting in the car. She paused a second in front of Max's Hardware and looked both ways to see where Lenny had parked. By 3:15 the campers were heading to the mountains for two nights at a campground near Independence, an abandoned ghost town nestled in the national park. At thirteen thousand feet the weather promised to be clear, crisp and cool, a beautiful summer weekend in the Rockies.

A tourist strolled down the sidewalk and paused to window-shop at Max's Hardware store. Directly above him was the second-floor apartment where Lenny and his family lived. As the man studied the power washer in front of him, he put his hand behind a shrub in a planter and palmed the red access card Allie had put there twenty minutes ago.

Once he had the card, Jim Gordon headed back to Denver, keeping his speed just under the limit. It was Friday afternoon, but traffic was still light on his side of the interstate. The outbound side was an entirely different story. Thousands of city folks were heading west to spend a weekend in the mountains. The next two days were slated to be perfect weather-wise and there were lots of boat trailers behind the cars and trucks. Jim set his cruise control at 68 mph. His mission was to get the access card back to headquarters as quickly as possible, but the risk of getting pulled over for speeding wasn't worth saving ten or fifteen minutes.

It was nearly six when Jim walked into a conference room next to Carlos's office, tossed Lenny's red access card onto the middle of the table and took the chair next to mine. I'd been told he was part of the plan from this point forward. There were three others in the room. Two were high-level lieutenants in the Resistance I'd met earlier and the other was a handsome guy not a lot older than I was. He was dressed in a black Enforcement Patrol uniform. Two days ago, sitting in a room with a cop and plotting how to rescue a prisoner would have surprised me, but now nothing did. I'd come to expect almost anything from these people, even a cop helping us spring my dad.

"How'd it go?" I whispered to Jim.

He gave me a thumbs-up. "She did great. Piece of cake."

"Okay, guys, let's get started," Carlos said, and the buzz in the room stopped. "We've been through the drill so much we should all know our parts by heart. Now it's time to make it happen. We have thirty hours to get the job done and put the card back. The cop whose card this is usually doesn't get back home until late Sunday afternoon, but I'm going to play it safe. The card will be back in the planter before nine Sunday morning and even earlier if everything goes perfectly. Everyone here knows his part in the plan and where to be."

He glanced to his side and spoke directly to the handsome young guy in a black Enforcement Patrol uniform.

188

His name tag said "Munro" and he had a corporal's stripes. "Patrick, every minute's going to count once you're inside the prison yard. You can't rush things – you can't make it look like you're in a hurry – but you can't waste even a second. If anything goes wrong while you're in the building, we won't be able to help you."

"Gotcha, chief," Munro answered. "Get the prisoner into the ambulance, get the hell outta there, ditch the wagon once we're two blocks away, and run like hell to the doc!"

Carlos smiled. "I like your enthusiasm. We can hope that's how it goes. You've got lots of help once you're out. Just take care of yourself inside."

Corporal Munro raised his fist into the air, picked up the red access card and shouted, "To freedom!"

Everyone in the room stood and cheered except for me. I prayed.

Munro and one of the lieutenants left the room to prepare for the mission later tonight. All that remained were Carlos, Jim, another Resistance leader and me. We would watch the events unfold from here.

CHAPTER THIRTY-EIGHT

We had over four hours to kill. Carlos sent someone to pick up pizza and then the others went back to work. I sat in the conference room alone, waiting impatiently for eleven o'clock and running through things in my head.

We knew Dad was in the infirmary, but we didn't know why. Carlos had access to some of the EP's database because his company maintained it. But he'd admitted they didn't know everything. I was also convinced there was someone inside headquarters who was leaking information to the Resistance, but with all that, we didn't have solid information about my father.

I wondered about Corporal Patrick Munro. He had the most important role in my plan. Was he really part of the Enforcement Patrol? What he really was didn't matter. There were a lot of people with vastly different backgrounds who were part of the Resistance, I'd learned. Some were chipped; others weren't. It was mind-boggling that all this existed.

At ten thirty everyone came back to get ready for the show. I glanced at my watch for the hundredth time. At last it was eleven and time for the operation to begin. We turned to a sixty-inch monitor on the opposite wall as the operation started. A map was in one corner of the screen so we could monitor the ambulance on GPS.

We had two sources of audio and video. Patrick was in the front seat, wearing the body camera every patrolman wore, and the ambulance had a front-mounted camera. Carlos told me the ambulance driver was a Resistance guy with a stolen white access card. It had been reprogrammed by someone inside the EP – that person no one talked about – and it worked perfectly. I learned that only white cards were ever reprogrammed; they were the lowest security and literally tens of thousands of people had them. Anything higher than a white card contained encoded security traps and couldn't be altered.

The dash camera recorded their approach to the EP's massive and heavily guarded headquarters. They took a road around the building to the back, following signs that read "Inmate Drop-off – Authorized Personnel Only." They pulled up to an entrance blocked by a heavy metal strip full of spiked teeth that could be lowered into the pavement. An officer stepped from a guard shack and took the driver's white access card. Patrick had his clipped to his shirt pocket in plain sight but, as everyone had been led to expect, the guard didn't ask for it. Everything went fine – the driver's card worked perfectly, as Carlos said it had done in earlier tests.

The spike strip dropped and the guard waved the ambulance through. We had finished the first step in a very risky plan. The stakes and the danger increased exponentially now that they were inside. The driver's access card was no good now. From here they had to use Lenny Vargas's card – a pilfered card registered to a captain but clipped to the pocket of a corporal. Everything depended on the situation being so routine no one would notice. We knew how things usually happened; we just didn't know what to expect tonight.

The ambulance moved slowly down a narrow driveway with tall whitewashed concrete walls on both sides. There was an eight-foot metal gate blocking the far end and another guard, a sergeant this time. Patrick handed over Lenny's access card and we held our collective breaths as we watched. The guard put the card up to his scanner and the gate swung open. We'd been told the guard wouldn't look at the scanner's screen, and that information was right. He never noticed the name and rank of the person whose card it was. If he had, the driver and the corporal would have been prisoners themselves within seconds.

They'd passed two hurdles – the easiest ones – and now they were inside the prison itself. They had two more checkpoints left, both unmanned, and then they had to get out again.

We had no idea that at that moment – 11:11 p.m. – a breach was reported to the security monitoring department four floors above where Patrick stood. The moment Lenny's access card was used, an alert was generated. Just like the last breach, this time Lenny was once again logged out and off duty for the weekend. His card should have been inactive, yet someone had just used it. Unlike the password breach earlier, this one was a major infraction. Following protocol, the man who logged the incident sent a priority message to his night duty officer two doors down the hall.

I hadn't been involved in the training, so I had no idea exactly how the rescue was going to unfold. My eyes were glued to the screen as a gripping movie that was terrifyingly real unfolded. I saw the driver move across a brightly lit courtyard. It was the middle of the night, but there were people taking a break and smoking cigarettes. Several EP vehicles were parked here and there. A sign ahead read "Infirmary Loading/Unloading Only" and the camera swept around as the driver backed into a parking slot.

From this point on we would watch the feed from Patrick's body camera. It had been reprogrammed to transmit video only to our screen and not to the Enforcement Patrol's monitors. He was officially off duty tonight, so no one would expect any transmission from his camera.

Four floors above the courtyard the night duty officer sat in the toilet, doing his business and reading the newspaper. Although the building was technically open twenty-four seven, the major activity at night was in the jail. That part of headquarters seemed to never stop and he was the senior man in the building tonight.

Before taking a bathroom break a few minutes ago, he had watched an ambulance pull through the entry area. He had no idea where it was from and he didn't care. It was just another in the constant flow of human traffic into and out of the Enforcement Patrol's incarceration center.

He had almost six hours to go on the graveyard shift and was having trouble staying awake. He took his time in the bathroom, unaware that a high-priority message was flashing on the monitor in his office.

His rubber-gloved fist full of papers, Patrick led the way into the building as the driver pushed a gurney he'd taken from the back of the ambulance. Patrick used the access card twice more, ending up in the infirmary, where he walked confidently to a nurses' station.

A pretty young nurse looked up, seemed to like what she saw and smiled. "What brings you here in the middle of the night, Corporal?"

He leaned on the desk as though he had all the time in the world and passed the sheaf of papers to her. "Why the hell they want to move prisoners at this ungodly hour is beyond me, but I didn't have anything better to do anyway."

"Dax, Daniel." She read the name out loud and a male nurse working next to her raised his head.

"They're moving Dax? He's in pretty bad shape."

Those words sent shivers down my spine. We hadn't known anything about Dad's condition until right now. *At least he's alive,* I told myself.

"Yeah, we're taking him to some specialized facility. The name's on there ..." He pointed to a fictitious entry. "But don't ask me. I just follow orders."

"Don't we all?" The male nurse laughed. "Come with me, guys. I'll take you down to the patient's room."

We saw an EP guard sitting outside the door and then Patrick was inside. It took the body camera a second to adjust to the room's darkness and then I felt a rush. There was my father lying in a bed! There were IV bottles hanging from a metal pole, and tubes ran to his nose and mouth. Dad looked up and saw Patrick's uniform. "What are you doing?" he asked weakly.

"It's okay, Mr. Dax. We're moving you to a different facility."

"Another torture chamber? Or is this one the death chamber? You bastards ..." He began to struggle and I noticed the restraints for the first time. There were broad straps across his chest, thighs and ankles.

"He's a fighter," the nurse said. "Better keep an eye on him. He's also considered a flight risk. I guess you all know that."

"Yep," Patrick replied calmly. He looked at his watch. "We can handle him, but I gotta get going. I'm supposed to have him delivered soon and I don't get a lunch break until afterwards. Plus they'll have my ass if I'm late."

"I hear you, man. Same story around here. Let's get him moved to your gurney. You can bring the straps back next time."

The three of them lifted Dad onto the wheeled conveyance and the nurse laid the IV bottles next to him.

"Sign here for the release," Patrick said, shoving a paper in front of the nurse. Then they took my father away. Two more swipes of Lenny's red card and they were back in the courtyard with Dad on the gurney. Six minutes had elapsed since they'd entered. In two more they'd be home free.

The man in the security monitoring department was becoming alarmed. In the past few minutes there had been four more unauthorized uses of Captain Vargas's access card, all in the infirmary downstairs. He wasn't allowed to leave his post, but he wanted to make sure his supervisor had seen the five alerts. He decided to give it a few more minutes.

Patrick and the driver hoisted Dad into the ambulance. Patrick climbed in the back with him and whispered, "Just stay calm, Mr. Dax. We're with the Resistance."

I heard the weak response. "I'll be damned. The cavalry's arrived at last."

I glanced at Carlos and could tell he was upset. "Why's Patrick in the back?" he exploded. "That wasn't the way we rehearsed it."

The driver pulled up to the first of the two gates between prison and freedom. He held out his access card and we all heard the guard's muffled voice.

"I need a red card. Where's the other guy who was with you a few minutes ago?"

"He's in the back. One sec."

On Patrick's body cam we saw a little window open between the driver's area and the back where Patrick and Dad were. "The guard needs your access card."

Carlos hit his desk with his fist so hard it shook. "Dammit! This is a huge mistake. Patrick should be sitting in the front seat! We went over this a dozen times!"

Patrick handed the card through the window and the guard swiped it. We could see the heavy gate opening, but then the guard said, "Captain Vargas, can you confirm where you're stationed?" He was looking at the readout on the scanner.

Carlos was livid. "He's checking the information on the card. This would never have happened ..."

"Uh, sure," Patrick responded. "I'm in Leadville."

Carlos murmured, "I hope to hell that sergeant didn't happen to take a close look at Patrick's uniform when they came in. If he did, he knows it's a corporal he's dealing with, not a captain."

"Sir, we don't see many local EP officers removing prisoners. You guys bring them in, but usually regional officers move them after that. Do you mind stepping out of the ambulance for a moment and letting me see your paperwork?"

My heart sank as the gate began to swing shut again.

To his credit, Patrick remained cool and composed. Instead of following the guard's order, he stayed where he was. "We're on a tight deadline to move this man to a medical treatment facility. He's from Leadville too; he was in my jail before he came here. He's very unstable and he's going to die without proper treatment. Here are the papers." He thrust them through the window and the driver handed them over. "My orders are to deliver him alive, Sergeant," Patrick said through the window, keeping to one side, out of sight. "If he dies right here, it'll be your problem to explain to my boss. We have to get him to the facility fast. The sooner we're out of here, the sooner this is my issue to deal with, not yours."

The guard was apparently considering his options. Nothing happened for what seemed to me like an eternity.

Then he said, "I'm sorry, Captain. Once I confirm everything's okay, we'll have you on your way. I have to call my duty officer. I need you to step out of the ambulance right now, sir."

CHAPTER THIRTY-NINE

Patrick opened the rear door, exited the ambulance and walked to the command post. The guard was inside, facing away from the door, reaching for a two-way radio. Patrick took a short club from his belt holster and hit the guard squarely in the head with it. The man crumpled to the floor.

He walked calmly out, passed the access card over the scanner and got in the right front seat as the gate began to swing open. No one was paying him any attention. The smokers were fifty feet away, still engrossed in conversation just like before.

As they waited for the gate, Patrick tried to calm the nervous driver. Just like he did, we all knew there were security cameras everywhere and any second there could be an alarm.

"We've got one gate to go. Just keep calm. Everything's going to be fine. Just move it!"

The night duty officer upstairs finished his bathroom chores and strolled back to his office. The clerk who'd sent him the alerts heard his boots coming down the hallway, stuck his head out and said, "Sir, I sent you some alerts a few minutes ago. Somebody's using a logged-out access card downstairs in the jail. They've swiped it five times so far."

"What color access card?"

"Red, sir."

Suddenly the duty officer sprang into action. This was a major issue and he had already let too much time pass. It could be as simple as a man forgetting to log back in after being off duty. It could also be a security breach. Regardless, he was the senior man on duty. The problem was his alone. He looked at the live video from downstairs and saw an ambulance sitting at Gate A, the outer of the two guard stations. Just then the clerk down the hall dinged him with another alert. The red card had opened the gate the ambulance passed through seconds before. He grabbed his radio.

Sweating profusely now, the ambulance driver went down the passage and stopped at the spike strip. The guard moseyed over, took the driver's white card, swiped it, and the barricade began to sink into the ground. He handed the card back and said, "Have a good one," as the driver stomped on the accelerator. The vehicle lurched forward and the guard yelled, "Hey! What the hell do you think you're doing?"

"Slow down!" Patrick told the driver. "We're out, man. Keep your cool! All we have to do is get around the building."

The driver eased off and Patrick gave a wave out the window to the guard. They were halfway around the building when klaxons began blaring and huge yellow searchlights on the roof beamed down. The driver began to accelerate again and Patrick yelled, "Keep your speed down."

Carlos picked up a two-way radio on his desk and spoke to the men in the ambulance via its onboard communication system.

"They're after you, Patrick. You have to move it. Can Dan walk?"

"No. I don't think so. Plus he's restrained in three places and we don't have time to untie him."

"Get the hell out of there! Keep your light bar and siren off."

The driver made the final turn, leaving the building behind and speeding toward the busy street. Patrick yelled, "There are two Suburbans just pulling out of headquarters. They're two blocks behind us and they're lit up!"

"Can you make it to the site?"

"I'm not sure we have enough of a head start ..."

"You have to make it! We have to get him unchipped! They're on your tail. You have to go!"

It never dawned on me that the EP could track Dad through his chip, so it wasn't part of my rescue plan, but Carlos had prepared for it, thank God. I asked how you could unchip someone, but he waved me off with a shake of his head. He kept his eyes glued to the monitor as he turned a dial on the radio and said, "Tomcat, get ready. They're almost there."

"Roger, boss." I heard the reply through a hiss of static.

Patrick watched the ambulance's GPS screen and fired instructions to the driver, sending him into one turn after another. We followed their path on our system as they zigzagged through an industrial area. "Slow down! Dead end ahead!" he shouted as we heard the squeal of brakes and tires and the vehicle began a careening turn.

"How close are the cops?" Carlos asked.

"I can't see them right now. Now I can! Maybe three blocks back."

"Turn off your lights," Carlos instructed. "You're almost there!" They were speeding through a dark warehouse district and I could see an intersection, a red light and heavy cross-traffic several blocks ahead.

"They're closing in on us," Patrick reported, telling the driver to turn again. "Keep your speed up." We heard the driver curse that he couldn't drive so fast with no headlights. Suddenly, ahead and to the right we saw a garage door, one of a dozen in a row of dark buildings, swing open.

The ambulance pulled in and the door immediately closed behind it, leaving the street as dark and deserted as it had been seconds before. We couldn't see anything outside now, but we heard wailing sirens as the two EP Suburbans sped past the building.

"Get him to the roof!" Carlos yelled into the radio. "Tomcat's waiting for you! I'm changing frequency!"

Carlos turned a knob on the radio and said, "Tomcat, they're in the building. Keep this channel open."

"Roger that, boss. We're ready when they are." It was hard to hear the response because of deafening background noise – something that was familiar but I couldn't quite place.

"What's going on?" I asked one of the men next to me.

"Helicopter," he whispered, putting his finger to his lips. Now I knew what the noise was. It was the sound of a rotor, the same noise I'd heard up at the ranch earlier.

Less than a minute later the whirring noise became louder and louder. Now there was the distinct sound of an engine revving as we heard, "Up and away, boys. Let's blow this joint!"

Carlos and the pilot exchanged several more communications as the chopper carried my father away. Before long the pilot said, "Bringing her down, boss. I can see the crew waiting for us."

I had been watching Carlos off and on since everything started, idly wondering how often things like this happened. Other than his frustration with Patrick, he had remained calm. He seemed accustomed to running dangerous operations, but the tension we felt was also visible in his pursed lips and his clenched fists. He picked up his phone, initiated a call and mostly listened for several minutes. When he finished, there was a sign no one could miss. His shoulders relaxed as he leaned back in his chair. His stress and anxiety were replaced by a smile and two thumbs in the air.

"It's all over," he said with a sigh. "Your dad's in a safe house under a doctor's care. And he's unchipped. They can't track him now." He looked at one of the guys next to me. "Where's that champagne we keep around here? If this isn't a time to break it out, I don't know what is."

After the others clinked glasses and made a toast, he sat down next to me. I was physically and mentally drained and an emotional wreck. I was trying my best to keep my composure in front of these professionals, but it wasn't going to last much longer.

"You asked me earlier about unchipping. Sorry I couldn't answer you then – you'd have rather had my mind on the exercise, believe me. There's a way to disable a chip using an electrical stimulation device. It's really simple, but it's irreversible. Once it's done, there's no going to the World Union and trying to explain what happened. You're an Outcast for the rest of your life. People do it for various reasons, usually to escape from the cops. We have doctors who work with the Resistance. One of them is the woman who's tending to your father. He's in a safe house – I won't tell you where because it's on a need-to-know basis. She unchipped him in the chopper so the EP can't track him. She'll stay with him as he regains his strength. Sometime later today I'll get a report on his condition and what she needs in order to treat him. As soon as I know, you'll know too."

It was a relief to hear good news for a change. Dad was alive and safe, even though he'd been in the infirmary and the nurse had said he was in bad shape. Hopefully it was nothing he couldn't recover from. I allowed myself to think about seeing him again. I hadn't let those thoughts into my head since he and Mom disappeared. But now I could.

The early November evening had turned crisp and chilly as the sun dropped behind the mountains and darkness enveloped the abandoned ghost town where they'd pitched their tents. Lenny, Mabry and Allie had eaten hot dogs grilled over the campfire and now, wrapped in blankets, they sat in lawn chairs, drinking hot chocolate.

Around ten they turned in, snuggled down in their sleeping bags and fell asleep to the sounds of night creatures in the darkness. At one a.m. the stillness was broken by the shrill ring of a phone. Lenny pawed through a rucksack to find it. "It's that damned Johnny Wheeler," he mumbled sleepily when he looked at the screen. "Doesn't he know what off duty means? And who the hell calls at this time of night?" He answered the phone and said nothing for what seemed to Allie and her mom like a long time. At last he spoke.

"I'm with my family, camping in the White River National Park, sir. I didn't bring my card. I left it at the house like I always do."

Allie lay in her sleeping bag, her body trembling with shivers that weren't a result of the falling temperature. She held her breath and tried desperately to think of a logical reason his card would be missing. And how she could put it back.

"Yes, sir," Lenny said, looking at his watch. "I'll be in your office as fast as I can – for sure in less than three hours." He put down the phone and began to pull on his shirt and jeans.

"What's going on, Lenny?" his wife asked, concerned because she'd never heard Lenny call his boss "sir" before. "Is there a problem?"

"Damn right there's a problem. Someone used my access card to break a prisoner out of the jail in Denver two hours ago. It was that political prisoner – Daniel Dax – the guy who was in Leadville until last Sunday. Two guys in an ambulance staged a jailbreak and took him away. I'm in deep trouble and I have to report to Denver ASAP. Get up and break down the camp. We're going back. Now."

CHAPTER FORTY

After the helicopter took Dan Dax away, Patrick Munro and the driver closed the roof access door, took the elevator down and fled on foot. Since no one knew yet who they were, their chips wouldn't give them away because no one was searching for them. Within a half hour they were picked up by a Resistance vehicle and unchipped.

By the time dawn broke, the cops were scurrying like ants through the abandoned garage two miles from EP headquarters. They'd strung crime scene tape around the perimeter of the dingy concrete-block building with weeds everywhere and a few rusting car parts scattered in a partially fenced back lot. The place obviously hadn't been occupied in years.

As the men worked, they realized what an enormous amount of planning it had taken to pull this off. A forensic team was going over the ambulance from bumper to bumper. It wasn't what it appeared to be; it was instead a refurbished cargo van that had been outfitted and painted to look like an ambulance. Its license plates had been stolen a month before. There were no fingerprints except those of the missing prisoner, Daniel Dax, and there was nothing that might have implicated anyone else.

They'd discovered the location while doing a building-to-building search of the three blocks where it had disappeared just before midnight. From tracks in the dust they could see that the rusting door had been opened recently. The building was owned by a corporation out of Halifax, in the Northeast Americas sector. They'd ultimately learn that the owners were a retired couple who lived near the ocean and said they hadn't been able to rent the building for a decade. The EP would finally conclude that they weren't involved, although in reality the two were secret Resistance sympathizers whose building was always available to the cause.

Investigators followed a trail along the dusty floor and saw that the gurney had been rolled into an elevator. They first took the creaky lift to the top floor and opened a door onto the roof. There were no tracks from the gurney's wheels here – in fact, there was no dust at all. The officers examined the second floor, found no evidence that the gurney had been there, and correctly surmised that the prisoner, gurney and all, had been whisked away by a helicopter whose rotors had cleared away the dust.

Calls to the local public and private airports would reveal that nothing was picked up on radar that night. If a chopper did come and go from the building's rooftop, it flew at a very low altitude. They went house to house in the shoddy neighborhood around the industrial area and learned that some residents recalled hearing a helicopter last night. The information reinforced their theory about the escape but did nothing to move their investigation forward. Daniel Dax had been successfully removed from a secure prison facility, taken to this building and spirited away.

The only substantive evidence they had were clear videos of the driver and his accomplice, a young man in an EP uniform, and several swipes of an Enforcement Patrol captain's access card that made the entire situation possible.

CHAPTER FORTY-ONE

Around the same time Lenny and his family returned to Leadville, Jim Gordon had slipped the access card back into the planter where he'd gotten it yesterday. Then he drove back to the safe house, his mission accomplished.

Wheeler and Abbott were already in the office when Lenny arrived. He'd spent a fruitless hour searching his house for the card. Without it he couldn't enter the building, so an officer escorted him from the parking garage.

Wheeler started to introduce Abbott, but the federal officer held up his hand. "I'm perfectly capable of telling Captain Vargas who I am." He pointed to a chair next to him and said, "Sit down. You're going to be here for quite some time, I predict." Lenny noticed the man's World Union lapel pin and blue access card. The latter was an indicator he was dealing with someone high up in the chain of command – there was only one level of card higher than the one clipped to this guy's pocket. He also picked up on the agent's arrogant attitude.

In words that Lenny considered an obvious but unsuccessful attempt to sound friendly, the man said, "I'm Heston Abbott. I'm a senior interrogator from the district office in Mexico City and it's fortuitous that I was in town already so I can lead our questions today. Not that Major Wheeler here isn't capable." He waved a hand at Lenny's boss as though he were brushing off a fly. "He just isn't trained in interrogation techniques. I, however, am considered a master by my peers."

I need to be careful, Lenny thought as he observed his boss sitting silently and looking like a whipped dog in front of the pompous ass doing the talking. *Think before you answer his questions.*

The federal agent continued. "Originally I came here to interrogate Daniel Dax. Dax is a man with whom you have a connection, isn't that right? Even before someone used your card to break him out of prison, I mean. He was in your jail in Leadville. How much direct contact did you have with Mr. Dax while he was a prisoner there? How well did you get to know him?"

Lenny was an officer himself and he deserved respect. Already he didn't like where these questions were going. It was time to stop things before they began.

"Just a minute. Before you start firing questions at me, I want to know what happened here last night. How the hell could my card have been used –"

Abbott interrupted, leaning forward in his chair until he was only inches from Lenny's face. "Only one of us is going to ask questions, Captain Vargas. Do you understand? I will ask and you will answer, completely and truthfully, or else you'll find yourself in far more trouble than you can imagine."

Becoming concerned, Lenny looked at his boss. "John, what's going on?"

Wheeler stared back, saying nothing but obviously uneasy with the situation. In reality, he was terrified. He hoped to God this interrogation wasn't going to turn ugly and he hoped he could stop things if it did. He also knew he had no power over this brutish man and his cruel techniques. That had already been proven.

"Major Wheeler is merely an observer," Abbott advised. "Your transgression is a federal matter."

"My transgression? I haven't done anything –" He rocked back in surprise as Abbott suddenly jumped up and yelled.

"You haven't done anything? Captain Vargas, until now I considered you at least marginally intelligent. You were a county sheriff and now are a captain, neither of which would mark an individual as particularly bright or capable." He calmed his words and for the first time Lenny saw the cruel smile that had made John Wheeler cringe in the basement interrogation room. "If you are, in fact, intelligent, then consider this. I have a man in front of me whom I suspect of providing the way for a traitor to our nation to escape from prison. That man is you, and you are an officer in the Enforcement Patrol, a man who took an oath to uphold and protect the World Union and its citizens. Until I hear something to make me think otherwise, I consider you as much a traitor, if not more, as Daniel Dax is. You are in very bad trouble, Captain Vargas. I don't know if you can comprehend that, but your job and much more – your very life, perhaps – are in my hands at the moment. And I don't like what I see. I don't like what happened last night, and I'm disgusted that an officer in the service of the Union is involved."

He paused and looked at Wheeler. "Get me some water," he commanded. Seriously worried what might happen if he left his office for only a moment, the major nonetheless jumped up and left the room. He left the door open on purpose, but before he walked five steps, he heard it slam. Wheeler went through the bullpen filled with cops at work, ran to the break room, grabbed a bottle from the fridge and rushed back, only to find the door locked. He rattled the knob and knocked.

"It'll be a moment," he heard through the door. He stood helplessly, locked out of his own office as everyone in the bullpen pretended they didn't notice what was going on.

Wheeler couldn't hear anything for a couple of minutes. Finally he heard the lock click and Abbott opened the door, taking the water as the major returned to his desk. Lenny was still sitting in the same chair. Wheeler raised his eyebrows, a signal to ask if his subordinate was okay, but Lenny just looked at him blankly. It was obvious, the major thought, that Lenny now realized he was dealing with something frightening.

"I've been discussing choices with Captain Vargas," Abbott said evenly. "In an attempt to keep an open mind about his involvement in the prisoner's escape last night, I've offered to continue our discussions here instead of down in the basement. Major Wheeler, wouldn't you advise the captain that talking up here in your office is a far superior idea?" He smiled grimly as Wheeler bobbed his head up and down like a marionette.

"Lenny, you don't want to go there –"

"That's enough, Major," he interrupted harshly. "All I needed was a yes or no. You may sit down now while I continue."

Abbott told Lenny he wanted to hear everything. And Lenny had complied, explaining that he hadn't even spoken once to Daniel Dax while he was in Leadville. He had intended to interrogate the prisoner, but when Major Wheeler assumed jurisdiction, Lenny's involvement was over before it began. The prisoner was moved to Denver a week ago and Lenny hadn't even been around when that happened. He and his wife were on a fishing trip last weekend – they went camping almost every weekend at this time of year. The only difference this time was that Vargas's stepdaughter, Allie, was along too.

"I agree it is convenient how you were never around when things were happening with Mr. Dax," Abbott said when he was finished.

"I never said it was convenient –"

Abbott screamed in fury, astonishing Lenny and causing John Wheeler to push his desk chair further away. "Shut up! When I want you to talk, I'll tell you. Here's what I see. Just days before your prisoner is to be moved to Denver, someone uses your password to access a seemingly innocuous file – a list of residents and businesses in your county. You were off duty when that happened, and on the surface, that was a relatively minor infraction, although it is an offense for which your superior officer should have reprimanded you." He looked at Wheeler and said calmly, "And for that I will deal with you later.

"Then, Captain Vargas, you take another weekend jaunt, carelessly leaving your access card where others can find it. While you are up in the mountains, miles away from Denver but with only your family to vouch for your whereabouts and activities, someone shows up here at headquarters last night, uses your card over and over, and whisks a dangerous criminal away to freedom. That man is chipped, but suddenly our tracking system can no longer locate him.

"Let's go over this one more time, Captain Vargas. This time I suggest you tell me the truth about what happened here. You are supposedly a trained, seasoned professional – albeit a careless and sloppy one, hence your rank of captain when a man of your age should easily be a major or more."

Lenny squirmed in his chair, wanting to lash back at this infuriating line of questioning but also seriously afraid of this man. It was easy to see that Johnny felt the same; he was cowering in his chair like a schoolchild hoping the teacher wouldn't call on him.

Abbott took a stack of photos from his briefcase, handed them to Lenny and said, "These are the two men who were in the ambulance last night. This man" – he pointed at a clear photo of a young Enforcement patrolman standing at the nurses' station in the prison infirmary – "is an EP corporal named Patrick Munro. He's the one who had your access card pinned to his pocket. Who is he, Captain Vargas? Do you know him? Do you know the other man, the driver? How did this man Munro get your access card?

"Tell me the entire story one more time and answer my questions. If you'd like to continue this absurdity that you aren't involved, then by all means, please give me your professional opinion as to who these people are and why they abducted my prisoner."

Thirty minutes later the people working outside Major Wheeler's office glanced up, then averted their eyes as the man in the black suit walked out of his office, shut the door behind him and went to the bank of elevators across the room. Then he was gone.

CHAPTER FORTY-TWO

Lenny had gone to Denver only after turning the house upside down. "Do you have any idea where it is?" he asked Allie.

She shook her head and Mabry asked her husband why he thought Allie would have it. He didn't respond – he simply kept looking. It would be great if he could turn up for the meeting with his card in hand, proving that whatever happened didn't involve him. But it wasn't to be. The card simply wasn't where he'd left it yesterday or anywhere else in the bedroom. At last he gave up and hit the road, telling his wife he'd be back sometime this afternoon.

Frantically hoping the card was back, Allie told her mother she was going for a walk. They'd only been home a little over an hour and it was still dark and frigid. "Are you sure, honey?" her mother asked. "It's not even five o'clock; the sun's not up yet. If Lenny upset you ..."

"It's not that. I can't sleep anyway," she answered truthfully. "I just want to get some fresh air. I'll be back in a few minutes." She put on a heavy coat, hat and gloves and went outside. When she'd agreed to all this, she had no idea Nate was going to use Lenny's card to stage a prison break. She had no idea who he was involved with; what had happened was huge and she prayed that he'd brought the card back like he promised. He'd told her it would be back by the time they returned from the camping trip, but obviously they were back far earlier than anyone had expected. She got to the planter, looked both ways, saw no one, and anxiously put her hand behind the plant. The card was there! She breathed a huge sigh of relief as she put it in her coat pocket.

There was no way Lenny could tie her to any of this. All she had to do was think of a logical place the card could have fallen where no one would see it, and put it there for Lenny to find. It would have to be in their bedroom and it had to be back before he got home. There would still be the mystery of whether Lenny's access card really was used in the prison breakout. But if the card was found in the house, it would make more sense that someone copied his information instead of stealing the actual card, then risking exposure by returning to put it back.

Freezing, she forced herself to walk another fifteen minutes and then returned. Mabry was cooking waffles and bacon and the house smelled wonderful. She went into her bedroom and stuck the card in the top drawer of her dresser under her socks until she could figure out what to do with it.

"Is Lenny going to be okay?" she asked her mom as they ate breakfast. "What's going on with his security card, and why did they want to see him in Denver so badly?"

Mabry told her daughter that this prison breakout was a huge deal – it was unprecedented, in fact – and the EP officials were looking at every angle. "We know he's not involved," she assured Allie, who knew it already. "He was camping with us. Nobody was in the house while we were gone. There's something else going on and they'll figure it out, I'm sure. Don't worry; Lenny will be home for supper."

Allie was worried for Lenny but also for Nate and herself. She was suddenly in the middle of something really big – something that wasn't going away.

CHAPTER FORTY-THREE

After Dad's harrowing escape, Carlos took me to the safe house. I was exhausted, but it was a wonderful kind of tired. It had been twenty-six days since my father and mother walked out of the house to run into town for supplies and lunch. I could never have imagined that afternoon that I would never see Mom again, the house and barn would be burned to the ground, and a plan I created would free my dad from prison.

It was close to three when I fell into bed. I was careful not to disturb Ben since he worked early on Saturdays. It wouldn't have been a problem – he was snoring like a steam engine – but I was respectful anyway. I never heard him leave; when I finally opened my eyes, it was afternoon.

Cassie and Maeve invited me to go with them to Wendy's for lunch and it felt good to accept without trepidation. Everything went smoothly; chipped Cassie paid the bill for the Outcasts and I walked through the screening machine like I owned the place. Being normal was something I was getting used to. It felt good.

They had to have known I was out almost all night, but no one asked. I appreciated that; I figured people living in a safe house had more secrets than others did, and maybe they had a different view on respecting the privacy of others. I knew very little about my housemates, but it turned out I was about to learn more.

After dinner everyone settled back in the living room as usual and Ben said, "Smitty and I owe you our backgrounds. All you know about him is that he works for the EP downtown. All you know about me is that I was descended from a line of noble pirates. Are you ready for the rest of the story?"

215

Maeve jumped in with a theatrical yawn of boredom. "I was hoping you'd forgotten. Nate's your roommate. Why don't you tell him your story when you're both in bed? It should put him right to sleep and save the rest of us the agony of hearing it again!"

"Protest all you want, baby. You and I both know you're as eager to hear it again as he is to hear it the first time! But I'm a gentleman. Smitty, you may go first."

I'd felt more comfortable around Smitty than any of the others from the beginning. I didn't understand why, since Maeve and Ben were as friendly as he was and Cassie was pleasant, although she was very shy. It was something about his relaxed attitude. I knew about Cassie's and Maeve's inner turmoil hidden just beneath the surface, and although I hadn't heard Ben's story yet, I felt his braggadocious attitude was a shield for something he was hiding too.

"My story, by Aristotle Smithins Hightower the fourth," he began. "I'm afraid you'll find mine boring compared to the others', but I feel fortunate not to have endured the struggles and heartache Maeve and Cassie did, and I'm blessed that my parents are safe and sound in London instead of in the brig for being pirates, like Ben's dad and uncle are. Mine are university professors.

"I grew up with a predilection for tablets, thanks to my parents' encouragement. I built one from scratch when I was eight, I taught myself the sophisticated code that major companies used to encrypt their data, and I learned how to hack into their systems. I went to work for the World Union after university. The aptitude tests they administered showed I should be in data processing or systems analysis, but I wasn't willing to accept a boring, nerdy desk job. I wanted something challenging and fun. I told my interviewer that I could hack anything. I don't think he believed me, but I convinced him to give me a test. He put me in a room with a tablet, a pad of paper and a pencil, and he told me to decode what was on the screen.

"It was a tough assignment, but modestly I'll say that in less than an hour I was finished and I had a job offer. I became a specialist first class in a department that had a cryptic name of its own: the ED Services Unit. Now I'm a senior ED analyst and a trainer for the World Union."

"ED – that means encryption and decryption?" I asked.

"Very good! Yes, as you might imagine, there are tens of thousands of messages a day that flow into and out of World Union offices worldwide, many of which are encrypted because of their confidentiality. My unit in London has the most sophisticated equipment imaginable to both encrypt and decrypt. It's fascinating work and I enjoy every minute of it."

I'd heard just enough to be completely confused. "You're chipped and you work for the government. So how did you end up in Denver living in a safe house?"

"I don't live in a safe house. I live in the spare bedroom of my uncle Jim's residence."

"Jim? Jim Gordon's your uncle?"

"Uncle-in-law, actually. He's not a Brit like me, but he's my mother's brother-in-law. Now to why I'm here, the World Union is installing decryption units in every EP district office worldwide. I'm on loan from the London ED Services Unit to help establish one here and train workers. It's a two-year program and I have eighteen months to go."

"So were you surprised when you got here and found out Jim was running a safe house?"

"I knew all about it; so did my parents. They're sympathizers, helping the cause in the jolly old Western European Area. Although I've always supported the concept too, I wasn't particularly interested in being a part of the Resistance itself, but I'm enjoying learning more and more about you strange half-breeds known as Outcasts. Until you came along, I thought Ben was a typical example of the male of your breed. Thank God I found you. Now I know there are normal Outcasts too!" Everyone laughed.

"Smitty and I have to be careful," Cassie added. "We're chipped and we work for the government. It would go badly for us if they found out what was really going on."

I asked what they would do if the EP ever came knocking at the door. The answer was simple – it never happened unless they had a tip or an idea there were Outcasts in a house. There was simply not enough time to do house-to-house checks.

"There's also a mole somewhere, I hear," Smitty whispered conspiratorially. "That person would let Carlos know if something was going down. The EP never does anything quickly. Planning to raid a house would take so long we could pack up and move before they got here. At least that's the theory."

It all made sense to me. Maeve asked Smitty if he was through and he made a magnanimous gesture toward Ben. "Only one story left, you son of a pirate!"

"When we last left Ben Creel," he began dramatically, "he had left Florida, heading west in a truck filled with everything he owned. He was escaping a past life and had to be sure the dreaded Enforcement patrolmen didn't track him down through the chip that had been embedded into his psyche as an infant."

"Oh, God," Maeve muttered. "It gets more outlandish every time."

"The brave and courageous young man had intelligently saved his World points, so he had plenty of money. He followed the interstate highways day after day until one glorious morning when he awoke to a view of the majestic mountains ahead. They beckoned him to come, to settle in an enchanted city called Denver. It was a beautiful place and there was a wizard ..." He paused, obviously enjoying the attention his tale was generating. "Oh, wait. There actually wasn't a wizard. That's another story."

Maeve continued for him. "You went online and visited a prohibited site, you learned there was a Resistance cell, you applied for help, they unchipped you, you joined the Resistance and the rest is history. That's the story. See how easy that was? Can we watch a movie now?"

He looked at her, pretending to be offended. "You ruined everything, you evil witch! Now there's nothing left to tell. You condensed my life into one sentence! How debasing!"

There was something I actually wanted to know out of all these antics. "What do you do now?" I asked, wondering what kind of jobs Outcasts might have.

"Okay, I'll be serious now. I work for the Resistance. I'm in military demolitions training, learning how to use explosives, make bombs and that sort of thing. My day job is working at a thrift shop."

I looked at the others and saw them nodding. He was telling the truth, but his answer raised more questions. "I don't understand either thing you said. How can you work in a thrift shop? You're an Outcast."

"This is no ordinary thrift shop, although you'd never know it if you weren't in on the secret. It's in a rough neighborhood – a place thrift shops ought to be if they want to help people – and the general public is our clientele. Chipped people who are down on their luck, homeless, hooked on drugs or booze or just needing a helping hand come shop with us. Other people shop there too. It's a place where Outcasts can get what they need. Everything you brought from Leadville went to the shop and some of it's already helping other people like us."

"But they can't pay. And the sensors ... what about the detection devices?"

"Outcasts *can't* pay, so they *don't* pay. Chipped people check out right next to them and never know that they're getting their goods for free. And the detectors? Well, for some reason ours are out of order. Always have been, as long as I've been around. Isn't that convenient?"

"Doesn't the World Union have inspection teams?"

"Sure they do, but think about it. How many detection devices are there in one block of stores? Maybe twenty? Multiply that by thousands of blocks and many thousands of stores just in metropolitan Denver alone. Multiply that by the whole Northwest Americas region. The World Union doesn't have the interest or the manpower to look for faulty detectors. Someday a random check might turn up the broken machine in our store. So what? We just tell them we'll get it fixed. And that's that."

"I get it. But the other thing you talked about – demolitions training – what's that about?"

"The Resistance has a top-secret training facility. Nobody knows where it is. I'm thinking I'll tell Maeve, though, so I'll have to kill her." He laughed as she shot him the bird. "Seriously though, it's a military-style camp where you can go on weekends and get training that'll help the Resistance. There are over a hundred of us who do this, and there are maybe ten different specialties. If you're interested, ask Jim and he'll tell you all about it."

CHAPTER FORTY-FOUR

"What the hell's going on, Johnny? Who is this guy? They can't hold me overnight! I haven't done anything!"

Wheeler wanted to tell him everything. He wanted to express how incredibly afraid he was right now, not only for Vargas but for himself. Heston Abbott was a lunatic, a deranged sadist who seemed most at ease when he was inflicting pain on others. But Wheeler kept most of it to himself. If Abbott ever found out he was trying to help, he could be charged with interfering with a criminal investigation. He had to be very careful what he said now. He would tell the truth, but only part of the truth.

Abbott had listened to Lenny's story the second time and his honest admission that he had no idea who Patrick Munro or the driver were. He also swore he'd left his access card in his house, which he'd come home to early this morning. There was no sign of forcible entry, but his card was missing.

Once he finished, the World Union interrogator told Wheeler that Lenny was being detained. "Lock him up overnight. No charges yet – he's under suspicion of aiding the Resistance. I want to continue our discussion tomorrow, downstairs."

Now John Wheeler sat with the man he'd worked for at the Lake County Sheriff's Office a long time ago. Neither of them particularly liked the other, but both of them were involved in something ominous and far-reaching – something neither of them understood. The World Union wasn't going to let this drop and their interrogator obviously believed Lenny Vargas was involved. That scared Lenny, but it scared John far worse because he'd seen Abbott in action.

"This is really serious, Lenny. I was an observer at Dan Dax's first interrogation just like I was at yours today. But his wasn't the same. The first time he was carried out by two officers. I missed the next one – I was busy, thankfully – but that one ended Dax in the infirmary. The guy's crazy. He's using techniques ... I can't talk about it, but trust me, you don't want this to happen.

"You have to admit your story doesn't add up. There are lots of holes. You just put your access card in a drawer and next thing you know it ends up being used to free a political prisoner? And no one even broke into your house? There's much more to this, and if you know anything, you have to tell him. For God's sake, Lenny, believe me. This guy's gonna hurt you."

As much as he despised following Abbott's orders, neither he nor his boss had any choice in the matter. It wasn't Johnny's fault; he was just doing his job. Lenny resigned himself to the fact that he would be here overnight.

Lenny asked to use the phone to call home, and Wheeler pushed it across the desk to him. Mabry was scared and began asking questions Lenny couldn't answer. "There were cops here this afternoon," she told him. "They went through the house, examined the locks and asked questions about who had keys."

He told her that was okay. They were investigating to see if the house had been broken into and the card stolen. That hadn't been the case, they determined, just as Lenny himself already realized. This wasn't a break-in. It was something else entirely.

He didn't really know what was ahead, but he optimistically told his wife he'd definitely be home tomorrow. Uncharacteristically empathetic, Lenny's boss said Mabry could call him if she had any questions at all. Lenny appreciated that small kindness, but it made him nervous. John was worried; he could tell.

A few minutes before six Captain Leonard Vargas was delivered to the intake desk, where he was booked, fingerprinted, photographed and strip-searched. Since he was an EP officer, he was sent to a solitary confinement protection unit for his safety.

John Wheeler walked out of his office fifteen minutes later, fearful of what might happen tomorrow. He went home, poured a stiff drink, then another and another, until he passed out on the sofa.

Lenny Vargas ate dinner off a metal plate that had been passed through a slot in the barred door. His hands trembled as he held the fork, picked at his food and sipped a lukewarm cup of coffee. He had a good idea who was involved with all this. He had no idea what was going on or why, but today during the interrogation, red flags kept popping into his mind. There was really no question who had taken his card.

He had to stay strong and keep his thoughts to himself. It would be disastrous if Abbott learned who Lenny thought was involved. When he got home, he'd sort this out, but he damned sure couldn't let this cold-blooded man get his hands on Allie.

He fell asleep in a place he never dreamed he'd be, a jail cell like the ones in which other men had found themselves thanks to the efforts of Lenny Vargas. This time he was the prey, not the hunter.

CHAPTER FORTY-FIVE

I sat at breakfast in the safe house Monday morning, expecting to be heading to Carlos's office soon. I was still exhilarated from my dad's rescue Friday night and news yesterday that his condition was steadily improving. I didn't know where he was, but the doctor had sent word that he was off the IVs and resting comfortably.

Friday Carlos took my phone – the one that had been the ranch's house phone – and gave me an untraceable burner instead. The old one would be destroyed; it was in the EP database and therefore trackable. As I sat at the kitchen table, Carlos called. I broke into a huge smile as I listened.

"I presume that was good news," Maeve commented afterwards. "You look like you're about to burst."

"I get to see Dad! Jim's taking me there; we're leaving in thirty minutes! I can hardly wait ..." I stifled a tiny sob; my heart was about to burst and I was embarrassed to be so emotional in front of everyone. But it didn't matter. She came over and hugged my neck.

"What wonderful news! Did they tell you where he is?"

"No. All that matters is I get to go there! I can't eat anything else. I've got to go get ready!"

I ran upstairs and shut the bedroom door. I was glad that Ben had already left for work so I could let my emotions go. My chest was so tight from anticipation I could hardly breathe. There was a time I'd given up, finally believing I'd never see either of my parents again. And now – soon – I was going to be with my father. I went to the bathroom, splashed water on my face, brushed my teeth and combed my hair. I wanted to look presentable for the reunion of a lifetime.

I was waiting out back when a car pulled in. I was expecting to see Jim, but it was Carlos instead. As I jumped in the front seat, he said, "This is going to be a great morning. I'll give you time alone with your dad, but I want to see him too. I hope you don't mind my tagging along ..."

I didn't mind anything. The whole town could have tagged along. The only thing that mattered was that he was alive and now we were going to be together again. What the future held, I didn't know. All that mattered was today.

As we backed out of the driveway, he handed me a pair of sunglasses and a wide-brimmed hat, apologizing but asking me to wear them. "I try to keep people from knowing any more about our activities than necessary. I trust you – this is a precaution in case you ever get detained. The less you know, the better off all of us are, you included."

I laughed as I put them on, telling him I'd wear a sack of manure on my head if it meant I got to see Dad. The glasses were tinted so deeply that I could see absolutely nothing, and I knew that was the idea.

As we drove, we talked about Dad's rescue. I asked where Patrick and the driver were and he said they were now unchipped and in hiding. The number of cops working on this case was unprecedented and the reward for information was the largest ever offered. Even with all that, Carlos's source told him there were no leads at all.

"There's something else you need to know," he added. "That EP officer from Leadville whose card we used spent last night in jail at headquarters. I don't know details, but if I hear more, I'll tell you."

That was disturbing news, especially if it involved Allie. When I had told Carlos my plan for rescuing Dad, all I said was that it might be possible to get Lenny's access card from his stepdaughter. He hadn't asked me how I could do that, and I was sure he figured something was going on between us. The only good things were that Lenny Vargas didn't know she took the card and that it was already back. Jim had returned it before dawn yesterday, long before the family was supposed to be back home.

I thought about what might have gone wrong until Carlos announced we'd arrived. I took off the glasses and hat as we went down a long paved driveway lined with Italian cypress trees ten feet tall. Ahead of us was a rambling white two-story building that looked like a resort. We pulled under a porte cochere and Carlos handed the keys to a valet. I walked toward the entrance, but Carlos waved me over to one side where a golf cart was parked and ready to go. We drove alongside the building and went over a grassy lawn toward a stand of huge oak trees and three isolated cabanas that sat in the shade under them.

Carlos parked in front of one and put his hand lightly on my arm. "Before we go in," he cautioned, "your dad's been through a lot. He's improved in forty-eight hours, but he has a long way to go. Don't be alarmed when you see him. He also doesn't know about your mother. The interrogator told him she was alive, then that she was dead, but he didn't believe him."

"When are you going to tell him?" I asked. Carlos said he would be told when the time was right and I'd be there too if I wanted to. His doctor felt Dad was just too weak to handle the shock at this point.

I promised I'd be fine. I absolutely couldn't wait to see him – my only concern was what I'd do if he asked about Mom. I asked Carlos what to do if Dad brought it up, and he said we'd deal with that if it happened.

"Can we go in now?" I asked, and Carlos nodded with a smile. We walked up three stairs to a little porch and he knocked on the door. A pleasant-looking lady in scrubs answered the door. She was one of Dad's full-time nurses, Carlos explained.

"Come on in," she said warmly to me. "Someone's been waiting for you!"

He was propped up on pillows in a bright, comfortable room. There was a tube hooked behind his ears that ran under his nose and there was a port in his arm to administer injections. His arms were a mass of bruises and one eye was swollen half-shut.

He held out his arms and I ran to him. "You look good, Dad," I said.

"Didn't I teach you not to lie?"

"Take it easy, guys!" the nurse scolded jokingly. "And no big hugs, either one of you! Dan, you watch yourself! You're still healing!"

"Hush, woman! This is my boy! I can hug him if I want to!"

I leaned over his bed, embraced him and felt his weak response. "I thought ... I thought I'd never see you again," I said through the tears I could no longer keep inside. "I thought you and Mom ..."

Suddenly I hesitated. I'd said it without intending to.

"Where is she, Nate? Have you seen her?"

I turned helplessly to Carlos. He came over and stood by the bed. "Hey, Dan," he said quietly, taking Dad's hand. "You look like you've been in a bar fight."

"If I ever see that bastard Heston Abbott again, wait and see what *he* looks like. Are you changing the subject on me, old friend? Where's Melanie? You have to tell me. Regardless of what's happened, you have to let me know what they did with her."

Carlos looked at me and I shook my head. I couldn't do it.

"She's gone, Dan. But not because she was arrested. They drew her lottery number. She was euthanized three weeks ago."

Dad clenched his fists and said nothing. A monitor by the bed began to beep loudly and the nurse said, "His blood pressure is spiking. The doctor told you this could happen!" She prepared a syringe and injected it into his port.

In a moment he sank back into the pillows resignedly and whispered, "I knew it. In my heart I knew she was gone. I could just tell – a feeling – does that make sense?" He wasn't talking to anyone in particular – he was just staring up at the ceiling – but then he looked at me. "I knew all this time you were fine. Somewhere inside I had a peace about you, but I never felt that way about your mother." He turned to the nurse next. "Just get me well and get me out of here. I have something to do as soon as I'm able."

Carlos nodded and said, "No one could blame you for how you feel, but you have to concentrate on getting well. You've been through a huge ordeal. You could have died if we hadn't gotten you out, and by the way, you have Nate to thank for the plan that made that happen. It's going to take weeks for you to recover. There'll be time for retribution and there are plenty of friends who'll help. Just let it go for now."

Dad's face turned dark. "Don't ever say that to me again, Carlos! I'll never let this go. Never. Not even when the ones who did it have paid. This is the kind of oppressive government we live under and I'll keep fighting until it falls or I do."

"Me too, Dad," I responded, squeezing his hand. "I'll be with you all the way. You have to teach me what I need to know."

He smiled weakly. "I will, Nate. It's just you and me now."

CHAPTER FORTY-SIX

At 7:30 Sunday morning Major John Wheeler was already at his desk. He often came in on the weekends, but today's early arrival was for an entirely different reason. Today at 10:30 Heston Abbott was going to continue the interrogation in the basement chamber where he'd questioned Daniel Dax.

Wheeler did a last scan of the high-priority email he was sending to his ultimate boss, Gregory Nail. Nail – a civilian who was deputy director of the Enforcement Patrol, NWA Division – was at the World Union's district headquarters in Mexico City. No one outranked Nail except his own boss, the director, who was in Tel Aviv.

Wheeler had never communicated with any EP officials other than his bosses here in Denver. It was a standing joke that the big-shot civilians at district headquarters made policy but didn't have any experience in law enforcement. Today he hoped a man he'd never met would choose to do the right thing, and do it in time.

He'd awakened on the sofa fully dressed at 2:30 a.m., hung over as hell and feeling miserable. He'd tried to go to bed, but nagging thoughts kept him awake. He hated traitors like Daniel Dax and he didn't care much for Lenny, but no one deserved treatment like Heston Abbott doled out. When Dan Dax was rescued, Wheeler had been secretly relieved. Hopefully the EP would arrest him again someday, but at least for now he wouldn't be beaten to death by a brutish monster.

For over an hour he wrote, crossing out sentences and changing words until it was right. He explained who he was, what his role had been in the Dax investigation, and what he'd seen. He spelled out in detail the horrific treatment the

231

man had received and that Abbott had deliberately delayed charging Dax with a crime so he could question the suspect before he was allowed counsel. An attorney would have stopped all this and Heston Abbott knew it. This wasn't the first time he'd pulled that maneuver. Questions first, lawyer later.

He also explained the situation with Lenny Vargas. Wheeler had been a part of many an interrogation in his career; like other officers, he'd developed a sixth sense about the veracity of what people said. It wasn't foolproof, but he didn't think Vargas was crafty enough to pretend he was clueless. His dislike for the man didn't stop him from believing he was telling the truth. He had decided Lenny really had no idea how his card had gotten into the hands of Dax's abductors.

At his desk, he put everything into an email. It was a damning exposé of the World Union man who'd brutally beaten one subject and was prepared to question another this morning. He didn't expect instant results. He really didn't know what to expect. He might end up with a reprimand – or worse – in his own file for insubordination. Maybe they'd start an internal investigation, or maybe there would be no response at all. He wasn't sure how things worked at district headquarters, but as a moral man sworn to uphold the law, he had to do something.

Less than two hours later Wheeler's phone rang. It was Nail's executive assistant, asking if he had a moment to speak with the deputy director.

The conversation went well, John reflected twenty minutes later. The man sounded sincere and said there would be no toleration of the things Wheeler had alleged. If – and this was a big if – Wheeler's story was true, the deputy director would personally guarantee the situation would be dealt with quickly and decisively.

There was an unspoken other side to the situation. If Heston Abbott could convince his boss Wheeler's allegations weren't true – he would be looking for a job at the least, and more likely facing charges.

Deputy Director Nail chose to believe Wheeler for now. He ordered that Vargas be released. According to John's email, Vargas had not been charged with a crime, he was being interrogated because someone stole his access card, and it was likely he wasn't involved with the prison breakout. Since Vargas was an Enforcement Patrol officer and had a family in Leadville, Director Nail accepted Wheeler's assurance that he wasn't a flight risk. If they needed to talk to him again, there was a very high probability he'd be around.

Meanwhile Abbott would be recalled to Mexico City today and the recordings of the basement sessions with Daniel Dax would be requisitioned. Wheeler breathed a sigh of relief when he heard that part; in the frenzy of everything he'd forgotten that every interrogation session was recorded for this very reason. The videos would confirm his story one hundred percent.

"Thank you for your concern," John told his superior. "If I may offer a suggestion, I'd ask that you move quickly. I think Abbott intends to resume questioning in less than an hour."

Half an hour later his office door burst open and Heston Abbott stormed in, his eyes full of fury. He closed the door behind him, walked to the desk, leaned across and said, "You've made a very serious mistake, Major Wheeler, very serious indeed. I'm not a man you want as your adversary, but you've chosen to do battle with me. You've achieved what you wanted – your friend is on his way home. Now I've got my sights on another person of interest. That person would be you. What caused you to run crying to district headquarters about my treatment of a traitor to our Union? What caused you to complain about my simple questioning of one of your officers yesterday? What do *you* have to hide, Major Wheeler? That's my next project and I promise you before it's over, you'll regret this day that you betrayed me."

Abbott turned and walked out. Once he was gone, John Wheeler closed his office door, took the recording device from his pocket and turned it off. This was just a little insurance. It wasn't much – the video recordings were the real evidence – but it was another example of Heston Abbott's modus operandi.

He sent a requisition request to the security department, asking for copies of videos from the basement interrogation room for October 29 and 31, the two days Abbott questioned Dax. He had no idea how long it might take for Nail to requisition the recordings and they were absolute proof that his allegations were true.

A few minutes later he saw a response in his mailbox.

The videos for those two days weren't available. By order of the World Union, they'd been forwarded to the district office and wiped from the database here.

"By whose order and when?" Wheeler fired back, a lump rising in his throat. He knew the answer to both questions.

"The order was issued yesterday at 6:12 p.m. our time by Heston Abbott. The videos were forwarded to him and expunged at 6:27 p.m."

He forwarded that exchange of emails to Deputy Director Nail and asked if he could do anything to keep those recordings from getting to Abbott. This time there was no response.

The damning evidence that could prove John Wheeler's accusations were true was gone.

CHAPTER FORTY-SEVEN

Lenny awakened to a trolley banging along the corridor outside his cell. He glanced at a clock hanging nearby; it was 5:20 a.m. Even in solitary he could hear noises from the main cell block – laughter, blaring music, yelling and cursing all night long. He'd gotten almost no sleep and he was emotionally and physically drained. He was in no shape to face what was coming this morning, but he had to be strong and get through it. He'd done nothing wrong – maybe Allie and that boy had, but he swore he wouldn't give her up. This guy Heston Abbott was a lunatic. If Allie was involved, he'd deal with her himself.

A guard pushed his breakfast into the cell, then moved on down the row. He ate as much of the bland meal as he could stomach, just to keep his strength up. He splashed water on his face, put on his socks and shoes, and sat on his bunk. An hour passed, then two. He began to grow apprehensive. What was going on? Why were they delaying this?

Shortly after ten an officer appeared at his cell door, opened it and said, "Get your things, Captain Vargas. You're being released."

As he drove home, he tried to call John Wheeler, but it went to voicemail. "Whatever you did, thanks," he said sincerely. This wasn't over by any means – that was partly evidenced by his new access card, a white one this time. For now they'd given him a basic access card like any new employee carried. It made absolutely no difference to him; he was simply glad to be free.

He struggled with how to deal with Allie – and her mother too. Mabry was understandably protective of her daughter, but he was certain all of this had to do with that

235

boy Allie had been seeing. Despite his wife's opinion, he had to hear Allie's story.

Mabry and Allie hugged him when he walked in. They listened as he explained everything that had transpired. And they cried as he told them about Heston Abbott's harsh questions and his insistence that Vargas was somehow involved.

"You have to admit it looks pretty bad," he continued. "My access card was used to break out a prisoner. My story is that I was out of town and left the card in the bedroom. There was no forcible entry to our house ..."

"It's even worse than that," his wife responded. "Look what I found under the dresser when I was vacuuming this morning."

She held up the red card and Allie gasped. She'd placed it there last night before dinner and didn't know her mom had found it already.

"I looked there. The card wasn't there yesterday. You know what this means ..." he began, but Mabry interrupted him with a furious outburst.

"No, Lenny. I *don't* know what it means! Neither do you! Maybe you knocked it off the dresser before we went camping. Maybe it fell off and you missed it when you were looking. Don't start making accusations. I won't let you do it!" She turned to her daughter and hugged her tightly as they both began crying. "She had nothing to do with it and I won't let you go after her!"

Allie ran to her bedroom and slammed the door. She fell on her bed, gasping for air between heaving sobs. What had she gotten her stepfather into? She hadn't meant for any of this to happen. She should have asked Nate what he wanted the card for. But she didn't. He told her if Lenny started asking questions, he didn't want her dragged into whatever was happening. It'd be bad enough if he caught me, Nate had said.

She should have paid attention to the hundred red flags, but all she'd wanted was to impress this boy – to give him what he asked for – because she was falling for him. It was as simple as that in the beginning, but it was crazy now.

She had no idea what to do, so she turned to the only person she could talk to – the same person who'd gotten her into this mess.

Allie tried to call Nate, but something strange happened. The call didn't go through but also didn't go to voicemail. It just clicked off. She tried twice more and got the same result. It wasn't like the phone was turned off – it was like it was no longer in service.

Suddenly she was really, really scared. What was going on? Had something happened to him? Or had he chosen to cut her off after he used her to get what he needed? She couldn't believe he was like that. He was different – more intense and more genuine than anyone else she'd ever known. But, she admitted, she didn't know him at all. She'd been with him less than two hours total. His father was in prison and she knew he would do anything to save him. She'd have done the same thing.

Her mother checked on her after supper, but Allie was in bed, lights off and covers pulled up to her neck. She pretended to be asleep until Mabry left, closing the door quietly.

Sometime in the night her door opened and a figure entered her room, moved stealthily to her nightstand and unplugged her phone from its charger. She was in a state between waking and dreaming and until morning she wasn't sure if it had happened or not. When she woke up and saw her phone was still plugged in where she'd left it, she decided she'd been dreaming. But it had seemed so real.

Her mom was drinking coffee at the table when she walked into the kitchen.

"Where's Lenny?" she asked.

"He went to the office early. I need to talk to you, honey. He's in really serious trouble. You know that, don't you? He's free for now, but the World Union people aren't finished with him. It's a major crime – a traitor was freed from prison using an EP captain's access card. He's a good man, Allie. He had nothing to do with any of this, but they don't believe him. He could lose his job. He could be charged with a crime. If you know anything about this – anything at all – please tell me. Please don't let them take Lenny away from us."

Lenny sat at his desk, checking the list of residential cellphone numbers in the county. One number had appeared on Allie's phone five times. Twice they were incoming calls and three times she had called the number. Two were made just before she'd sneaked off to meet that boy last week. And she'd called again yesterday when she went to her room after their blowup. That call lasted only seconds; obviously she didn't talk to him then.

There were also voicemails. On one a week ago a young male voice said, "Hey, it's me. Please call me when you can. I have a question for you." At 3:01 p.m. that day, Allie had called him back. The minute she got out of school. The very minute.

The number she had called over and over was a cellphone registered to Daniel and Melanie Dax.

CHAPTER FORTY-EIGHT

There had never been a fight in their short marriage like the one today. Lenny had spent the morning planning his strategy and deciding how to convince Mabry her daughter was in the middle of a very big problem. He went home for lunch and tried to reason with her, explaining all the evidence. Allie had secretly met the boy after lying to Lenny about a debate practice. They had exchanged half a dozen phone calls. Lenny had seen him and heard his voice. Most damning of all, the phone belonged to Dan Dax.

"I'm going to talk to her this afternoon," he said at last, after every attempt at reasoning with his wife had failed. "I know you'd like to protect her and I understand that, but she's into something really bad and she's dragged me into it as well. I promise you Abbott's not finished with me. I got a reprieve somehow, but this isn't over by any means. Until I know what's going on, I can't respond to allegations against me.

"You know me. You know I'm not going to throw her under the bus," he said earnestly. "We can work something out once I know what she's involved in and who the boy is. He has Dax's cellphone. Why? My access card disappeared, then miraculously reappeared after being used in a prison breakout. How? Who's behind all this? What was so important about Daniel Dax that they went to such lengths to rescue him? She knows something about this. You know it and I know it. I have to talk to her. Period, end of discussion."

She paced back and forth in the tight kitchen. "No," she said at last.

"Is that how it's going to be?" he said quietly. "Allie or me, and you're choosing her? It doesn't have to be like this —"

She exploded. "I love you, Lenny, but I'm not going to subject a sixteen-year-old girl to a cop's questioning. You went through an interrogation Saturday in Denver; of all people, you know how stressful it can be even if you're innocent. I'm simply not going to put her through that. I'll ask her about it myself and I'll let you know what she says."

Lenny dropped the conversation and started eating the now-cold pizza in front of him. His career was hanging by a thread. It looked really bad for him – there was no reasonable way to explain how his access card was somehow taken, then returned, without forcible entry. He didn't blame Heston Abbott for wanting answers, but he did take serious offense at his high-handed tactics. Johnny Wheeler had told him what this guy was capable of and he had to find out what Allie knew so he could fix things. If he didn't, and if he was called in for one of Abbott's beatings, he feared he might break and give her up. That simply couldn't be allowed to happen. Mabry couldn't talk to Allie herself. She didn't even really know what to ask.

"I'm sorry, but you're going to have to do this my way," he said as he carried dishes to the sink. "I have to know what she's doing. This isn't just about her anymore. She's brought me into it too. I'll be here when she gets home from school."

Without another word between them, he went back to work. At a quarter to three he returned to wait for Allie. As soon as he opened the door, he knew something was wrong. The place seemed unnaturally quiet.

"Mabry?" No response.

He walked into the kitchen and saw a note on the table. They were both gone. He ran into the bedroom; some of Mabry's clothes were missing from the closet. He jerked open her dresser drawers and saw they were empty.

Lenny glanced at his watch; it was five minutes until school let out. He ran down the stairs two at a time, verified that her car was gone and jumped into his. There were lines of cars waiting to pick up kids; ordinarily Allie wouldn't come out this way since she walked to and from school, but today he knew Mabry was picking her up.

Just as he double-parked the Suburban and got out, the bell rang and students began pouring onto the sidewalk. He walked up and down, looking for his wife's car but not seeing it. Several people waved at him as he went down the line of idling cars. As he passed one, the tinted passenger window came down and a voice said, "Lenny! Are you looking for Mabry?"

He glanced inside. It was a good friend of hers, the wife of a guy Lenny hunted with now and then.

"Yeah. I needed to give her something."

The woman seemed confused. "You know they were going out of town today, right? I called her an hour ago and she couldn't talk. She said she was picking up Allie early because they had to go to a family dinner in Denver. Did you forget ..."

"Yeah," he said, the enormity of the situation suddenly beginning to weigh heavily on him. "Yeah, I knew that. I just forgot."

She was concerned now. "Are you okay? Is there something I can do –" Just then her daughter ran to the car, said hello to Lenny and jumped in.

"No, no. I'm fine. I've been busy today and it just slipped my mind." He waved and walked back to his SUV. He wasn't fine. He wasn't fine at all. He was overwhelmed, scared, angry and defeated. Everything was falling apart and he couldn't do anything to stop it.

CHAPTER FORTY-NINE

I spent all the next morning with my dad. Jim brought me out this time and I wore the same hat and glasses so I wouldn't know where I was going.

Once we were alone in his room, he pointed to a video monitor mounted high in the corner; it might or might not have audio capability, he cautioned, so we spoke in whispers.

He told me things I needed to know – where I could find the master password, what was on the thumb drives, and all about his interrogation. It was hard to hear about the brutal torture – something civilized people in the twenty-first century wouldn't believe could happen to a citizen – but he assured me that Heston Abbott was a dangerous man. Dad believed Abbott would have killed him to get information, but I knew he would never have given me up.

"What if they'd given you truth serum?" I asked. I'd read about sodium thiopental. It had been the means of extracting information in many a twentieth-century spy movie, but I didn't know if it actually worked or if anyone used it anymore.

"I thought he might do that very thing," he revealed. "Carlos thinks the World Union cops use it. Since I worked undercover for the Resistance, I took a long-lasting antidote several years ago just in case. I want you to get that antidote too. If these people capture you, I'm afraid what might happen. I've already learned firsthand that rules sometimes don't apply. But then I knew that already. It's why I've helped the Resistance all these years."

For over an hour he explained the work he'd done for the cause and how he and Carlos Fine had become inseparable friends. I told Dad it was easy to tell how much

Carlos cared for him from watching his face during the rescue. He was scared, he was determined, he was resolved, and in the end he was relieved that his friend had made it out alive.

Before I left, I had to confide something to my father, something that was weighing on me and had consumed me since all this began. "I want to kill two people," I said softly. "The first one is Sheriff Vargas. He arrested you and Mom, and if that hadn't happened, she might be alive today. The second one caused you to be lying here in a hospital bed, beaten half to death. I'm going to kill that World Union agent who questioned you. I want to do this. For you, but for me too. Please don't try to talk me out of it." I patted his hand. "I hope you understand, Dad."

"I understand your thinking, son, but you won't accomplish anything by doing it. Think about it logically for a minute. Lenny's the only one you can even get close to. He walks the streets of Leadville every day, so theoretically – just theoretically – you could make something happen. So let's say you do it. What did you gain except a little satisfaction? You've rid the world of a mid-level EP officer who was just doing his job. If they catch you, then I've lost not only your mother but you too. It's one thing to fight for the cause, but you have to be smart about it. Lenny Vargas is a tiny cog in a very big wheel.

"The other guy – Heston Abbott – is the one that deserves killing in this deal if you ask me, but there's no way I'm suggesting you do it. You'll never get near enough to make it happen, no matter how hard you try. He works and lives in Mexico City – for you it might as well be a million miles away. The Resistance might help, but killing a federal agent would bring so much public outcry that the cops would never stop looking for the perpetrator. It might just bring the Resistance down. Both those guys are part of the cancer that infests our government, but killing them doesn't help. It'll give you satisfaction – I understand that – but is the risk worth it?"

I squeezed his hand and didn't answer him. He smiled weakly and murmured, "Like father, like son, I guess."

That evening Carlos stopped by the safe house. He took me away from the others and said, "I need to give you the truth serum your dad told you about this morning."

I rolled up my sleeve as he pulled some liquid from a bottle into a hypodermic. "What else did Dad tell you about what we talked about?" I asked.

"Nothing," he replied, his voice guarded. "Why? Is there something I need to know?"

I shook my head and smiled. "All good here."

CHAPTER FIFTY

I waited to call Allie until I knew she would be out of school, but got her voicemail. I half-expected that; she wouldn't have recognized my new phone number. I asked her to call back and it didn't take more than a few minutes.

"Hey, Allie," I said, surprised how happy I felt when I heard her voice. "How's it going?"

She paused a moment and replied, "Corey! I was wondering when you were going to call. I'm out of town for a few days, so you're going to have to work on the science fair project alone until I get back. I'm sorry about that."

"You know who this is, right?"

"Sure, that'd be great. How about I call you around five? I can give you what you'll need to keep working on the project. It won't be a big deal."

"I'll wait for your call." I knew what she was doing. She wasn't alone and she didn't want whoever she was with to know who was calling. She also was out of town – I wondered where she'd gone, since it was a school day. When she called back, she explained. I thought she'd ask why I changed phones, but today she seemed in a hurry to get things off her chest. She told me what had happened on the camping trip, how Lenny had been questioned by a World Union agent, and how she had put the card back in his bedroom. As soon as he got home, he'd started questioning her and she was scared.

Her mom had pulled her out of school this afternoon after a big fight with Lenny, she continued. They were spending the night in a hotel in Vail. She didn't know what was going to happen next, but she was afraid. Not afraid for herself, but that he might force her to tell him what she knew about Nate.

247

I was sorry for the trouble the card had caused Lenny and her too by association. That it couldn't be helped didn't make things better. I'd taken advantage of her, using her vulnerability and her interest in me to accomplish a mission. My dad was free, but her stepfather had taken his place. At the moment Lenny was home, but until there was a good explanation about his card, they'd keep after him. His story didn't make sense, but it wasn't my problem now. I had other things to deal with, like Dad.

Even though I had used Allie to get the card, I didn't realize the EP security people tracked them so closely. Maybe Carlos had known that – he probably had, but it didn't matter. Getting Dad out, whatever the cost, had been the goal, and my relationship with Allie – whatever that meant – had made it work.

Like before, there was this thing nagging in my brain. I knew I should walk away and never contact her again. I should let Allie's stepfather – the bastard – get whatever the feds threw at him. Same for Allie. So what if Lenny was going to question her? She didn't know enough about me to tell them anything and I was safe in the hands of the Resistance. She meant nothing to me. I had used her and it was over.

"Memorize this number," I told her before we disconnected. I recited the Resistance number Dad had given me and made her repeat it back. All I said was that these were friends who would help. Just in case, I told her. Just in case things got really bad for her, call that number.

Why was I still trying to help her?

CHAPTER FIFTY-ONE

That night after Mabry and Allie left was the longest night of Lenny's life. The house was empty, like it had been before they came into the picture. It was a hollow, sad feeling being alone again. He'd been lucky to find Mabry, and even with a teenager in tow, he couldn't imagine life without her. He called her phone a couple of times, but she didn't answer and he didn't leave a message. Finally he gave up.

He sat in the dark, drank a couple of beers and thought how much had changed in just four days. He was certain Allie was involved in something sinister, something way over her head that she had no idea about. Most likely this was the work of the Resistance using her to get information from his office.

He hadn't understood why when he saw the order from headquarters to arrest the Dax couple. They were ranchers living outside of town, seemingly normal individuals. Then the wife's number came up and she was shipped to Denver to the euthanization camp. That was one thing, but then his boss, John Wheeler, suddenly took over the case and moved Dax to Denver. Yesterday Wheeler told him it was actually Heston Abbott doing the questioning. What about this guy Dan Dax warranted sending a World Union agent up here from Mexico City? Who the hell was he, and what was this really all about?

Around six he reached across the bed like he always did, to pat his wife before they got up to start the day. But the bed was empty, just like it had been the dozen times he'd awakened during the night. He'd tossed and turned, getting very little sleep and trying to figure out a way to make all this good again. For his own sake as well as hers, he had to hear Allie's story, but now she was gone.

Mabry fixed breakfast every morning. Today there was an empty table he couldn't handle, so by 7:30 he sat at the counter in the Silver Dollar Café, the same place where he'd arrested the Dax couple a few weeks back.

"Don't see you in here for breakfast much. Mabry kick you out of the house?" The owner grinned, coming out of the kitchen when he saw Lenny walk in.

The words hit home and he struggled to return the banter. "Yeah, she said if I don't like her coffee, I can try the crap you serve instead. So here I am."

The man laughed heartily, then asked, "Whatever became of those people you arrested in here the other day? You know, that couple and then that boy that was asking about them?"

The boy! With everything going on, Lenny hadn't thought much about the boy who had said the couple were his relatives. The investigators found fingerprints in their Jeep and also at the ranch house, but there was no match in the system. They'd decided he was an Outcast who had been at the ranch and who had also moved the Jeep after the Dax couple were arrested. They didn't know who he was, but it really didn't matter. What little they knew about him had been put aside.

Suddenly everything clicked. That boy was the one Allie was involved with. It made perfect sense.

Lenny told the proprietor about Melanie Dax's euthanization and said Dan had been transferred to Denver. He let it go at that. Right now he wanted to stop talking, finish breakfast and get to the office. He wanted to pull the file on the incident with the boy and see if there was anything they'd missed.

A couple of hours later his phone rang. He glanced at the screen and fumbled to answer it quickly.

"Mabry! Mabry, where are you? I have to talk to you!"

Her words were concise and even, without a hint of emotion. "I'm home. We're both home. We want to talk to you."

"Two minutes! I'll be there in two minutes!"

She looked as bad as Lenny felt; she obviously hadn't had much sleep either. "I'm glad to see you," he began as he joined them at the table.

"Don't talk, Lenny. I hadn't planned to come back this quickly, but now you need to be quiet and listen. Allie has something to say. Go ahead, honey."

"I'm so sorry about all this. If I had known what he'd do, I'd never have let Nate have the card. You have to believe me, Lenny! I would never do anything to get you in trouble."

Lenny resisted the urge to start questioning as Mabry said, "Start from the beginning. Tell him what you told me last night."

She had made up her mind to tell almost everything but his name. "I met this boy – Nate Jackson – and something just clicked between us. He said he was here on spring break, visiting relatives. I can't tell you why, but I liked him instantly."

Lenny knew that already – he'd seen her all over the boy when he observed their secret meeting.

"I felt sorry for him. His mom had been euthanized not long ago by the Population Control Council. I thought of how awful that would be if my mom was gone. I wanted to comfort him and be with him, but he was only going to be here for a few days."

"Where'd you meet him?"

"Downstairs across the street. He was sitting on a bench one day, writing in a journal. It was some kind of school project about Leadville's history. Then I ran into him again a couple more times. The last time he asked me if I could help him."

"He asked me if he could borrow your access card. I know it was stupid, but I said I'd get it the next time you went camping. I had no idea what he wanted it for, but I know now. He must work for some underground group –"

"The Resistance," Lenny interjected.

She paused. Nate had never mentioned that name. "I don't know what that is, but maybe so. Anyway, he must have given the card to the bad guys who rescued that prisoner."

"Stop a second," he said. Mabry tried to interrupt, but he held up his hand. "You have to let me say something here." She didn't stop him and Allie became fearful.

"Nobody *rescued* anybody, Allie. The prison breakout wasn't a good thing, even though it's obvious you think it was. The 'bad guys,' as you call them, went in there and freed a traitor – a man they'll execute for his crimes someday. Presuming they can find him, that is, now that my access card freed him and he's disappeared. Who's the boy, Allie? Tell me the truth. Who's the boy? I already know he was using Dan Dax's cellphone when you two talked back and forth. Dan Dax's wife was euthanized recently by the PCC. She was your friend Nate's mother, right?"

Mabry's eyes widened – she was stunned. A tear trickled down Allie's cheek.

"Mom," she pleaded.

Her mother spoke softly but with determination. "Allie, it's time to tell the truth, like Lenny says. Tell us what happened."

I drove Jim's car west on I-70 and took the exit south to Leadville. The .38 special and a box of ammunition were in the backpack beside me. I was on a mission and I kept my speed even with the cars around me – not too slow, not too fast. Of all days, today wasn't the one to get pulled over. The fact that I didn't have a driver's license was my least worry. My Outcast status and generic chip were felonies, but possessing a gun and ammo was a much larger issue. That would put me behind bars for a long time.

I wished it had been Heston Abbott I was about to kill, but Dad had been right. I didn't know his whereabouts or how to get close to him. I couldn't drive to Mexico City; there were checkpoints along the Rio Grande that used to be the US border. So I had to do first things first. By arresting my parents, Lenny had started the whole thing. Today I was going to settle the score with him, regardless of the risk.

THE OUTCASTS

I told Jim and Carlos I wanted to see Allie again. They didn't think it was a good idea and Carlos only agreed if I'd allow Jim to drive me there. I hated what I had to do, but I hoped they'd understand once it was over. While Jim was in the shower, I went downstairs, took his keys and drove away.

My phone rang six times while I was driving, but I didn't answer. There was no doubt who was calling – Carlos, Jim or both. When I got to Leadville, I checked the phone – every call was from a blocked number and there were six messages. I deleted them all. No one could talk me out of this. Today would be the last day of Lenny Vargas's life.

I sat in plain sight on a bench across the street from the Enforcement Patrol office, the fully loaded gun ready in my jacket pocket. I had nothing to hide since Vargas and his people had never laid eyes on me. My silenced phone vibrated. This time it was her.

Instead of answering, I waited for her message. She was sobbing. "Nate! Nate, what are you doing? Don't do it! For God's sake, please don't. It's a trap!"

What the hell is she talking about?

I walked around the corner and called her back. She answered in seconds.

"Nate, thank God I saw you."

She saw me? Impossible. She's in Vail.

"Lenny knows about you! My mom made me tell him. They knew I was lying. He's seen you too, Nate. He spied on us when I met you last time and he knows what you look like. You're in terrible danger. Get out! Hurry!"

"How do you know where I am?"

"I can see you from my window! Mom and Lenny will kill me when they find out I called you, but I saw you sitting there. I know what you're getting ready to do, but don't do it. He's ready for you!"

I glanced up – there she was in the window. I had to move quickly; I turned to run and saw Lenny Vargas and another cop just behind me, guns drawn.

"Drop the phone and put your hands up," he yelled.

He picked up the phone, glanced at the number and said, "Hello, Allie. Your friend's in a lot of trouble. So are you. I'll see you when I get home."

"Don't hurt her!" I screamed.

"I think at this point you'd better be worrying about yourself instead of my stepdaughter."

CHAPTER FIFTY-TWO

I sat in a cell, wearing an orange jumpsuit a size too big that had the words COUNTY INMATE on the back. An EP sergeant lounged in a chair just outside my door; there had been someone guarding me every minute since I came.

I hadn't said a word since I arrived. They'd found the .38 special and the bullets, but I had no identification. I was glad I'd left Jim's keys in the car two blocks away. I didn't worry about it; he'd come get it once he heard about me.

They used a wand to read my chip. All they got was my "name" – Robert Cane – and the fictitious ten-digit ID number. They knew immediately it was fake; Carlos had already prepared me for that. But they didn't know who I really was.

I heard the sergeant's radio hiss to life and a garbled message. He got up, told me to put my wrists through a slot in the door and handcuffed me. Then he walked me to Vargas's office.

"Sit down, son," the sheriff said. My phone was on the desk in front of him. "Sergeant, you stay here too. Mr. Nate Jackson is going to have very close attention from us while he's our guest. We don't want this one getting away."

As much as he regretted it, Lenny had to tell his boss that Allie was involved. Now that this kid was under arrest, he couldn't cover it up anymore. The boy had used Dan Dax's cellphone to call her. She had given him Lenny's access card. He wasn't one of the men who'd broken Dax out of prison, but he undoubtedly knew who did. He'd come to Leadville with a pistol, most likely intending to kill Vargas.

Once Nate was booked, Lenny prepared a report to headquarters, outlining everything he had so far.

255

Now I sat in front of the man I'd come to kill. He picked up my phone and said, "I guess Allie helped you out again, didn't she, Nate? Were you planning to shoot me? Was she going to help you? Is that what brought you back to Leadville, packing a .38, even though you could have stayed safely in Denver with your renegade friends who broke that despicable traitor out of prison?"

He watched for my reaction. I was boiling inside, but I averted my eyes and kept quiet.

"If your real name is Nate Jackson, where did you get a chip that says you're Robert Cane? You didn't get it from the World Union and it's not a fully functioning chip. Where did you get a phone that's registered to Daniel and Melanie Dax? You're awfully young to be involved in something so sinister, boy. You can make things much easier if you tell me the truth from the very beginning."

"I want a lawyer." Those were my first words to him. I didn't know if I could get a lawyer or not, but I'd seen enough movies that it seemed like a smart thing to ask for.

"I'll bet you do. You damn sure need one. But let me explain something to you. The way the World Union works is that we do some preliminary investigation to decide whether or not to charge you with a crime. Now in your case, that's going to be pretty easy to decide, since you were caught with a pistol and a hundred rounds of ammunition. That in itself is worth thirty years. You also gave my access card to someone who committed a federal crime. That's forty or fifty more. You know, you'll be old by the time you're out. Allie won't even be interested in you anymore. She'll be a grandmother by then. Know what I mean?"

"I want a lawyer."

"Shut up! Until you're charged, it's all preliminary and you're not entitled to an attorney. Lawyers only screw up things anyway. People who want to do the right thing tell the truth. I bet your parents taught you that; Allie's did, and that's why she decided to come clean about you. So you don't need a lawyer telling you what to say. You're going to tell me the truth."

The phone on Vargas's desk rang and he pressed a button, which must have sent it to someone else because it stopped ringing. In a moment there was a brief knock on the door and a lady stuck her head inside.

"Major Wheeler's on the line, sir. I told him you were interviewing a prisoner, but he insisted on talking with you immediately."

Lenny was disappointed. He knew exactly why his boss was calling. Once his report hit the World Union database, word had spread fast that someone tied to the Dax case was in custody. This was a huge deal; this prisoner wouldn't be in Leadville for long.

He knew this was coming. He had just wanted a little more time to find out how Allie was involved. Now that Nate was behind bars, he could make her talk. As fragile as she was, he could break her easily, but he was afraid he'd lose his marriage if he did it that way. He wanted to hear it from Nate Jackson, not his stepdaughter.

Lenny asked the sergeant to take Nate outside for a moment. He answered Wheeler's call and was immediately ordered off the case. Johnny told him to cease all communication with the prisoner and prepare him for transfer to Denver. EP officers would pick him up in two hours.

In a moment Lenny asked the officer guarding Nate to bring him back. The man seated Nate and started to take a chair. "Hey, Sarge," the sheriff said affably. "Why don't you grab a cup of coffee and let me talk to the boy for a few minutes? Pull my door shut when you go, please."

The man looked confused, but he did what he was told.

"Now it's just us, Nate. Just you and me. Now you're going to tell me about Allie."

It was ironic that we drove past Carlos's building on the way to the EP's prison. I saw SECURITY BRIDGE

CORPORATION and thought about how close they were, yet how far from being able to help me now.

At EP headquarters the Suburban drove through the same two gates and across the same courtyard where my dad had been rescued last Friday night. I saw the sign for the infirmary, but we went in another direction to an intake center. They booked me again and I was put in a holding cell. I heard one of the guards say I was supposed to go to Wheeler's office, whoever that was. Shortly a cop cuffed my wrists behind my back and took me to the third floor. There were nice offices up here; whoever this guy was, he was apparently pretty high up in the chain.

"I'm Major Wheeler," he said. "Sit down."

He released the guard, looked at some papers and said, "Nate Jackson. Is that your name?"

I said I wanted a lawyer.

"As soon as you're charged, you can have a lawyer," Wheeler explained in a more reasonable tone than Lenny Vargas had used. "It won't be long, but we have to get more information before we get to that step.

"You had a pistol and ammunition with you at the time of your arrest and you have some kind of rogue chip inside you that says you're Robert Cane. Let's talk about those things first."

I said nothing and refused to look at him.

"If you're trying to play some kind of game with me, I strongly suggest you reconsider what you're doing. Do you know Daniel Dax?"

I glanced up, immediately wishing I hadn't.

"Ah, yes, I see that you do. Maybe you know he escaped a few days ago. He didn't do it by himself, as I'm sure you know. He was in too bad shape to walk out of here. Do you know why?"

There was a long period of silence as I stared out the window.

"Look at me!" he said earnestly and I turned back to him. "Daniel Dax was interrogated by an agent from the World Union. I'm giving you some good advice. Trust me, you want *me* questioning you, not him. You want to cooperate with me. You have no idea –"

Wheeler's door suddenly flew open and a man in a black suit walked in.

"Speak of the devil," he muttered. The boy's time was up.

"Hello, Major. I hear we have a new arrival."

CHAPTER FIFTY-THREE

Lenny hated what he had to do next, but for Allie's sake he had to question her before the people in Denver did. The report he'd sent left no doubt she was involved, and everything would happen quickly now. He only hoped Mabry would understand. Allie wasn't really complicit in all this. She'd been used. He desperately wanted it to be that way.

He called a lawyer friend of his and went through hypotheticals, never telling the man his stepdaughter was the one in trouble. He offered to meet with Lenny, but confirmed what the sheriff had always known. Questions first, lawyer later. That was the law and that was how it went. If you were never charged, you were not entitled to representation by counsel. You could get it on your own, but the lawyer wouldn't be allowed to sit with you during interrogation or stop a line of questioning. Lenny – and Allie – were on their own.

He found Allie and her mom in the kitchen. Mabry hugged him around the shoulders. "I'm so sorry, Lenny. She's made some huge mistakes, and she knows it."

They talked for twenty minutes. He fired questions and she answered every one. She only knew Nate was back in town when she saw him, she said truthfully. She realized what he was about to do and told him to get away.

"How's he tied to Dan Dax? Why did he use you to get my card? You have to tell me, Allie. They'll interrogate you in Denver. We have to go over these questions so you'll be comfortable answering them truthfully."

"In Denver?" Mabry's face registered shock – Allie's too. "You can't let them take her to Denver!"

261

"I can't stop them." He sighed, his shoulders slumping. "It's gone too far. She's right in the middle of the biggest federal case in this district in years."

His phone rang – it was a Denver number.

He couldn't miss the gloating voice. "Captain Vargas, this is Agent Heston Abbott. I'm sure you remember me. We have a little unfinished business, it seems. I'm ordering you and your stepdaughter, Allie Cooper, to report to me no later than four this afternoon. Don't be late, Captain. We have a lot to talk about."

"We'll be there."

He looked at Allie and told her what was coming. "I'm so sorry," he said, far more concerned about her than himself. "I'd give anything if it could all just go away."

He went back to the office after telling Allie he'd pick her up at two thirty. He had several loose ends to tie up before what he expected would be a prolonged absence. He might never be back, he thought wistfully.

John Wheeler sat at his desk. There were two sheets of paper in front of him, both bearing the signature of Agent Abbott. One was an order remanding Nate Jackson to the custody of the World Union. That was bad enough – he was worried about the boy's welfare – but the other one made him literally sick to his stomach. Abbott had ordered Lenny and his stepdaughter to report for questioning this afternoon at four.

Obviously Abbott's recall to Mexico City – which had lasted only a couple of days – was nothing more than a slap on the wrist. He was back and nothing seemed to have changed. Deputy Director Nail had intervened last time, but now things were different. The situation had escalated. Now Abbott was cutting Wheeler out and taking charge himself. That was deeply disturbing. Wheeler had seen the horrible things Abbott had done to Daniel Dax. He knew Nate Jackson, just a child himself, was next on the man's agenda.

Then Abbott was going to question a sixteen-year-old girl! He couldn't imagine what the sadist had in mind for her.

He couldn't let it happen. It was morally reprehensible. There had to be a way to stop this.

Lenny walked in a little after two, ready to pick up his stepdaughter. He could hear the sobs as soon as he opened the door. He hated this for Allie ... but it wasn't Allie sobbing. It was his wife.

"She's gone, Lenny. I don't know where she's gone, I swear! She told me she had to go to the drugstore. She left over an hour ago and she never came back. A few minutes ago I found this on her bed."

It was a brief note. "Mom and Lenny, I'm sorry for what I've put everyone through. It's better if I leave. I'm afraid for me and afraid for Lenny too. I hope they don't blame him because I left. It's my decision and that's why I gave you this note – so he can show it to the people in Denver."

"She's a good girl, Lenny. I have no idea where she would even go. She's just a child and she didn't mean to do anything wrong. She even left a note ..." She drew heavy breaths through her sobs. "She left a note to try to help keep you out of trouble. She's gone, Lenny! Oh my God, she's gone!"

Thank God, Lenny thought to himself, hoping that boy had told her how to get help.

Allie had been hiding for over an hour when a car pulled up. It was the make and color she'd been told to expect. She walked to the driver's window and saw two people – a friendly-looking older guy and a cute girl.

"Allie?"

She nodded.

263

"Hop in. I'm Jim Gordon and this is Maeve Perkins. Let's get you out of here. We have a quick stop to make in Minturn; then we're off to Denver."

"Where's Nate? What's going on with him?"

"He's locked up in Denver, Allie. The World Union took over his case."

She cried, hoping everything she was doing was the right thing for her ... and for Nate too.

Lenny waited until after three before he called John Wheeler. He wanted to give Allie as much head start as possible; they'd run her chip as soon as he called, and maybe she could get away in the meantime.

"I'm not allowed to talk to you," his boss said somberly. "It's out of my hands – this is a federal case. I can transfer you to Agent Abbott –"

"Wait a sec, Johnny. What's going on here? Why isn't it your case anymore?"

"It's a long story," he replied after a pause. "Short answer is, I reported Abbott for the way he treated Dan Dax, so now I'm on his list. Apparently his superiors don't care how he works because he's right back at it. Now he's out to get me too. I can't tell you how relieved I am that Allie's gone. I hope you didn't have anything to do with it because you're going to regret it if you did. Even if you weren't involved, he may use his techniques on you. He's a maniac – I tried to tell you that the other day. I'm glad Allie's not here. If they track her chip, they'll bring her in, but maybe – somehow – she can manage to hide."

"I swear I don't know anything about it," Lenny replied. "But *she* does. We both know that, and I agree with you that it's a good thing she's gone. I just hope she's safe. I have no idea who she'd turn to." Lenny was surprised that he had agreed with Wheeler about something. That hadn't happened in years. Maybe Johnny wasn't such a bad guy. It sure seemed like he was trying to make this right.

"Are you going to turn yourself in?" Wheeler asked. Lenny said he had no choice. He wouldn't be there by Abbott's four p.m. deadline, but he would be there tonight.

When they were finished, Wheeler transferred Lenny to Abbott, who merely listened as he learned the girl was gone. "I presume you've initiated a chip search for her," he said when Lenny was finished.

That was exactly what Lenny had expected him to ask.

"No, sir, I didn't. This isn't my case or my jurisdiction. This is a federal case and I didn't want to do anything to interfere with your investigation."

"I see," Abbott replied tersely. "You may think you're clever, but that was a mistake, Captain Vargas. Allie Cooper is your stepdaughter and she's involved in something very, very bad. We will discuss it further when you arrive. I promise you I'll have the girl back in custody soon, and as you and I chat, I'll keep in mind your failure to assist in apprehending her. I expect you here as quickly as possible. Report directly to me and speak to no one else. Do you understand?"

Lenny understood and he didn't care about himself anymore. Now it was only about her. He hoped she was safe.

On the short ride up to Minturn, Jim chatted with Allie to make sure she understood her decision to leave came with far-reaching consequences, the immediate one being that she had to be unchipped. "They'll find you in no time if we don't," he explained. Bringing Maeve along had been a great idea – *her* idea, actually – because she was closer to Allie's age and could make her feel comfortable about what was ahead. Allie would have faced years in prison for conspiring to rescue Daniel Dax. Jim told her she would be among friends now, and how lucky it was that Nate gave her the number. She was embarking on a new journey, but others had done it too and they would be with her every step of the way.

"What are you all exactly? All Nate gave me was a phone number. Are you a bunch of Outcasts?"

Maeve laughed but let Jim answer. Carlos had said not to tell the girl much until they knew more about her. Jim explained they were a group of people who felt the government was too restrictive and who thought the population control program was inhumane. "We're sort of like freedom fighters," he continued, adding that some of them actually were Outcasts while others were chipped.

Soon they arrived in Minturn, a village nestled between the ski areas of Vail and Beaver Creek. Jim pulled into a parking spot in front of a store offering electrolysis. They all went in and within five minutes Allie was an Outcast.

Fuming, Heston Abbott slammed his fist on the table and yelled into the phone, "What do you mean, you can't locate her chip? She's somewhere around Leadville, you idiot! Find her now or you'll wish you had!"

He turned back to the young man strapped to a chair in front of him. "Seems your little girlfriend's disappeared," he said. "Do you happen to know where she might be?"

I said nothing, which seemed to infuriate him even more this time than before. So far he hadn't laid a hand on me, although I knew from seeing Dad's bruises that it was inevitable.

"Unless you're deaf, which I doubt, you can hear me. So I'm going to give you one more chance." He turned to the table behind him and laid out several things from his briefcase. "Let's see, this should do the trick." He turned around and held up a curling iron. He plugged its long cord into a wall outlet.

"It's getting really warm," he said after a few seconds. "Here, feel how hot it's getting." He stuck the tip of it on my hand and I jerked away. It wasn't that hot yet, but still it left a tiny mark.

He smiled broadly and I realized he was really into this. This wasn't just his job; it was a passion. He loved it. "I'll let it warm up for a minute while we talk. If you still don't want to cooperate, I'll let you feel it again."

I was terrified. I wasn't brave like Dad. I didn't think I could do this and I didn't want him to hurt me.

"What do you want to know?" I said at last, defeated.

"That's better. First of all, who are you?"

Abbott hadn't spent much time with the boy in this first session. It had been a long day. It was getting late and he was looking forward to dinner at his favorite restaurant in the area. There was plenty of time. The kid wasn't strong like his father. The mere hint of pain had been enough to get the boy talking. By five Abbott had sent Nate back to his cell and the records were updated to reflect his actual name: Nathan Dax.

John Wheeler was working late tonight. He was usually out an hour ahead of his assistant, but now it was after six and he hadn't emerged from his office since that federal agent left hours ago. On her way out, she knocked softly and then stuck her head in the door to make sure everything was okay.

He was leaning back in his chair, feet propped on his desk. The overhead light was off and the room was bathed in gray. The only illumination – lights from offices in the building across the street – trickled through the windows.

"Sir, are you all right?" She'd never seen him like this before.

"Yes. I've never been better, in fact. Thanks for everything you do for me, Carina. I don't take the time to tell you that often enough, but I deeply appreciate all the help you've given me over the years."

Something was wrong.

"You're welcome. Major, is there anything I can get for you? Should I stick around a bit longer? I was about to go ..."

He shooed her away. "No, no. Go on home and go on with your life. You've been here long enough today."

Everything he said sounded strange and different, but he seemed in good spirits. She didn't know anything else to do, so she told him good night and left.

CHAPTER FIFTY-FOUR

It was eight p.m. and Heston Abbott was wrapping up dinner in his favorite establishment in the Northwest Americas, a sophisticated continental restaurant on the sixtieth floor of a downtown building. He was a wine connoisseur and he had been surprised to find a place in Denver that offered his favorite white burgundy for under a hundred World points a bottle. Until he'd discovered this place, Abbott had never had a decent meal in Denver, which he generally considered a wild-west cow town full of hicks.

Tonight the federal agent had treated himself to a quiet evening, lingering for two hours over cocktails and soft piano music and then ordering fresh Copper River salmon flown in this morning from the Pike Place Market in Seattle. The burgundy had paired perfectly with the entree and he was savoring the last tasty morsel of fish when his phone vibrated. He surreptitiously removed it from his pocket and glanced at the screen. It was the office and it could wait. He wouldn't answer calls in a restaurant – he considered that the height of boorishness and tsk-tsked when other diners did it.

Lenny Vargas hadn't shown up by the time he left the office, so he'd issued instructions to place him in a holding cell when he arrived. After this wonderful evening he wasn't going to spoil things with business matters. He would deal with Vargas tomorrow.

He sipped the wine as his server removed the dishes. He ordered a double espresso, sat back in his chair and reflected on how good life was. He was truly enjoying every minute of it. Then his phone vibrated again.

That was irritating. He summoned the waiter and ordered him to hold the coffee and keep his wine chilled until his return. He stepped into the lobby, returned the call and said curtly, "This had better be something important."

He listened for a moment then hung up without saying a word. He returned to his table and cancelled the coffee order. He slugged the rest of his wine as his check was being prepared. He walked five blocks to EP headquarters and stormed into the night duty officer's office, slamming the door so hard it rattled the floor-to-ceiling window next to it. The terrified officer cowered.

"Can I not leave you imbeciles alone for two hours?" he screamed. "Can I not enjoy a dinner without something going wrong? Tell me. Tell me how in hell this happened."

The officer explained that the second person from the top at the facility, Major Wheeler, came to the inmate lockup at 6:37 p.m. and presented papers that would release Nathan Dax into his custody. The prisoner was brought from lockup in handcuffs. Wheeler had ordered the cuffs be removed – he had brought his own plastic ties and he secured the boy's wrists. Then he took Dax away. No one gave it a second thought until the eight o'clock headcount, when the guard doing the tallying asked when the detainee would be back.

"I called Wheeler's office, sir," the frightened duty officer explained, his voice shaking. "I needed to know how much longer it would be." The guys upstairs told me he'd been gone for nearly two hours. He never came back after he picked up the boy. I contacted the desk officer. The two of them walked out of the building immediately after Major Wheeler took him from here. I didn't know what else to do, so I called you, sir."

"Who signed the order to release Dax? Let me see the papers," Abbott snarled.

"Uh, you did, sir. Here they are."

There was his scrawled signature at the bottom of the form. It wasn't actually his, of course, but the night duty officer wouldn't have known that.

"Dax doesn't have a functioning chip. Did you run the locator on Wheeler's chip?"

"Yes, sir, right before I called you. There's something strange about that. Major Wheeler's chip is deactivated, sir."

"Deactivated? Like it was disabled?" He thought of Nate Dax's strange chip and wondered if Wheeler had been in collusion with Dax and the Resistance all along.

"No, sir. His chip deactivated itself. We got the notice right before you arrived. It appears Major Wheeler's dead, sir."

I'll believe that when I see his dead body, Abbott thought. "Get me a car and driver. Take me to the location where his chip deactivated. Now!"

The driver followed the GPS coordinates to a one-story ranch-style house in Westminster. Since the guard had notified no one else, Abbott was the first person from headquarters to arrive. They pulled into the driveway and parked in front of a garage door. As soon as he got out, Abbott could smell exhaust fumes. The car was apparently still running inside.

John Wheeler's death was presumed to be suicide by asphyxiation, a finding that the medical examiner would confirm the next day.

Meanwhile the traitor Daniel Dax's son, Nate, was missing, along with his girlfriend, Allie Cooper, who was the stepdaughter of Captain Vargas. Neither had functioning chips, so they couldn't be traced.

And speaking of which, in all the hubbub he'd forgotten Vargas entirely. He called the night-duty officer and confirmed that Vargas had arrived and was confined in a temporary cell for the night.

"See if you idiots can keep him there," he snapped.

He went to bed thinking how he'd start his interrogation tomorrow morning. He had some new toys to try out and was looking forward to it.

CHAPTER FIFTY-FIVE

As they drove toward Denver, Allie continued to question Jim about Nate. "What will happen to him? Is my stepdad's boss, that Major Wheeler, going to interview him? Is that who's doing it?"

"I can't answer that. Ever since Nate's dad was rescued, this has been a federal case. That makes me think Wheeler won't be the one. We'll keep you informed about Nate if we hear anything." He didn't mention Heston Abbott.

They took Allie to a different safe house. It was in Aurora and it was only used in special circumstances. There had been several logistical considerations in deciding where to put her. Carlos wanted to talk to Nate before getting them together and he had no intention of putting them together in the same safe house.

Carlos had to be careful with her. Even though she'd agreed to be unchipped, Allie's real motives were completely unknown. She was only sixteen and she had walked away from her mother and her life. That was a jarring, traumatic move – would it last? There was no way to tell, and she'd always be free to return if she wanted. As long as the World Union was involved in the Dax case, she could be in grave danger, but it would be her choice whether to stay.

The possibility she might return meant Carlos had to isolate her from the Resistance. She couldn't be allowed to see and hear things that might get others in trouble. She wouldn't be tossed into the mix as Nate Dax had been because her circumstances were entirely different. She didn't choose this life. She was escaping possible imprisonment and torture. The World Union could put pressure on her. They could use Lenny Vargas as bait to make her turn herself in. If that happened, the less she knew about what was going on, the better.

Her temporary residence was a quiet bungalow twenty miles from Nate's house. Jim promised someone would contact her tomorrow and left her in the hands of a housemother. The forty-something lady welcomed her and helped her settle in to the place that was her new home for now.

Allie had arrived with nothing but the clothes on her back, so the lady made a phone call. Around six p.m. someone delivered a boxful of freshly cleaned, gently used clothes that fit her perfectly. That someone was Ben Creel, who made the routine delivery on his way home from the Resistance thrift store he ran and never met the person for whom the clothes were intended. He had no idea the package was going to his roommate's friend Allie.

CHAPTER FIFTY-SIX

I still couldn't believe I was sitting in Carlos's office. He seemed relieved and grateful for my release, although nothing made any more sense to him than it did to me. He called the facility where Dad was recuperating and told them to pass along the news that I was safe.

"You need to know something about Allie Cooper," he said. He saw the look of concern on my face and assured me this was positive news. "We have her. Heston Abbott demanded her stepfather bring her to Denver for questioning and she left. She called us, Nate. She told us you gave her the number; good job on that. They'd have caught her in no time if you hadn't." He explained how Jim had picked her up and took her to a sympathizer, a registered nurse in Minturn, who had unchipped her.

"What about Lenny?" I felt sorry for him even though I had planned to kill him just this morning. "I guess he doesn't have anywhere to go, and he's not even involved in this."

"You're right, and Abbott's bound to bring him in. I haven't heard anything yet, but I'll let you know if I do."

"Where's Allie? When can I see her?"

Carlos explained she'd been taken to a secure location for tonight. "I want to talk with you in the morning once I have more information," he continued. "There are some things about her situation that are totally different than yours. We're going to keep her isolated for the time being. It's all good; she's in a safe house too and she'll be well cared for. You've been through a traumatic experience. We'll talk about her tomorrow, but right now I need to know exactly what happened to you; then I'll take you home so you can rest."

I was happy to talk because only an hour before I'd wondered if I'd survive the interrogation tomorrow. Somehow now I was free. I told him everything.

I had been sitting in my cell, ashamed that I had confessed who I really was without Abbott's having to do much at all. He'd touched a curling iron to my hand and it hurt a tiny bit, but that hadn't scared me as much as the evil radiating from this guy. He was going to have fun doing whatever he had in mind and I wasn't strong enough to resist.

I hated the man; I'd never felt this kind of intense, deep hatred – not even in the moment of passion when I killed that guy in our living room or when I was plotting to kill Lenny – but I knew it now. I knew what he'd done to my father and I wanted to kill him, but now there was no way to do it. Look how I'd botched my plans to kill Lenny Vargas, I admitted to Carlos, who said, "I told you so," and smiled.

Abbott only kept me an hour. I told him who I was and that I lived at the ranch. Then he started grilling me on what Dad's relationship to the Resistance was. I lied about that part and said I didn't know anything about it.

"Of course you don't," Abbott had replied smugly. "At least not now. I'll jog your memory tomorrow and you'll remember."

When he was finished for the day, Abbott had said, "I really look forward to seeing you tomorrow, Nate. You may be his son, but you haven't one tenth the strength of your father. You're a weakling, a coward. Your father endured a lot without giving me anything. Then you and your friends rescued him before I was finished. He'd have talked – of that I have no doubt. But now it's just you. Tomorrow I'll give you some of what I had planned for him. You should sleep well tonight thinking about that. Like father, like son. One traitor breeds another. I'm anticipating what you're going to tell me about the Resistance."

Just like that, he walked out and a guard took me back to my cell. I was terrified; Carlos said it was understandable. I didn't eat any of the unappetizing meal they gave me. I just sat there on my bunk and wondered if I could be half the man Dad is. I knew the guy was right, but

I would try to be strong, for Dad and for my mother's memory.

I continued the story. "Around six thirty a guard took me to the front, where there was an EP officer – a major – waiting. He told them to take off my handcuffs and he put plastic ties on my wrists. He walked me to the front of the building, used his card to get out, and we walked a few blocks away from headquarters."

"What happened then?" Carlos asked, thinking how bizarre this story was.

"He cut the ties on my wrists and asked me if I had somewhere to go. I could see your building and I said yes. Then he handed me this – it's a chip from a recording device." I passed it to Carlos. "Then he said to get copies of Abbott's interrogations in the basement. Abbott deleted the originals, he said, but there are backups of everything that goes on in that building. Find those videos and you can take him down."

"Then he looked at me and said, 'Now go. Run. Get away and hide!' and he walked away."

"I didn't know what was happening, but I didn't waste any time. I ran as fast as I could. I stopped and backtracked a couple of times because I was afraid it was some kind of trap, but finally I just gave up and came in your lobby. The night guard called you and here I am."

"So you'd never seen this EP major before. What was his name – do you remember?"

"I glanced at his nameplate. It might have started with a W – I don't remember." I asked him if the message about finding the videos of interrogations made sense. He nodded and simply said, "I'll work on that and the recording chip too."

He gave me a new burner phone and drove me back to the safe house. It was only a little after nine, but I was absolutely exhausted and ready for bed. Unfortunately that didn't happen for some time. Carlos had called ahead and told them I was free. Maeve was waiting by the garage when we pulled up. As soon as I got out, she ran to me and started crying. She threw her arms around me and planted a big kiss right on my mouth. That was a surprise – not unpleasant by any means, but a surprise.

"Nate, I've prayed for you every night and now here you are! I've ... we've all been so worried about you. Thank God you're back with us! Come on in. The others are waiting to see you!"

Everyone had heard about my situation and how I was rescued from Heston Abbott. It was another exhausting hour before I could finally go upstairs.

I was in bed and half asleep when I heard the ding of a message on my new phone. It had to be Carlos; no one else knew the number.

His message read, "Vargas voluntarily turned himself in to EP tonight, being held in Denver."

In a moment there was another ding. "News from EP: John Wheeler, a major and second-in-command at Enforcement Patrol headquarters in Denver, was found dead at his home tonight. Preliminary reports indicate he took his own life. Medical examiner's report to follow."

Wheeler. That was his name; I remembered it now. "That's him," I texted back.

I had no idea why he'd chosen to rescue me before committing suicide, but I said a little prayer for him. He'd probably saved my life.

Meanwhile, Carlos sent a message through the usual channels to the mole inside the EP. He needed to know if it was possible to determine the days and times Heston Abbott had interrogated individuals in the basement and if there were videos of those interrogations.

CHAPTER FIFTY-SEVEN

This morning Abbott and Vargas met in Wheeler's office. After keeping Vargas locked up overnight, he had chosen to begin the morning's interrogation here for a couple of reasons. First, he was on thin ice with his superiors over his interrogation of Dan Dax. He didn't need any more crybabies. Today he'd use a less hostile environment instead of the dungeon-like basement room with its metal chair and leather restraints. Second, he had some revelations for Vargas, things he hoped would unsettle the man and make him reconsider his unwillingness to cooperate.

"Last night was a busy time around here," Abbott began after making sure they each had a bottle of water. It was an uncharacteristically cordial gesture, Lenny observed.

"Did you hear the news through the prison grapevine?" He smirked; there was, in fact, a reliable system of information distribution throughout the jail, but Vargas likely would have been out of the loop since he was in solitary confinement.

"Why don't you tell me so we'll both know?" Vargas stated flatly.

Abbott ignored the sarcasm. "Your boss did something very out of character last evening. He forged my signature on a release form and walked Nathan Dax out of the building."

Lenny took a deep breath and smiled.

"Does that sort of treason make you happy, Captain Vargas? An officer in the Enforcement Patrol – a man sworn to uphold justice and the government – became a traitor. I'm beginning to understand now that you're a traitor too. It's obvious from your attitude. What do you know about what happened? You called Wheeler yesterday; he transferred your call to me. When you talked to him, what did he tell you about his plans for the boy?"

"Where are they now?" Lenny asked.

That infuriated Abbott. He stood and bellowed, "*I'll* ask the questions! You have one minute left before you push me over the limit, *Captain* Vargas." He spat the title like it was rotten meat. "I'm doing my best to treat you with respect and civility, but believe me, there are other ways we can chat. Now, one more time. What do you know about Major Wheeler's actions?"

Lenny refused to throw Johnny under the bus. "I called him to tell him Allie was gone and I'd be late because I was looking for her. She left a note – I gave it to the people downstairs who booked me last night. I had nothing to do with it and I tried to explain that to Johnny, but he cut me off. He said it was a federal case and it was out of his hands. He told me he would transfer me to you. And he did."

"Did he seem distraught or overly worried about the situation?"

Where's this going? Lenny wondered. *What's he after?*

"He sounded like his usual self. Why?"

"Because, Captain Vargas, John Wheeler committed suicide a few minutes after releasing the boy. Now why do you think he'd do that? Is there anything you can say to enlighten me on what this is all about, since I strongly believe you're as much a traitor as your boss was?"

Lenny's mind was reeling. This was absolutely bizarre. He'd underestimated John Wheeler. He'd considered him a weakling and maybe he was. Maybe that was why he did all this, so he could keep both Nate and himself out of the clutches of this demonic individual.

"Well? Are you going to cooperate, or shall we take things up a notch?"

"I didn't do anything, Agent Abbott. You'll learn that eventually, whether you beat it out of me or you just believe what I'm telling you. Now that he's dead, I'll tell you what John Wheeler really said. He said you're a maniac and you were out to get him too because he reported you to the World

Union for your brutal techniques. John was glad Allie had run away, even though he said her chip would give her up eventually.

"Once Johnny told me about you, I was glad for her too, just like I was glad to hear you say Nate Dax got away. I was thankful I didn't have to bring my sixteen-year-old stepdaughter down here and deliver her into your hands. As badly as you treat grown men, who knows what you'd have done with a beautiful young girl?"

Abbott looked at Vargas, disgusted. What kind of human being did this fool think he was? He was an educated, refined gentleman, accustomed to a good lifestyle and the things that came with it. He had no prurient interest in Allie Cooper. His interview with her would have been strictly business and strictly aboveboard.

The situation today was another thing entirely. He was under pressure from his boss in Mexico City after the call from Wheeler. He was being watched closely and he couldn't afford any more problems. Furthermore, he actually believed Lenny Vargas. He didn't think the man knew anything more. Regardless, he'd been less than forthcoming about his stepdaughter and that made him a traitor in itself.

"So it pleases you that the World Union has temporarily lost three traitors. I see. All right, *Captain* Vargas. I will call you that, but I believe it will be the last time anyone does. You earned that title, but you didn't deserve it. I am recommending you be charged with high treason, aiding and abetting the enemy, espionage and subversive activities. Those are four crimes, each of which carries the death penalty. You can only die once, tragically, because a man such as yourself should have to endure it more than once. You know the process these days. It doesn't take long from start to finish. I predict you'll be in hell in ninety days."

"I predict pretty soon I'll see *you* there."

Abbott smiled. "Perhaps. We have all sinned, but at least I'm no traitor to my country. That's the lowest form of human being on the planet, in my opinion."

Abbott's recommendation for charges was approved and within the house Lenny was in a cell with two other prisoners. He had been stripped of his rank pending trial and he would no longer be in protective custody. Now he was in a crowded cell block with a heinous mixture of violent and nonviolent criminals from all walks of life. Abbott would be sure every one of them knew Vargas was both a former sheriff and a traitor. Heston Abbott knew even murderers didn't like traitors ... or former sheriffs. Everything would work out fine now.

Meanwhile, Abbott had one more loose end to tie up. He was impatiently waiting for an important document to arrive, something that might bring all the missing chickens home to roost.

CHAPTER FIFTY-EIGHT

Smitty was feeding sheets of numbers into a scanner. In a few minutes there would be output on his screen. They would be numbers no longer – it would transform into the World Union's daily briefing summary intended for the commander.

Before the government established a decryption unit here, the daily briefing report would either come unencrypted or it would require hours of decoding by hand, entrusted to one person who had a high security clearance. After six months, Smitty was pleased with how well his unit was performing. They were receiving and sending a few dozen text and video messages every day. The three people who reported to him – two women and a man – still had the lowest level clearances, but that would change as they grew in their jobs. Smitty held the highest clearance given to anyone outside the World Union's Tel Aviv headquarters. Someone had to see everything, and he was that person.

He glanced at the translation as it began feeding out. The daily briefing was like an online newscast, covering the economy and the stock exchanges but also providing top-secret information about security, military strength and technology. One story caught his attention. It discussed recent increases in Resistance activity in the Northwest Americas sector, especially in the Denver area. There was a call to action – the commander was ordered to create a task force. It would investigate domestic terrorism and formulate a plan for stopping the Resistance in the Denver area.

Interesting, he thought, making a mental note to tell Carlos. He emailed the report to his boss and went back to work.

An hour later an aide came over. "Take a look at the email I forwarded you," she said. "It just arrived in the top-security mailbox. Have you ever seen anything like it?"

Smitty hadn't. It was encrypted, but in all his training he'd never seen something that looked like this. It was nothing but squiggles and arrows, shapes and colors. The top three lines were in English. The first gave the recipient's name – Heston Abbott. He'd heard that name from Nate.

"Why didn't they just send it directly to this guy Abbott instead of coming through us?" she asked.

"Because that's not protocol." This was a training opportunity. He called the others over. "See this line?" he pointed to the second line at the top of the document on his screen. "This was sent to us from the Las Vegas ED Services Unit/Commander's Office. It's from the head of the Enforcement Patrol there, but it was handled by our counterpart in Vegas. That ensured the highest security on their end and the highest security on ours. From here, we forward it to the person it's meant for."

"Look at the crazy code," someone said. "What the hell is it?"

"That's not our business," he said. See the third line? 'TOP SECRET. FORWARD DIRECTLY TO RECIPIENT. DO NOT DECRYPT.' We have to send this one on just as it came in."

He sent them back to work and gazed at the three unencrypted lines at the top. Writing "do not decrypt" was like putting catnip just out of the cat's reach, Smitty thought with a tiny smile as he forwarded the mail to Heston Abbott's secure internal account.

At five p.m. his staff went home and Smitty went to work. He'd been fidgeting all day, trying to stay occupied as he counted the minutes until he was alone. He wanted to know what this document was about. The EP's network was secure, but a few top people – including him – could see all traffic. He'd installed the program that made that happen, so it was easy to temporarily disable it. Now it was just him, the cryptic document and the EP's powerful Galaxy network at his disposal.

He entered a few keystrokes, powered his tablet off and on again, and brought up the email from the secure folder where he'd saved it. So far he wasn't breaking the rules. Every document received by his unit was archived in highly encrypted folders in case they were needed in the future. The rule-breaking would begin if he opened the document.

Without hesitation he opened the page and saw the hodgepodge of symbols and lines. He brought up a program he'd invented at university. Decoding this might be his biggest challenge yet, but he loved challenges. They kept life interesting.

The usual decoding process wasn't working this time. The document was an enigma; attempting to decode it only created another set of numbers and figures entirely different from the first. He ran that second set through the program and the result was yet another jumble, all letters except for a mass of binary code at the bottom.

There was one more thing he could try. Using an "all-languages" command, he ran the third decryption through the computer again. This time he came up with a recognizable format with words, spaces, sentences and periods. Where all the code had been at the bottom, there was now a color picture of a woman he didn't know.

He didn't recognize the language, but if it were real, that part should be simple. He ordered an English translation and within seconds a message appeared. The document was being translated from Tagalog, a language of the Philippines, into English. This had been one well-encrypted document, he thought to himself, but it was no match for the brain of Smitty Hightower. He glanced at it and decided it might be important. He made a copy and stuck it in his pocket. He closed his programs and files, reactivated the top-brass access he'd turned off earlier, shut down his tablet and opened his office door. He was startled by a man in a black suit standing directly in front of him, blocking his path.

"Good evening. I presume you're Mr. Hightower. I'm Agent Heston Abbott from the World Union. May I have a moment?"

CHAPTER FIFTY-NINE

Smitty squirmed in his chair, the paper burning a hole in his pocket as though it were literally on fire. The agent was as sinister as he'd heard and now he was two feet away. He'd walked in, ordered Smitty to sit down and pulled up another chair for himself.

He cleared his throat and tried to quash the nervousness. "What can I do for you, Agent Abbott?"

Abbott waited a moment and said, "What's your role here, Mr. Hightower?"

"Er, I'm a senior analyst, sir."

"A senior analyst for whom? The Enforcement Patrol?"

"No, sir. The World Union. I'm a senior encryption/decryption analyst. I'm on assignment here to set up this unit and train the people."

"Ah, so we both work for the federal government. That makes me a bit more at ease. Did you personally handle the encrypted document you forwarded to me earlier today?"

"Yes, sir. One of my people brought it to my attention and I –"

Abbott interrupted. "Brought it to your attention? Could you explain exactly what you mean?"

"The document came in from the ED Services Unit in Vegas, our sister unit there. It was highly encrypted –"

"One moment, please. How do you know it was highly encrypted?"

His questions were making Smitty very uncomfortable. He was very, very far out of his comfort zone and he had to be extremely careful. "My co-worker pointed out the unusual code on the page. She'd never seen it before.

I've been doing this work for years and I hadn't either. It was different – that's all. Just something we'd never seen."

"And then what happened?"

"I told her I'd handle it. I forwarded it to you and that was the end of it."

"Did you retain a copy of it?"

Does he know I have a copy in my pocket? Smitty wondered in horror. "No, sir. I mean, yes, there's a copy of it that the system automatically retains in the Galaxy, but I had nothing to do with that. It happens every time, just in case you need to retrieve the document in the future. It's still encoded, just like it was when I sent it to you. Nobody decoded it ..." He realized he had to stop talking. He was going too far. *Just answer the questions.*

"*Could* someone have decoded it?" Abbott asked quietly. "You, for instance. You strike me as an intelligent man. *Did* you decode it?"

Smitty was sweating profusely now. "No, sir. I couldn't have decoded it. It was too complicated –"

"How do you know it was complicated? Am I making you nervous, Mr. Hightower?"

"Yes, all these questions are making me nervous. I handled your document just like we handle them every day. I'm sworn to secrecy. I took a loyalty oath when I was hired. I don't care what's in the things that pass through here. My job is to get them where they belong and to encode and decode things if I'm asked to. If you want to keep questioning me, I want to talk to my boss because I don't know exactly what you're looking for. I haven't done anything wrong."

"It would be hard to talk to your superior right now, wouldn't it? You work for the World Union, not the EP. Your boss is in London, where it's the middle of the night. If you insist on speaking with someone higher up, then perhaps I can arrange to accommodate you here overnight until that person is available. Would that be satisfactory, Mr. Hightower?" He smiled mirthlessly.

Smitty was suddenly aware that his pants were wet. He was petrified with fear.

"I didn't look at your document, if that's what you're after," he answered shakily. "I don't want to stay here overnight. I didn't do anything wrong. I just want to go now."

"Then by all means go," Abbott said, gesturing toward the door. "I never said you couldn't leave."

Smitty walked out, leaving the man sitting in his office. That in itself was a breach of protocol, although that was the least of Smitty's concerns. Embarrassed about his accident, Smitty kept his hands in front of his pants as he left and hoped no one would notice. He ran to the street, barely made it to the curb and threw up. He'd never been so scared in his life and he had no idea if this was over or just beginning.

He entered a number on his phone and said, "I'm in trouble." He told them what street he was walking on. Five minutes later a sedan pulled alongside and the tinted passenger window went down.

"Hop in," Carlos said.

They drove aimlessly as Smitty described the strangely coded document that Abbott received. It was the most highly encrypted thing he'd ever seen. He'd decrypted it, made a copy and was leaving when Abbott stopped him and then grilled him relentlessly.

"I'm afraid to go home," he admitted. "What if he's following me?"

"That's why we're driving around instead of going to the office. I've kept an eye out. No one's following us except one of my guys who's been on our tail the whole time. Once you said you were in trouble, I brought backup just in case. I want to pull over and take a look at the document. Do you know what it's about?"

"No. I didn't read it. I just printed it off and stuck it in my pocket. It's some kind of order from the World Union and it has a woman's picture on it." He handed it to Carlos.

His eyes were immediately drawn to the picture. She was a beautiful woman even though now her face showed nothing but fear and sadness. How many good times they had spent together and how often he'd thought what a lucky man Dan was to have found a wife like Melanie.

There was a full page of information about the person in the picture, a forty-year-old female named Jane Doe, real name unknown, who had been held in the Las Vegas female detention center for the past three weeks at the request of Heston Abbott, an agent with the World Union in Mexico City. Her chip had somehow gotten deactivated and she appeared to have amnesia. She could remember nothing about her past.

The final paragraph of this document was the bombshell. It was an order of transfer. Heston Abbott was going to take custody of the Jane Doe prisoner. Not only was Melanie Dax alive, but in a few days Abbott would be taking her to Mexico City. Carlos was certain Abbott knew who his prisoner was; he had probably created her fake euthanasia in the first place.

Smitty was right, Carlos mused. He couldn't go back to the safe house, but for a different reason than he thought. This wasn't just about Smitty's safety. It was about keeping this quiet until Carlos could decide how to deal with it. Carlos trusted Smitty, but it would be simple human nature to want to relate tonight's harrowing events. If Smitty described the woman in the picture, Nate would pick up on it immediately. There would be time to let him know – soon – but he needed a plan first. He was going to set a trap.

As he dropped Smitty at a suburban motel for the night, Carlos asked if he knew how to access the backup interrogation tapes, the ones Wheeler told Nate to find.

Smitty smiled and said, "Do you have any doubt that I'd know how to find something in the EP's database? Of course I can access backup tapes! Your wish is my command."

CHAPTER SIXTY

When I came downstairs for breakfast, something felt strange. Everyone was there except for Smitty, and everyone was in deep conversation, but the minute I came into the room, it stopped and no one made eye contact with me. I felt like the odd man out.

"Morning," I said cheerfully. "Am I interrupting something?"

"No, of course not," Maeve said flippantly. "Did you sleep well?" Everyone else fiddled with their food, staring down at their plates like they were about to crawl away and needed supervision.

I actually had slept well and I felt rested for the first time in days. All day yesterday I'd stayed around the house. I wanted to see Allie and Dad, and I wanted to talk to Carlos about what happened, but Jim had asked me to stay put and rest for twenty-four hours. There were things going on, he said, things that involved me. Carlos and I would talk soon.

The whole episode the night before last when that EP officer simply let me go was bizarre, but just as crazy was what had happened afterwards. Jim told me the guy went home and killed himself. What the hell was going on? I hoped Carlos would know.

After a day of relaxation and hitting the sack early, I felt more refreshed than I had since I left Leadville. It was good to be home, if that was what you could call this quasi-dormitory, and it was good to feel safe again.

"Where's Smitty?" I asked. He didn't have to be at work until nine and he never failed to show up for Maeve's sumptuous breakfasts. Jim said he had stayed with a friend last night after working late.

"Carlos asked if you could come downtown today," Jim informed me. "I'm going in this afternoon at two. Can you join me?"

That was fine with me. I hoped I could see Allie today. She was going through a lot and I wanted to assure her that things would be all right.

The first thing I asked Carlos was how she was doing.

He said she was fine. He told me why she was isolated and expressed his thoughts that she not learn about the Resistance, at least for now. I could understand his reluctance to reveal secrets that might compromise everything if she revealed them. Even I didn't know her well enough to comment. I had no idea if she was strong enough to leave her life behind. She hadn't been an Outcast nor had she seen tragedies like most of the others at the safe house. She didn't have parents who were sympathizers or a family member who died for the Resistance. She was just a girl caught in the middle of a terrifying situation, all because she agreed to help me. And now I had to help her if I could.

Maybe tomorrow, Carlos said when I asked if I could see her. He was going to meet with her later today and assess the situation. Then he changed the subject.

"Nate, I have something to tell you – something that's going to wrench your emotions in every direction. I want you to promise me before I start that you'll take my advice on this one and not act on your own. It's imperative we play this one my way."

"It's Dad, isn't it! What's happened to him? Did they ... did they capture him?" Dear God, I didn't want this to happen again. I knew we would never be able to rescue him if it had.

"It's your mother, Nate. She's alive."

I sobbed uncontrollably for maybe five agonizing minutes. I didn't know one human being could have this many tears inside him.

"Where is she?"

"She's in custody. Apparently she has been all along. I only found out last night and I didn't tell you until now because I wanted to have a plan before I did. I worked all night and I think I know what to do. From what our source at the EP can determine, the World Union people pretended to euthanize her when her lottery number was drawn. They deactivated her chip and sent you the emails, but they kept her alive in case they wanted to use her to break your father. It would have worked; we both know he'd have done anything to keep her safe. But fortunately it didn't happen because of your plan to break him out."

"Are you going to rescue her?"

"I'm going to try to bring her back." He explained that he couldn't give me details or even tell me where she was. He said the fewer people who knew the whole story, the better, and I had to agree. I trusted his judgment, as I would have trusted Dad's, and I was confident that if anyone could help Mom, he could.

It was dark by the time we left his office. Jim had gone off earlier to run errands, so Carlos gave me a ride home. But instead of going the usual route, he headed in a different direction entirely.

"Where are we going?" I asked after a few minutes on unfamiliar streets.

"How about we go out to a restaurant for dinner? I want to treat you to Denver's best Mexican food."

I told him that sounded great, and it really was exciting to me. I'd never eaten dinner in a restaurant before and the only Mexican food I'd ever had were Mom's enchiladas.

We pulled into the parking lot of a busy place with a huge red and green neon sign that said "El Rancho." He drove to the back and parked near a door with a sign saying "Banquet Room."

"I thought for your first time eating out, it might be quieter in our own room," he explained as we walked down a hall and opened the door to a darkened room. He flipped on the light and things went crazy.

"Happy birthday to you ..." A roomful of people started singing. I had totally forgotten it was November 10, my eighteenth birthday. With what was happening in my life, celebrating a birthday didn't seem high on the priority list. But these people had done it for me.

I felt light-headed as my father shuffled up to me on a walker. "Light hug," he whispered, tears rolling down his face. "I'm not ready for a bear hug yet. We'll save that for when we see your mother." I got a little weepy too. "Go see your friends now," he told me. "We'll talk in a little while."

Allie ran up and hugged me tightly. "I'm so glad to see you," she said. "Everyone's been so good to help. Thank you for saving my life, Nate."

"I'm sorry about everything," I said, but she shushed me and moved away so the others could see me.

"Eighteen years old," Maeve said, giving me a big hug and a kiss. "You're only four years younger than I am now. You need a mature woman, not that little girl." She laughed, pointing to Allie. "Hey, sorry about the freeze-out when you came down for breakfast this morning. We were just finishing our plans for tonight and you interrupted us!"

Smitty was there, and Ben and Cassie and Jim. All the friends I had in my new world were together in one room. Except for Mom, and I was confident she'd be with me soon.

We ate and talked and ate some more, and then it was time to open presents. This was strange; I'd never had presents before. They all had chipped in to buy me a tablet of my own, and I also got a shirt, some e-books and games.

Carlos stood and made a toast. Everyone raised beers except for Dad, Allie and me. We had water glasses.

"To tough, resilient people like Nate and his parents. To people who are willing to fight for what's right in this world. To Nate, who's been through more in eighteen years than most people will experience in a lifetime."

"To the Resistance!" Smitty bellowed.

I stayed and talked with Dad until he grew tired and had to go back to the facility. He didn't know anything more about Mom than I did, but he told me how much he believed in Carlos and his ability to make miracles happen. "Pray for her, son," he told me, although he didn't need to say that. I'd been praying ever since I heard.

Allie and I talked for over an hour. She was scared about everything that was happening in her life. She knew Lenny was in prison and she was afraid for his safety. She was worried about her mother too, and I wondered for a fleeting moment if it had been a mistake to bring her to this party, to allow her to see the faces of people who were working against the government. The only ones she'd even met were Dad, Jim, Maeve and me, but I still thought it was a risk. She was so young, so fragile and so dependent on her mother. Regardless, I was glad she was allowed to come tonight.

It was late when Ben and I finally turned in. "Nice evening," he said. "Did you have fun?"

I told him it was the most wonderful party of my life, and it was, since there hadn't been any like it before. I loved restaurant food, I loved being out in public with my friends, and I loved the feeling of belonging. All I needed now was my mother's freedom.

CHAPTER SIXTY-ONE

Three days after he got the transfer document, Heston Abbott stood at the front desk of the Las Vegas Prison Intake Facility. He was dressed impeccably as always in his signature black suit. A clerk studied the sheet, compared it to one they'd received earlier from the World Union office in Mexico City, and time-stamped it.

She picked up a phone and said, "Bring the Jane Doe to the front desk."

Wearing an orange jumpsuit, the prisoner tottered up. Abbott was surprised how gray and pale she was. Her eyes were sunken and it appeared that her hair hadn't been washed or combed in days. She looked at him blankly and said nothing as he signed the form that gave him custody of the amnesiac prisoner and took a small bag containing her toiletries and the civilian clothes she'd arrived in.

He put her in the backseat of a black World Union sedan, climbed in beside her, and the driver sped off to the area at McCarran International Airport where private planes landed. She seemed dazed and confused when he told her to climb the steps of a Learjet 24 and buckle her seatbelt, but she did as he asked.

The pilots finished their preflight checks. One opened the cockpit door and asked if Abbott was ready to go.

Abbott nodded. "How long will the flight be?"

"An hour and a half to El Paso, a quick stop for fuel and to stretch your legs, and a little over two more hours to Mexico City after that. Just relax and enjoy the ride. There are soft drinks and chips in the drawers under your seats."

She appeared to be asleep from the moment the plane took off. Abbott took a packet out of his briefcase, prepared a syringe and filled it from a small hypodermic bottle. He dabbed a cotton swab in alcohol and shook his prisoner until she opened her eyes.

"I'm going to give you something," he said. "Give me your arm."

She obediently raised her arm and he lifted her sleeve. He eased the tiny needle in and injected the fluid. "Go back to sleep now," he commanded, and she closed her eyes. He glanced at his watch. The drug would take effect in less than thirty minutes.

He was sipping a Coke when he saw her eyelids pop open. She shook her head, looked around and said, "Who are you, and where am I?"

"Good afternoon, Mrs. Dax. It's nice to have you back. My name is Heston Abbott. I'm a federal agent entrusted with your custody. May I call you Melanie?"

"Who the hell are you? What's going on?"

Abbott found the confused look on her face an understandable reaction to all that was happening. She had been in a drug-induced state for almost a month, since the day they had supposedly euthanized her.

All this had been Abbott's idea. It was a lucky break that her lottery number was drawn, but he had no intention of losing his queen in this game of chess. He'd secretly removed her to Vegas after injecting her with a strong opiate that caused perpetual drowsiness and induced a state of amnesia. He'd kept her on that medicine until today, and now she was herself again.

Of course she was confused. She had gone to sleep in a prison cell in Denver and awakened on a private jet with the man who'd imprisoned her in the first place.

"Where's Dan? Where am I?" She fired questions in a voice tinged with fear.

"Calm down, my dear. You're in safe hands. You've been ... away, shall we say, for quite a long time, almost thirty days. Your husband's still in prison in Colorado and I'm afraid he isn't doing well. In fact, you're the only one who can help him and your son, Nate."

Her eyes opened wide in astonishment.

"You're surprised I know about your Outcast son? Of course I do. He's in custody too." He was lying, of course, since he didn't have either one of them, but he had to keep her under his thumb. He could tell this one could be dangerous and he had to keep her in check.

"Where are we going? Where are you taking me?"

"We're going to Mexico City, to the World Union district headquarters. There are people who want to hurt you. The Resistance people want you dead, Melanie, to keep you from talking about all those subversive activities you and your husband have engaged in for years. But I promise I'll keep you safe."

The fog in her brain was clearing quickly. She'd been away somehow for thirty days? He had to have drugged her, given the way she felt when she woke up. She was wearing an orange jumpsuit; she'd obviously still been in prison somewhere, although she didn't believe a thing this slick individual said. She decided to pretend to cooperate until she could make a move. Maybe that wouldn't be possible, but she'd be ready. She flexed her hands and extended her legs, getting blood flowing and making them feel more like normal.

The cockpit door opened again. "We'll be landing in ten minutes, sir."

"Are we there already?" she asked.

"We're refueling in El Paso. You can get off, walk around for a minute and enjoy the fresh air. You haven't experienced any in quite some time, I'm afraid."

The plane taxied to a fixed base operator's terminal and the pilots went inside to check the weather along the flight path as two men in black overalls began to refuel the sleek jet. Unsteady on her feet, Melanie climbed slowly down the stairs and the agent followed behind her. He walked toward the tail of the plane and pulled out his phone.

The sun was fiercely bright and she squinted to let her eyes adjust. Suddenly one of the men doing the fueling darted under the rear fuselage and struck Abbott from behind with a baton. The other moved next to her and said, "Resistance, Melanie. Come with me. Hurry."

In less than five minutes the pilots returned to the plane to find one of their passengers unconscious on the tarmac by the plane. The other passenger – the woman prisoner – had vanished. The two fuel jockeys were gone too, leaving the hose still connected to the plane's fuel tank.

One of the pilots splashed water in Abbott's face while the other called for an ambulance. In a moment he was awake. He shook off the pain in his head and screamed, "Lock the airport down! Don't let them get away!" But it was too late. With the brief head start, the two Resistance operatives were speeding away in a van that had been waiting in the parking lot. Melanie had already changed into a sweatshirt and jeans Carlos had sent for her.

Despite establishing extensive highway checkpoints and inspecting every aircraft leaving El Paso, they couldn't track Melanie Dax without a chip. It would be pure luck if they found her, and their luck had finally run out.

CHAPTER SIXTY-TWO

Carlos Fine had spent most of the morning in meetings with his lieutenants at the Ciudad Juarez office of Security Bridge Corporation, just across the border from El Paso, Texas. It was one of his smaller satellite locations, but it handled a lot of traffic for customers from San Diego to Houston and south to Monterrey. As the meetings progressed, he had anxiously awaited the message that finally appeared on his phone. She was free and they were in the safe house.

It took the taxi less than five minutes to get from his office to the spacious apartment in the Campestre district, an area that once suffered from the drugs and violence that had consumed this city. When the authorities clamped down on the drug lords, Campestre recovered and was once again the most fashionable part of town.

She ran across the room and hugged him tightly. "God, am I glad to see you," she exclaimed. "From what I hear, I've been sedated for days. Abbott told me about Nate and Dan, how they're still in prison. Are they okay, Carlos?"

He asked her guards for time alone with her. Once they were gone, he said, "It's good to see you too and I have a lot to tell you. Nate and Dan are fine. They're not in prison; they're with us in Denver. Allie too ... but then you don't know about her. I'm getting ahead of myself. Let me start from the beginning."

That evening he returned to Denver. While the police were searching for her, she had to remain in place, but he promised to speak with her every day. She had talked to Dan and Nate and the tearful long-distance reunion made Carlos realize yet again why he had dedicated his life to the Resistance.

Heston Abbott sat in the expansive office of the commander of the World Union's Mexico City operations. Abbott had been here several times before, each one for a dressing-down by the big boss. This was no cordial meeting and it wasn't going well. He had never seen the commander this livid and his invectives were aimed directly at Abbott, a man whose arrogance and self-esteem made him loathed by those under him and tolerated by those above. Abbott feared he had gone too far. He might not be able to talk his way out of this one.

He'd spent the last hour explaining why he had removed a federal prisoner, rented a private jet and then let that prisoner escape, all without the knowledge or approval of his superior officers. His plan had been to move her to a safe location – Mexico City – and use her as bait to bring in her traitorous family. He would force her to make a videotaped appeal and they would turn themselves in.

"If you had sought approval for that mission," the commander said, "I might – I stress *might* – have approved it. Instead, you struck out on your own, knowing as usual that you were smarter and more clever than anyone else in this building. This is serious, Agent Abbott. It isn't the first time you've had a blemish on your record and this egregious one puts you way over the top in my books."

He paused, and Abbott smoothly said, "Commander, I have only had the interests of the government in mind as I have performed my job over the years. I'm very good at what I do. I'm the senior interrogator in the office and I get more results than anyone."

"You're right about that," the man conceded.

Abbott leaned back, relieved that he was beginning to get the upper hand.

"You do, in fact, get more answers than anyone else. Let me show you something interesting. I received this from an anonymous account at the World Union office in Denver yesterday. I've had a team trying to track down where it came

302

from, but so far whoever sent it has proven to be very elusive. Once you see what I'm going to show you, you might understand why. I think he or she might be afraid of what could happen if you knew who the person was."

He clicked a button on his tablet and a video appeared on a screen behind his desk. He turned and moved his chair so Abbott could see too.

He, Major Wheeler and Daniel Dax were in the basement interrogation room. He watched himself take out a stick and slam it onto the prisoner's thigh, eliciting screams of agony. The video went on and on. Major Wheeler sat to one side, clearly horrified. Then he had vomited and Abbott called him a disgrace to his uniform.

The commander clicked off the video. "According to the anonymous person who sent me this – and I take anything anonymous with a grain of salt – this was a backup video. The original was destroyed via an order signed by none other than yourself, Agent Abbott. This and one other video. I watched it too. The first time you interviewed that prisoner, he was carried out by two men. The second time apparently Major Wheeler couldn't make it. You got to do that one alone. You almost killed the man and he left on a gurney. Oh, and you ordered that video deleted too. Why did you do that? Were you afraid we might object to those little playthings you keep in your briefcase? Were you afraid I might be offended if I knew exactly how you get all that good information from prisoners?"

The commander clasped his hands in front of him and said, "I've never liked you and your holier-than-thou attitude, but that didn't mean you weren't a good, solid, loyal agent. I heard rumors and I called you on the carpet a few times before, but I had no idea you were involved in something like this. This is unconscionable, immoral. It's cruelty and you seem to enjoy it. You're a sick man, Agent Abbott. I hope you can get help."

He picked up the phone and in a moment the two agents he'd kept on standby entered the room. "Agent Abbott is under arrest for attempted murder and kidnapping a federal prisoner. Take him down and book him."

CHAPTER SIXTY-THREE

Six months later

Dixie and I are riding the fence line of the west pasture to be sure everything is secure. The last snows of winter are over and we'll move the cattle up here in a month or so once there's plenty of grass. I turn her back and go to the ridge to look down at our place in the valley below.

I can see the metal roof of the new house gleaming in the sunlight, clouds of smoke pouring out of the chimney. It's a crisp, cool day and Mom always enjoys a fire in the fireplace right up until it gets warm. Dad and two helpers are working on our new barn; the framework is almost done and they'll be in the dry soon.

Everything that happened since November made us celebrities, at least for a little while. My family and I have a new respect for our government and are actively working to help make things better between the World Union, the Enforcement Patrol and the Resistance.

The Resistance hasn't gone away by any means. It's still the same as always. Unbeknownst to the authorities, Carlos is still running things in Denver, and he is continuing to make progress in the name of freedom. But things are different now. The secrecy, the underhanded tactics, the bullying brutality of people like Heston Abbott – for now all those things are over. Dad says he hopes they'll stay that way, but everyone knows that bad people sometimes revert to their old ways once things die down and people forget.

One person who won't revert is Heston Abbott. He was found guilty on all charges and was euthanized a month ago. I never felt pity for the man. I only knew him at his worst and I felt nothing but relief when I knew he would no

longer mistreat others. I believe that man who rescued me –
that EP major – didn't die in vain. He gave me the key to
everything. He told me to find the backup videos. I didn't
know what it meant then, but during the trial everyone in the
world found out what kind of animal Abbott was, thanks to
Major Wheeler.

I haven't seen Allie or her father since Mom, Dad and
I got pardoned in late November, although I know they were
both cleared of any wrongdoing. Their family is still in
Leadville and Lenny's still the man in charge. Dad told me
they offered him a post in Denver, but he turned it down.
Too much bureaucracy, Lenny told people.

I don't know if I'll ever see Allie again. I rarely go
into town because I don't want to run into her, at least not
yet. We went through a lot but it was a scary, dangerous
experience for two people as young as we are. I don't know
if either one of us will ever make the move to start things
again.

I'm chipped now and Mom got hers back too after
they made the unprecedented move to let her live even
though her lottery number was drawn. The World Court is
looking into population control overall; Mom's situation
brought the issue to the forefront so people would feel
comfortable speaking their minds. We were on TV a lot
before things quietened down.

Along with our pardons the government gave us
compensation for our burned house and barn and people to
help build them back. They said we didn't have to reveal
anything about the Resistance – that in a free society people
should be able to exercise the right to protest. I've spoken to
Carlos; he said he'll believe that when he sees it, and he's
keeping things just as secret as always. Maybe someday that
can be different too.

Watching people in the government stand up for
what's right has restored my faith in our world. Leaders come
and go, good ones, mediocre ones and bad ones. At least
we're free, Dad says, and for the first time in my life, I truly
am free. It feels wonderful to be normal.

Bill Thompson's next exciting novel,
The Black Cross,
will be available in March 2017!
You'll see the dark side of New Orleans that the
tourists laugh about. Is voodoo real? Find out
soon!

Would you like to know about its release
in advance?

Just go to
billthompsonbooks.com
and click "Sign Up for the Latest News"

ABOUT THE AUTHOR

Bill Thompson, whose first book *The Bethlehem Scroll* won the prestigious EVVY award for fiction, is a former corporate entrepreneur and an avid student of history. *The Outcasts* is his tenth novel.

He's traveled extensively and particularly enjoys the ancient Mesoamerican sites in Guatemala, Honduras and Mexico. When he's not writing he's often off in the remote jungle where there's plenty of adventure. (There also has to be a martini at five o'clock. That's a requirement.)

Bill, his wife and a bunch of dogs live in Dallas, Texas.

Thank you!

Thanks for reading The Outcasts. I hope you enjoyed it and **I'd really appreciate a review on Amazon, Goodreads or both.**

Even a line or two makes a tremendous difference so thanks in advance for your help!

Please join me on:
Facebook
http://on.fb.me/187NRRP

Twitter
@BThompsonBooks